THE
LOST
WONDERLAND
DIARIES

THE LOST WONDERLAND DIARIES

J. SCOTT SAVAGE

SHADOW
MOUNTAIN

Chapter epigraphs from Lewis Carroll, *The Annotated Alice* (New York: W. W. Norton & Company, 2000).

Visit us at shadowmountain.com

Library of Congress Cataloging-in-Publication Data

Names: Savage, J. Scott (Jeffrey Scott), 1963– author. The lost Wonderland diaries (Series) ; bk. 1
Title: The lost Wonderland diaries / J. Scott Savage.
Description: Salt Lake City : Shadow Mountain, [2020] | Series: The lost Wonderland diaries, book 1 | Audience: Grades 4–6. | Summary: "When Celia and Tyrus discover the four lost diaries of Charles Dodgson (a.k.a. Lewis Carroll), they are pulled into Wonderland and must solve riddles and puzzles to stop the Queen of Hearts from opening a door and taking over our world"—Provided by publisher.
Identifiers: LCCN 2020010134 | ISBN 9781629727868 (hardback)
Subjects: CYAC: Characters in literature—Fiction. | Imaginary places—Fiction. | Riddles—Fiction. | Puzzles—Fiction. | Kings, queens, rulers, etc.—Fiction. | Dyslexia—Fiction. | Diaries—Fiction.
Classification: LCC PZ7.S25897 Lo 2020 | DDC [Fic]—dc23
LC record available at https://lccn.loc.gov/2020010134

Printed in the United States of America
Lake Book Manufacturing, Inc., Melrose Park, IL

10   9   8   7   6   5   4   3   2   1

To Jennifer Savage,
the Cheshire to my Hatter, who has been
inspiring, encouraging, and making me laugh
for more than thirty years.

Contents

CONTENTS

CHAPTER 1
The Right Time

"Oh dear! Oh dear! I shall be too late!"

Is it time?

Is it time?

Is it time?

The question bounced about the Rabbit family warren like a well-hit croquet ball.

Uncle Lop Rabbit tugged his greatcoat tightly around his shoulders, despite the weather being unseasonably warm, and held a single glass lens up to his eye to examine those around him with great scrutiny mixed with a dash of befuddlement. "I've heard the Arithma Sea is as purple as an eggplant and the schools of numbers are in a tizzy. It must be time."

Aunt Angora Rabbit squirmed in her corset and flicked one long ear. "I've heard it's twice as purple as a plum. Creatures of enormous size and questionable integrity are rising from the depths. High time, I'd say."

"Past time, if you ask me," Cousin Lilac huffed. "The

queen has declared a quarantine over all of Wonderland. She's locked the castle gates, and the Cards are seizing anyone trying to get in or out."

"The Cards," whispered the rest of the family, twitching their noses and thumping their feet.

"Have you heard about what happened to . . . you know who?" asked Nephew Rex.

"He was attacked by a beast," whispered one voice.

"A monster," murmured another.

"A demon."

"A phantasm."

"A fiend."

"A hauntstrosity," Grandmother Sable said with a shiver. "It got everyone at his house. And now . . ."

"They've gone madder than mad," Niece Satin said around a mouthful of carrot.

"It's getting worse every day." The twins, Perlfee and Pannon, spoke in unison like always. Although they were well-known as the gossips of the family, it was universally recognized that what they said was almost always true. "The gryphons turned savage in the middle of the last Lobster Quadrille and ate the entire class. Something's been horrificating the Avians. Rabid beasts have been reported in the Duchess's woods."

The two of them pressed their heads together, long ears quivering, as though sharing information, then nodded in unison. "Everyone is saying the end of Wonderland is near."

"The end of Wonderland?" Mother Marten squeaked.

Father Fauve's applewood pipe fell out of his mouth,

spreading hot ashes across his feet, but he barely noticed. "The *end* of Wonderland."

"The end of Wonderland."

"The end of Wonderland."

"The end of Wonderland."

It quickly turned into a chant, and the sound of thumping feet echoed for miles. The whole Rabbit family might have fled in a panic if Great-Great-Great-Grandfather Gotland Rabbit hadn't chosen that moment to shuffle out of his den in a checkered bathrobe and a worn pair of bunny slippers, which bore a striking resemblance to fussy Aunt Rhinelander.

"Can't a rabbit nap in peace around here?" he complained, rubbing the top of his bald head. "It's bad enough that my bladder is bashful and my liver is laughable. Now I must put up with the ruckus of rambunctious relatives rioting above my room. What's all this ruminating?"

"It's the end of Wonderland," shrilled Pika. No one was entirely sure how he was related, or if he was actually a member of the Rabbit family at all, but everyone nodded.

"A run on underwear, you say?" Grandfather Gotland asked with a scowl.

"The end of Wonderland," Satin shouted, spraying bits of chewed carrot everywhere.

Grandfather Gotland flicked an orange sliver disdainfully from his robe. "Why would anyone want to listen to a *thunder band*?"

"For lettuce sake," Great-Great-Great-Grandmother Gabali Rabbit said. She lifted one of Gotland's floppy ears and yelled,

"The family thinks it might be the end of Wonderland. They. Want. To. Know. If. It. Is. Time."

Grandfather rubbed his ear. "You don't have to shout." He twisted left and right—his spine cracking in at least a dozen places—then tugged up the waistband of his pajamas. "Bring out the clocks."

"The clocks," the family murmured as a pair of well-muscled rabbits in matching uniforms turned to two large wooden doors that hadn't been opened for as long as any of them could remember.

It took the clock-keepers several minutes to figure out which of them had the key, and when they did, the lock was so rusty it refused to turn at first. But eventually it clicked, and the huge doors swung open with a squeak of rusty metal hinges.

A moment later, the rabbits rolled out a strange-looking contraption made of hundreds of differently shaped gears, dozens of springs, several pipes, numerous levers, and two large clock hands.

"The Clock of Dithering," Uncle Lop whispered, studying it through his monocle.

Grandfather Gotland waggled his whiskers as the great mechanical clock was rolled up before him. "I seem to recall . . ." He reached for a lever with a red knob, but hesitated. "Or was it?" He began to twist a silver crank then shook his head. "That's not right."

After several minutes of starting and stopping, he finally grabbed the biggest handle he could find, closed his eyes, and tugged.

Springs sprung, gears whirled, pipes spewed clouds of smoke and whistled ear-piercing screeches. The two clock hands whirled until they were nothing but a blur before stopping abruptly with a loud double *clonk-clonk*.

Great-Great-Great-Grandfather Gotland studied the clock, tilting his head first one way, then the other.

"Well?" Cousin Lilac asked, wringing her paws. "Is it time?"

"I would say . . ." He shuffled his slippers. "That is . . . If I were to hazard a guess . . ."

Finally, Great-Great-Great-Grandmother Gabali elbowed past him and studied the placement of the clock hands. "Good news," she announced. "It is not quite time to panic."

There was a general sigh of relief from the family, followed by a feeling of unrest.

"You told us what time it *isn't*," Mother Marten said. "But what time *is* it?"

Grandfather puffed out his chest, resuming his spot at the front of the crowd. "Don't be ridiculous. The Clock of Dithering only tells what time it is *not*—an excellent choice when you are early enough to dawdle or late enough that there's no point in bothering. To learn what time it *is*, we will need the Clock of Action."

Once again, the soldiers marched through the doors. A moment later, they rolled out an enormous wheel of—

"Cheese?" Father Fauve asked.

"The best carrots can buy," Grandfather said.

"Created by a team of skilled artisan mice," Grandmother added as the clock-keepers wheeled the cheese clock into place.

Sunlight shone through hundreds of holes in the large wheel, creating dozens of overlapping circles of light on the ground. The numbers on the clock face began at $1\frac{3}{4}$ and ended at $13^{10}/6$. A silver butter knife pointed at $7\frac{1}{2}$ while a tarnished cake fork sat halfway between $3^{1}/3$ and $4^{7}/10$.

"The finest Swiss craftsmanship," Aunt Angora said approvingly.

When, at last, the wheel was in place, Grandfather waved his hands. "A little to the left."

The rabbits rotated the cheese wheel. The circles of sunlight in front of the clock began shifting toward one another.

"A little more," Grandfather said.

Slowly, the rabbits moved the wheel until all the holes lined up just right to form a single perfect circle of light on the ground. A loud chime came from somewhere deep inside the cheese. Click by click, the fork and knife moved until they both aligned at the top.

Grandfather Gotland's eyes widened. His ears flapped, and his whiskers wilted. "It. Is. Time."

He reached into one of the holes in the cheese wheel and pulled out a sheet of parchment so old it looked like the barest breeze would tear it to shreds. It was covered with folds, wrinkles, and small tears. Several spots had clearly been glued back together.

"Many, many years ago," Grandfather Gotland said in a trembling voice, "the outsider predicted that after he left us, Wonderland would one day face grave peril. On that day, he said, we should call another from his world—one who would come to Wonderland and save us all."

A hushed silence fell over the family as Grandfather unrolled the parchment. "The one who will save us is . . ." Narrowing his eyes, he turned the paper one way and then another. Finally, he pulled a pair of gold spectacles from his robe pocket and nodded. "The one who will save us is the . . . *Alice*."

"The Alice," the family murmured.

"We must go far and wide, telling everyone in Wonderland to stay strong," Grandmother said. "The Alice is on the way."

"But who will summon The Alice?" one of the rabbits shouted.

"It should be the one who met the last outsider," Grandfather said. "The queen's original timekeeper. The one who gave the Rabbit family our great purpose in the first place."

Pika's round ears quivered. "You mean Whi—"

"Shh," the rest of the family hissed.

Grandfather shivered and rubbed at a cabbage stain on the sleeve of his bathrobe. "Is anyone willing to speak to . . . ?"

All the Rabbit family members looked at one another, shaking their heads.

"He's in no shape to call anyone," the twins said in unison.

"Someone else must take his place," Grandmother said. "Do we have a volunteer?"

"I have a, um, pressing engagement to . . ." Uncle Lop said, edging backward.

Aunt Angora shook her head. "I'd be happy to if I didn't . . ."

"Under other circumstances, you see . . ." Cousin Velveteen began.

One by one, each mother, father, brother, sister, cousin,

grandmother, grandfather, child, in-law, and fiancée slipped away, each making half-hearted excuses, until only one rabbit was left.

Sylvan, one of the youngest members of the Rabbit family—barely out of her bunnyhood—had been sketching pictures in the dirt with a stick. Not paying attention to what was going on around her, it wasn't until the last of the relatives had disappeared that she looked up to discover her great-great-great-grandparents staring at her.

"Did someone say something?" she asked, having no idea what she was about to get herself into.

Great-Great-Great-Grandmother and Great-Great-Great-Grandfather looked at each other and nodded.

"She'll do perfectly."

CHAPTER 2
The Last Week

"Who in the world am I?"
Ah, that's the great puzzle!

If I could have chosen one place to spend my final week of summer vacation, the library would have been last on the list. Lower than last. Negative one hundred sounded about right. Better yet, the square root of negative one hundred—a number so imaginary the option wouldn't have existed at all.

Unfortunately, I didn't have a choice in the matter, any more than I'd had a choice about moving from Grand Forks, North Dakota, to San Jose, California—more than a thousand miles away. My mom accepted a job as head librarian at the Santa Teresa Library and that was that.

The painters had taken over our new house, changing the walls from a boring shade of white to an equally boring shade of beige, and since we didn't know anyone in California, I got to spend the last week before school with Mom.

In the library.

"How do you like the new circulation desk?" Mom asked,

waving at a line of computer screens as if she'd installed them herself. "The skylights are nice, don't you think?"

I must not have looked properly enthusiastic, because she shifted the box under her arm and nudged me in the ribs. "They're books, not prison bars, Celia. Try to smile a little."

I forced the corners of my mouth up, sure it looked more like a grimace than a smile. "When you said we were moving to California, you talked about going to the science museum and the beach—places that are actually *fun*."

"And we will, but this is a new job. I can't afford to take time off right now."

As if she'd taken time off from her last library job. Books had always been my mom's thing, but after my dad died three years ago, she'd taken her literary devotion to a whole new level. I would never have said it out loud, but I was halfway convinced she loved reading more than she loved me.

She put an arm around my shoulders. "I know you miss your old friends, but maybe you'll meet some new ones here before school starts."

Considering that ninety percent of the library's patrons appeared to either be kids under five looking at picture books or senior citizens reading newspapers, that didn't seem likely. Then again, the fact that Mom thought I had friends back home showed she didn't know me as well as she thought.

I shrugged. "I'm sure all the kids my age are hanging out back in the Biographies."

Mom sighed and set down the box of books. She handed me a sheet of paper filled from top to bottom with books and authors. "Here's your reading list. Pick at least three, and make sure one is a classic."

"Couldn't I do some math instead?" I loved numbers as much as she loved words. I could happily solve math problems forever.

Mom frowned. "I don't want you anywhere near the math section until you've read at least three chapters from one of the books on the list. She held out what looked like a mix between a TV remote and laser pointer. "Don't forget your reading pen. I think it's going to make a big difference with your IEP this year."

"Mom!" I bit the inside of my cheek—a nervous habit I did so much that I had a callus inside my mouth. "You promised I wouldn't have to do an IEP right away. I want to try things on my own first."

"We'll see," she said. But I could tell she'd already turned her attention to an elderly woman examining the young adult romance new releases.

Angry, I snatched the pen and the list from her hands and stepped directly into the path of a boy wearing a backpack so big it made him look like a tortoise.

He bobbled the stack of books he was carrying before catching his balance again. His eyes were brown behind the thick lenses of his glasses. "Sorry. I didn't mean to run into you. I was just . . ." He held out the books as if that explained everything.

I peeked at the covers, felt my stomach grow queasy, and looked away. "It wasn't your fault. I wasn't watching where I was going."

Although he was shorter than I was, he seemed about my age. "I haven't seen you here before," he said, glancing at the plastic pen in my hand.

I quickly hid it behind my back. "My mom's the new librarian."

His brown cheeks rose into a dimpled grin. "Your mom's a librarian? That's the coolest thing ever."

He thought having a librarian for a mom was *cool*?

Any interest I'd had in talking more dried up like an apricot in the California sun. I was hoping to make friends here, where no one knew who—or *what*—I was, but I wasn't about to start with a book nerd. "I better let you get back to your research."

He pushed his glasses up on his nose. "Research?"

I waved at his books. "You've got two science fiction novels, something about architecture, an art book, and what looks like *The Magic School Bus*. Either you have really weird reading tastes or you're researching something."

His cheeks dimpled again. "You read fast."

I didn't bother telling him that it would have taken me at least five minutes to puzzle out what the letters said. Besides, the covers told me everything I needed to know. Figuring out context from pictures was something I'd gotten good at over the years.

"So . . ." I said, wondering how quickly I could leave without seeming rude. "Looks like you're busy."

"Oh, yeah." He licked his lips, and his eyes flickered toward the front desk. "I guess I better get back to my, uh . . . research."

As I began to turn away, he raised a hand. "See you around." Balanced on one arm, his stack of books shifted, and two of them fell to the floor with loud bangs. Several people turned in our direction, and I took the opportunity to make my escape.

Finding an empty spot as far in the back as possible, I plopped into a chair and slumped forward. Seeing the reading pen clutched in my hand made my anger flare all over again, and I nearly smashed the annoying gadget on the table. But then my mom would have to buy another one, which we couldn't afford.

Moving halfway across the country between my seventh- and eighth-grade years was bad. But maybe it could be a new chance for me. At my old North Dakota charter school, we all wore the same uniform of khaki skirts or pants paired with shirts in the approved school colors—a sea of sameness where anyone who was different stood out.

Here, in San Jose, the kids I'd seen back-to-school shopping at Target were much more diverse. Their clothes ranged from fashion-model dressy to flip-flops and shorts. Looking at so many different faces and styles, I dared to hope that maybe I could fit in here—be just another kid.

But that hope would disappear in a middle-school second if the other students found out I had an IEP.

Individualized Education Programs—IEPs, for short—are supposed to help kids like me, who struggle in school for one reason or another, find different ways of doing our assignments. The teachers learn what's hard for us, and we complete our work in whatever way we can. Win-win. Everybody's happy.

At least that's how it had been explained to me at my old school.

Instead, I had to take a bunch of tests and answer a million questions just to figure out if I really had a disability. After the tests and interviews were finally done, I thought I'd made it through the worst part. It turned out it was only the beginning. Once the teachers learned about my IEP, I could tell that a lot of them were annoyed by having to make changes to the way they normally taught.

Not all of them, of course. Some were great about working with me, and the changes we made together seemed to help. But just when it felt like things were starting to click, the other kids discovered that I was different.

That's when the looks started. Then the jokes. Kids who used to be my friends stopped hanging around me. Even kids I didn't know looked at me funny. I wasn't "the kid with the reading disability." I was "the weird kid." The *stupid* kid. After that, it didn't matter what I did or said. I never managed to find a way to fit back in.

I wasn't about to let that happen at my new school, which meant making sure no one knew I had "issues." Pushing aside the reading list and the stupid pen, I gazed around the room.

In the children's section, a couple of four-year-old girls laughed at a picture book about dinosaurs dressed in Halloween costumes while two women I assumed were their moms chatted about romance novels. A college-aged guy with dreadlocks pulled books from the shelf while a girl with long blonde hair leaned against the wall with a magazine.

All of them sucked words from their books as easily as

people slurped spaghetti noodles—none of them knowing how much easier their lives were because reading came naturally to them.

With a disgusted snort, I turned away only to see a pair of brown eyes peeking out at me from above a nearby row of books. As soon as I noticed them, the eyes disappeared, and a hunched figure scurried around the corner and into the reference section. But not before I recognized the thick glasses.

The boy with the giant backpack was spying on me.

CHAPTER 3
The Library Thief

"Stolen!" the King exclaimed, turning to the jury,
who instantly made a memorandum of the fact.

I couldn't believe the little snoop was stalking me.

Half of me wanted to get up and confront him. But that meant talking. And talking—like reading—wasn't something my brain was very good at. Especially in stressful situations, which this would be.

Instead, I pulled out my phone to play Minecraft. It's a great game for kids like me because you can play by yourself and there's no dialogue to read.

I spent most of my game time in the Nether—an area filled with flames and lava—where I'd built a giant castle to hang out with the zombie pigmen, the outcasts of the Minecraft world. Unlike most of the aggressive creatures, as long as you leave the zombie pigmen alone, they leave you alone. It's a life philosophy I relate well to.

I was upgrading my castle when I spotted Backpack Boy

near the front of the library. He wasn't spying on me anymore, but he was clearly up to something.

Glancing over his shoulder like a spy in a movie, he eased toward the front desk.

What was he doing?

Standing to get a better view, I slipped behind a Dr. Seuss display and watched him make his way to a metal cart filled with returned books. Waiting until no one was looking in his direction, he quickly grabbed an armful. After a furtive look at the covers, he darted into a row of nearby shelves.

No way!

I rubbed my eyes, barely able to believe what I had just seen. The dorky kid was a spy *and* a thief. What kind of person would steal random library books? Maybe it was a California thing. There couldn't be a lot of money in it. Still, catching a library thief sounded a lot more interesting than hanging out with zombie pigmen.

I hurried into the row of shelves he'd entered, wanting to catch him before he could add the books to his already overloaded pack, but the aisle was empty. Peering through an opening between two shelves, I spotted him a couple of rows over.

He was quick for a kid wearing a backpack bulky enough to stop a crossbow bolt, but I wasn't about to let him get away. Ducking out the other direction, I circled around and approached from the opposite side. I saw a stooped figure through a rack of paperbacks.

I leaped into the aisle and shouted, "Gotcha!"

Unfortunately, it was an old woman browsing a stack of

mysteries. She threw her hands in the air, books flying every-where, and stared at me, her lips quivering. "What do you want?" she asked, clutching her purse to her chest.

My tongue stuck to the roof of my mouth like a lump of peanut butter. My brain shorted out. "I, uh . . . sorry," I muttered, hurrying away.

When my mom heard that her daughter had accosted a harmless old lady on my first day at the library, I'd be grounded for life.

Unless I could catch the library thief red-handed.

The kid might be one of those serial criminals who committed the same crime over and over. Who knew how many books he'd stolen? There could be a reward for his capture. Searching the main room for the telltale sign of his giant back-pack, I spotted him in the children's section. But when I got there, he was somehow clear across the building, disappearing into the reference shelves again.

He was like a library phantom, slipping in and out of the stacks through secret passages only he knew about. Taking a wide detour around the mystery section to avoid the old lady I'd scared, I hurried into the reference area, which contained books that were too expensive to check out. This was probably where Backpack Boy stole the good stuff.

Tiptoeing quietly, I peeked from one row to the next. He had to be somewhere close, and when I found him, I was going to make him return everything he'd taken. I might not be big, and I might not get good grades in school, and I might not have any friends, but I had a strong right punch.

At least I hoped I did. I mean, it wasn't like I'd ever

actually punched anyone. I'd wanted to after Paisley had started teasing me at my old school. Instead, I'd stomped into the bathroom, glared in the mirror, and told my reflection everything I wanted to say to her.

But if the book-stealing pip-squeak wanted trouble, I'd be ready to give it to him.

Moving quietly from shelf to shelf, I heard something coming from the back of the building. As I went to investigate, a voice called out, "Hello?"

It didn't sound like the library thief. It sounded like a much younger kid.

"Can anyone hear me?" the voice called.

What was a little kid doing this far from the children's section? Probably got lost looking for the bathroom. It'd happened all the time at the library where my mom used to work.

"We need help," the voice called again.

We? How many kids were back there anyway?

I headed toward where I thought the voice had come from—the library thief could wait—but there was no one around.

"Hello?" I called. "It's all right. You can come on out."

The only thing that far back in the library was an emergency exit with a sign warning that alarms would go off if you pushed the door open and an office with a plate on the open door reading HEAD LIBRARIAN.

I looked inside the office, spotting a bunch of moving boxes, stacks of books, and a desk that had already started collecting fast-food wrappers. Definite signs that my mom worked there. No kids though.

"Hey, guys," I called, using my talking-to-puppy-dogs-and-babies voice as I walked back through the shelves. "Are you lost? Do you need someone to take you to your parents?"

Whoever they'd been, they were gone now—along with Backpack Boy, probably. Except when I returned to my table, I saw the library thief himself standing beside my chair. He was holding my reading list and looking at my pen.

Spying on innocent people and stealing library books was bad enough, but taking my private belongings was going too far.

"Hold it right there," I yelled, grabbing him by the pack and spinning him around.

My voice echoed through the quiet library, and several people glared in my direction, but I didn't care.

"Put my things down and step away from the table slowly," I said in my best grown-up voice.

At least that's what I meant to say. What came out of my mouth was "Put my table down slowly and things away from the step."

As usual, my brain fritzed out when I was stressed.

Backpack Boy stared at me, his mouth hanging open either because I'd caught him in the act of stealing or because he didn't understand a word I'd said—possibly both.

I tried again. "What are you doing with my stuff?" This time the words came out right.

He handed me back my things. "I thought you must have left them behind. I was going to return them to you."

Exactly the kind of thing a thief would say. Obviously, he'd had practice lying.

I took a deep breath and rehearsed in my head how I was going to respond. My brain had plenty of tricks it played on me, but I had a few tricks of my own. Practicing in my mind what I was going to say before I said it helped me speak when I was stressed.

"I suppose you *weren't* spying on me a few minutes ago from behind those books?"

Backpack Boy ducked his head. "I *was* watching you. But I wasn't spying. I just wanted to see what you were reading. There aren't many kids our age who come to the library during the summer. Especially not ones who are so smart and pretty."

As though realizing what he'd just said, his dark cheeks flamed nearly purple. "N-not that I'm saying you're pretty," he stammered. "That is, you *are*. But it's not anything I noticed. I mean, not in a way that . . ." He pulled off his glasses and rubbed them furiously on his shirt.

I didn't know what to say. I'd never been called smart or pretty by anyone except my mom. And definitely not by a boy my own age, who I'd just met.

"You're a library thief," I sputtered, trying to ignore the burning in my cheeks. This was not the way I'd expected my big confrontation to go.

Apparently, it wasn't the response he'd been expecting either, because he put his glasses back on and blinked. "What?"

"Don't . . . try . . . to . . . deny it," I said, choosing my words carefully so I wouldn't mess them up. "I saw you take books from the return cart."

"Oh. That." He dropped his head again, the guilt plain on

his face. "I didn't take them. I mean, I *did* take them. But I didn't steal them."

I hadn't had this long of a conversation with someone my age for years, and it was getting way too awkward. I grabbed the zipper of his pack and yanked it open. Books spilled out like juice from a freshly cut watermelon.

"How do you explain that?" I demanded, pointing to the jumbled pile of paperbacks and hardbacks on the floor. For a brief moment, I felt the thrill of adrenaline rushing through my veins. He might be a good liar, but there was no way he could explain his way out of the evidence right in front of us.

Then, as I looked closer, a horrifying realization dawned on me. His pack was filled with books—I'd been right about that—but none of the paperbacks or hardbacks on the floor had stickers or plastic covers.

The books in his pack weren't from the library.

CHAPTER 4

The Bookish Tortoise

"And what is the use of a book," thought Alice
"without pictures or conversations?"

"Celia, what are you doing?" my mother hissed in a tone only a librarian who was also a mother could achieve.

Heat spread down from my face and cold shot up from my belly to meet in my chest so explosively I thought my heart would stop from the shock. I looked from my mother to Backpack Boy to the pile of spilled books and could think of no response to adequately explain everything that had happened in the last hour since I'd entered the library.

I chewed the inside of my cheek and muttered. "I, um . . . Well, what happened was—"

"It's my fault," the boy, who was apparently *not* a library thief, said. He pulled off his pack and began shoving books into it. "I dropped my things, and your daughter was helping me."

Mom looked at me with a doubtful expression, and I

dropped to my knees, keeping my face down as I picked up books and handed them to the boy.

"I couldn't help noticing your reading list," Backpack Boy said as I handed him books. "You have excellent taste. *The Phantom Tollbooth* is one of the best children's books published in the 1960s. Right up there with *Charlie and the Chocolate Factory.* And *A Wrinkle in Time* . . . Well, that's a classic. But you also have contemporary series like Percy Jackson and Wings of Fire. Not to mention the nonfiction."

What kind of kid talked like that?

Mom ate it up though. She put her hands on her hips and smiled. "It's a pleasure to meet another bookaholic."

"Addicted to reading and proud of it," the boy said. At that moment, if Mom could have traded him for me, I was sure she would have done the deal in a heartbeat. Putting the last of the books in his pack, the boy stuck out his hand. "Welcome to the library. It's a pleasure to meet you."

"Welcome yourself," Mom said, shaking his hand and beaming brighter than the skylights. "You see, Celia, I knew you'd meet new friends."

I had no comment.

Mom glanced over her shoulder at the group of older ladies. "You guys didn't see anyone running through the library scaring people, did you?" she asked us.

"No," the boy said, zipping his pack. "But if we do, we'll let you know. Libraries are places of learning, not scaring."

As my mom turned and walked to the front desk with a bounce in her step, I shot him a dark look. "'Libraries are places of learning, not scaring'?"

He shrugged. "Would you rather I told her you nearly gave that woman a heart attack in the mystery section?"

I clenched my fists. "You *were* stalking me."

"No. I mean, I was *watching* you. And I did follow you."

"Without my permission. That's called stalking."

He pulled off his glasses and polished them again although there wasn't a speck of dirt on the lenses. "I think we got off on the wrong foot. I'm Tyrus Weller."

"Celia Lofton," I said, plopping back into my seat. "What's with all the books? Are you a genius?"

"I wish," Tyrus said, sitting in the chair across from me. "My parents have threatened to ban me from the library if I don't get better grades this year."

I tried not to groan. Clearly the two of us should have been switched at birth. "What grade are you in?"

"Eighth," Tyrus said. "Or at least I will be when I start at my new school."

I tilted my head. "Bernal Middle?"

"You go there?" he asked. "What's it like?"

"No idea," I said. "I just moved here."

Tyrus grinned. "Me too. This is great! Now we'll each have a friend."

I covered my pen with my reading list. "About that. You seem nice, and it would be great to have a friend at my new school, but maybe the two of us shouldn't, you know, hang out."

"Why not? Is it because of our earlier miscommunication?"

I couldn't help laughing. "You don't talk like most kids our age."

"I know," he said. "My parents say I'm the youngest eighty-year-old they've ever met. I think it comes from all the reading I do."

I looked around to make sure we were alone. "Why did you take those books from the cart?"

"And you think *I* was stalking *you*?" Tyrus asked. He adjusted his glasses before pressing his hands flat on the table. "I know I'm not supposed to touch the returned books, but sometimes I can't help myself."

I hunched forward, fascinated. "What do you do with them?"

He bent across the table and paused before whispering, "I put them where they belong."

"What?"

"I put them where they belong. You know, in their spots?"

I raised an eyebrow. "You *reshelve* them?"

He nodded.

"Do you *work* here?"

He shook his head.

I knew I had problems reading, but my hearing was just fine, and yet, I found it almost impossible to believe what my ears were telling my brain. "Back up. You sneak to the front desk, steal books off the return cart, and then put them where they go?"

He blew out a long, slow breath. "That's right."

"Why?"

"It's fun. I just really love books. But since I'm not an employee, I'm not allowed to shelve them. So, I sneak."

I shook my bangs out of my eyes. "Now, I'm positive we can't be friends."

His face drooped. "Why not?"

I waved at his backpack full of books. "I'm not a reader. At least, not if I can help it."

"But you're at the library during summer break. And your mom works here. And you have an amazing reading list." He shook his head. "How can you not be a reader?"

"Long story." I sighed. "Look, it was great meeting you and all, but it might be best if you go back to stealing books and I'll go back to wishing I was anywhere else but here."

He folded his arms across his chest. "Not happening."

I wasn't sure how to respond to that. I hadn't made many friends, but I had plenty of experience losing them. When someone said they didn't want to hang out with me, I slunk away and tried not to show how hurt I felt. I'd never considered telling them "No."

"I'm not sure I understand," I said. "I don't like books, and they seem to be your favorite thing in the world. That doesn't give us much in common."

"Doesn't matter." Tyrus raised a finger. "We've already established that we're both new here. We're going to be attending the same school. We've both committed library crimes. We can't just ignore those kinds of connections because we feel differently about books."

He made a good case.

"What do you want to do?" I asked. "I mean, ordinarily we'd have more options than books. But since we're in a library . . ."

He pointed at my phone. "What were you doing on that? When I was, um . . ."

"Stalking me?" I grinned and opened my screen. "I was playing Minecraft. It's a video game."

He shook his head. "Not really into video games. I prefer worlds I can see in my head when I'm—"

"Reading," I finished for him. "Okay, so no books and no video games." That didn't leave us a lot of choices.

"We don't have to *read* books," Tyrus suggested. "We could talk about them."

"Pass."

We sat silently, looking at everything but each other. I felt bad. He seemed like a nice kid—for a book nerd. Under other circumstances, we probably could have found *something* in common.

I glanced toward the front desk and an idea occurred to me. I couldn't believe I was considering it, but Tyrus was right. Friends were rare enough that they were worth sacrificing for. It was the least I could do after he'd covered for me with my mom. Besides, I couldn't wait to see his face if my mom said yes to my plan.

"Come on," I said, jumping up from the table.

"Where are we going?"

I shook my head and walked to the front of the library where I found my mom talking to a teenager about different Star Wars books. It was amazing how much she knew about so many different things. If she ever went on a TV game show where they asked you questions, we would probably be millionaires.

After the boy left with a book in hand, I tapped my mom on her shoulder. She narrowed her eyes. "I told you we aren't leaving until—"

"It's not that," I said. "Tyrus and I were wondering if it would be okay if we helped you out by shelving the returned books. There's a pretty big stack, and the rest of the librarians seem busy."

I might as well have asked her if I could clean the house, take out the trash, and rub her feet. "You want to . . . *shelve books*?" she asked.

Tyrus's face lit up like it was Christmas and he'd discovered Santa had brought him everything he asked for, complete with an electric train circling the tree.

"If it's okay with you," I said.

Mom put a finger to her lips, slowly regaining her composure. "Do you know the Dewey decimal system?"

Tyrus straightened so quickly he nearly bounced out of his shoes. "The first three numbers represent the main class, division, and section of the book's subject. Like, in 724, the 7 stands for arts, the 2 is the archeology division, and the 4 means it's a book about archeology after the 1400s. After that, there is often a period followed by—"

"All right, all right," Mom said, laughing. "You know your stuff. Go to it."

Tyrus waited until Mom had turned away then pulled me into a bone-crushing hug. "You are the best friend ever."

CHAPTER 5

The Roller-Skating Fish

"But I don't want to go among mad people," Alice remarked.
"Oh, you ca'n't help that," said the Cat: "we're all mad here."

Watching Tyrus work was like watching a cheerful little book-sorting robot. He shuffled titles like sections of a Rubik's Cube, muttering book categories under his breath as he organized and exclaiming with delight when he found what he was looking for and was able to put a book where it belonged. As he finished each stack, he nodded with satisfaction and returned for more.

Eventually, I felt silly watching him and sorted a few myself. As long as I focused on the numbers on the spines of the books and not the letters of the titles, I was all right.

As we walked through the fiction section where books were organized by author name instead of numbers, Tyrus studied the L shelves.

"You've never read *A Wrinkle in Time*?"

I smirked. "You know that book is older than both of us combined."

"But it's a classic," he said.

I shrugged. "I've seen the movie."

"Not nearly as good." He grabbed the book from the shelf and held it in front of my face.

I looked at the letters for a moment then turned away. "I thought the girl who played Meg was great."

"She was," Tyrus agreed, flipping through the pages. "But they got the theme completely wrong, and they cut out some of the best scenes and replaced them with stuff that wasn't even in the book."

The problem with not being able to read well is that, no matter how many times you tell yourself you aren't stupid, you still find yourself feeling that way. I knew Tyrus wasn't attacking me personally but having him lecture me on how much better the book was than the movie made me feel like he was. I had to show him I was smart too.

I took a deep breath. "They did a terrible job of explaining the tesseract."

"The wormhole thing?" Tyrus asked.

It wasn't a wormhole, but I was impressed he didn't think I was talking about the blue box from the Marvel movies like most kids would have.

"Not exactly. A tesseract is a four-dimensional cube. Instead of having six sides, it has eight cubicle cells. Only, in the story, a tesseract is the fifth dimension, after a line, a square, a cube, and time. They use it to create a shortcut through space." I was speaking math now, so my words flowed, but when Tyrus just blinked at me, I realized how far off topic

I'd strayed. Tyrus was talking about a story, and I'd gone all quantum physics on him.

"It's also a great analogy for Meg and Charles Wallace," I said, trying to bring things back around. "No one understands them, just like no one understands time and space the way Meg's parents do."

Tyrus stared at me, and I thought maybe he was reconsidering his choice to be friends. Then he gave me his dimpled grin. "Wow! Now who's the brain?"

I studied him through my bangs. "Trust me, I'm the farthest thing from a brain. I just like numbers."

We shelved the last of our books, and he pulled me into the math section of the library. "How many of these do you understand?"

I checked around to make sure my mom wasn't watching then ran my fingers lovingly over the covers. "These are algebra, which deals primarily with sets and numbers. Those are calculus, which includes things like derivatives, functions, rates of change. This is geometry. Those are logic and number theory."

Tyrus shook his head. "Have you taken all those classes?"

I shrugged. "They don't offer anything above algebra in middle school, and Mom says I can't take more advanced classes until—"

"Until you do more reading," Tyrus guessed.

I exhaled slowly.

"But you love math so much," he said. "I can tell."

I was beginning to feel uncomfortable. "Not as much as you love books."

He shuffled his feet. "They're the only place I fit in."

I snorted to myself. *What do you know about not fitting in?*

Tyrus stared at me, and I realized I must have spoken out loud. I don't know if it's because my brain short-circuits or just a quirk of who I am, but occasionally I say things without meaning to.

My stomach churned. "I am so sorry. I didn't—"

"It's okay. I get it. At my old school, I was Mr. Popularity. You know, captain of the football team, class president, prom king. I completely understand you being jealous."

He said it cheerfully, but under the upbeat tone was a bitterness I hadn't heard from him before. It made me feel sick knowing I'd been the cause of it. I bit my lip, wishing I could take the words back.

He snorted a laugh that sounded more like a moan.

"I'm hoping it'll be better here. But where I used to live . . . Well, let's just say I wasn't into sports, didn't hunt, play video games, or play any musical instruments. I wasn't even geeky enough to hang out with the nerds."

I nodded silently, not trusting myself to say that I knew the feeling of being alone in a sea of other kids.

He rubbed his palms on his pants. "I got picked on every day. Kids threw rocks at me after school, and a couple of jerks smashed eggs on my head. I should have told my teachers or my parents, but . . ." He flapped his hands; he didn't have to say anything else. Once kids decide to target you, nothing grown-ups do seems to make any difference.

"That's when you found the library," I whispered.

Tyrus took off his glasses. "I didn't go to read at first. It was just a place to hide out. But once I was there, I started opening covers. I still remember the first time I found a book about a kid like me who didn't fit in."

Inside my head a firework popped as the pieces of the puzzle slid together. "*A Wrinkle in Time.* That's why you love it so much."

He shrugged, but his cheeks dimpled, and I knew I was right. "Stories were where I discovered I wasn't alone. It sounds stupid saying it out loud, but books gave me the friends I didn't have anywhere else. By the time my parents told me we were moving, things had gotten a little better, but I'm not exaggerating when I say books saved my life. That's why I think you're lucky to have all this around you, and a librarian for a mom. You have no idea how good you have it."

I don't know what made me do it. Maybe it was the honesty he'd shown, opening up in a way kids our age didn't with each other. Maybe it was the way his pain and loneliness echoed my own. Or maybe it was just that I was tired of holding in such a big secret, such a huge part of my life.

"I'm dyslexic."

Tyrus had been putting his glasses back on when the words left my lips. He held them a few inches away from his face, making his eyes look gigantic as he stared at me. It would have been funny if I hadn't been so terrified of what I'd said. I'd come here determined to fit in, and now I'd told a person I'd only known for a couple of hours a secret that could destroy everything.

"You mean the thing where it's hard to read?" he asked. "Like Percy Jackson?"

Now it was my turn to laugh. "That's like saying a fish has a hard time roller-skating." He looked confused, and I wished I'd never said anything, but I couldn't go back now. Not after what he'd told me.

I grabbed his hand and led him back to the table.

"Do you have something to write with?"

He gave me a pen, and I flipped my reading list over to the blank side of the paper. "Grab one of your books and open it to a random page."

He did, and I forced my way slowly through the first paragraph, working out the words and trying to copy them the way I saw them onto the blank sheet. By the time I was done, my head was pounding, and I felt like I was going to throw up.

"Read it," I said, sliding the paper across the table to him.

Tyrus stared at the lines, frowned, and then turned the sheet around slowly. "I can't. There aren't any words here. Just mixed-up letters and weird symbols."

"Welcome to dyslexia," I said, setting my page and his book side-by-side. "This is what every single page of every single book looks like to me."

Tyrus rubbed his jaw. "I thought dyslexia meant seeing the words move around on the page."

I shook my head. "That's called visual stress. For me, some letters seem normal, and some of them look like they are upside down or only half there. Some just look like alien symbols, which makes it hard to sound out words. Most of the time, I have to memorize the patterns they make."

"How can you read at all?"

"There are strategies I use, like focusing on small sections, taking breaks, changing fonts on my computer, or using audio-books when I can. But they don't always work. Most of it's memorizing patterns and forcing my way through. That's true for most people with dyslexia, but it's not just reading, though. Trying to spell anything new is almost impossible. Even when I do read, I forget lots of it."

Tyrus glanced down at the pen sticking partway out from under my reading list. "I guess that's not a mini lightsaber."

"It's called a reading pen," I said. "It helps me learn words I don't recognize. But if other kids see me using it . . ."

Tyrus nodded silently.

I could feel my face getting hot and wished I hadn't said anything. "I also get the added bonus of mixing up my words when I talk."

Tyrus rubbed his jaw, realization dawning in his eyes. "That's why you switched around your words when we were talking before."

"I'm not stupid," I snapped.

"I know you're not," he said.

"Well, you're the only one." I felt tears trying to force their way out of my eyes and blinked them back. I'd never spoken this openly about my reading disorder before. It was like lifting a boulder off my back while at the same time ripping open a hidden wound. "At my last school, no one would sit by me. They said my brain was broken and they didn't want to catch stupid. The teachers put me in special classes where they talked to us like we were five. The principal tried to hold me back a grade because she said I was slow."

Tyrus scowled. "I've only known you for a few minutes and I can already tell that's a load of garbage."

I wiped the back of my arm across my face feeling awkward. "You got eggs smashed on your head. I got my clothes taken out of my locker and thrown across the hall during gym class. I had parents uninvite me from their kids' birthday parties. I was told I wasn't trying hard enough. I got called every version of *stupid* you can imagine. But the worst part is, I convinced myself they were right."

Tyrus looked at the shelves of books around us. "For you, being around all this must feel like . . ."

"Like a person who can't swim—who is terrified of drowning—living in a swimming pool." I hiccupped and nearly choked. As if dumping my story on someone I barely knew hadn't been embarrassing enough.

Tyrus burst out laughing.

"You think it's funny?" I demanded, hurt and angry.

"It's hilarious," he said, not even trying to hide his guffaws, although several people were staring at us. "We're probably going to be two of the biggest outcasts Bernal Middle School has ever seen, and yet we make friends with each other a week before school even starts. I don't know what the odds are. You're the math genius. They're like a million to one, right?"

"There aren't a million kids in the school," I said. "At best, it's five hundred to one."

"Five hundred to one!" Tyrus bent over, holding his stomach like I'd told the funniest joke in history.

I didn't want to laugh, but it was impossible not to with

the way he was cracking up. Before I knew it, my anger was gone, and I was laughing so hard my ribs hurt.

Tears spurted from the corners of his eyes. "We're both fish in roller skates."

We were making so much noise we moved from the table to the back of the reference section where no one could hear us. We collapsed on the floor to catch our breath.

I was about to tell Tyrus we'd have to keep our giggles under control, or my mom would never let us shelve books anymore when the voice I'd heard before called out.

"Hello, can anyone hear me?"

CHAPTER 6

The Intriguing Puzzle

"Curiouser and curiouser!" cried Alice.

"Did you hear that?" Tyrus asked. "It sounded like a little kid."

I nodded, feeling a strange trembling in my stomach.

"The Alice," the voice called. "Are you there?"

It *did* sound like a kid—scared and lost—but at the same time, it didn't. There was something different about it. Something almost . . . *not human.*

"Are you trying to find your mom?" Tyrus called, getting to his feet and looking between the shelves.

I stood and followed him through the stacks. We ended up at the door of my mom's office without seeing anyone.

"Weird," he said, glancing back at me with a frown.

"Yeah," I muttered. It had to be the same kids I'd heard earlier messing around. Maybe they'd figured out how to talk through the vents. There had to be a reasonable explanation. So why did I keep imagining ghosts or aliens?

He peeked through the door. I knew he'd find the office empty since my mom was still at the front desk, so I nearly jumped when he exclaimed, "Wow! Check that out."

I pushed past him, looking around, but everything looked like it had the last time I'd been in the office.

"It's not usually this messy," I started before shaking my head. Who was I kidding? Her desk—and our house—always looked like that.

"My mom's amazing when it comes to books and trivia, but she doesn't like to clean, and she's not a great cook." Not that I held it against her—*much*. We got enough to eat. It would just be nice to occasionally have a meal where they didn't ask you if you wanted fries or onion rings with it.

But Tyrus wasn't looking at the mess, he was sifting through a stack of my mom's books. "I had no idea there were so many biographies about him."

I saw the picture on one of the covers he was examining and rolled my eyes. Charles Dodgson, aka Lewis Carroll.

"Do you know who this is?" Tyrus asked, holding up a book.

"I should," I muttered. "I'm his great-great-great-grandniece." I'd been told I resembled the pensive, dark-eyed man, but I didn't think we were anything alike.

I might as well have told Tyrus I was secretly Wonder Woman. His jaw dropped open like it was on a hinge. He lowered the book to the desk. "You're related to the author of *Alice's Adventures in Wonderland*?"

"And a bunch of other stuff." Being related to Lewis Carroll was another thing I preferred people didn't know about me. It would have been okay by itself—maybe even a little bit cool—but when people found out I was a descendant of one of the best-known authors in the world, it made it even worse to have them discover that I hated reading.

Tyrus pulled out book after book, sorting them into piles. "These are about his personal life. These are about his novels. This one is about his puzzles. This is about his writing."

"Someone please answer me," the strange kid's voice called out.

Tyrus and I both spun around. It sounded like the voice had come from near the floor.

"Hello?" I said, looking under a chair, but all I saw was a cardboard packing box my mom had probably brought from home.

"Maybe they're outside the building," Tyrus suggested, pressing his ear to the wall. Something rattled by his feet, and he reached down to pick up a package. It was wrapped in brown paper that looked brittle around the edges, and instead of tape, it was secured with fraying twine.

"Where did you get that?" I asked. For a split second, I had the crazy idea the voice had been coming from the package.

"This looks old. We probably shouldn't mess with it."

But as Tyrus set it on the desk, the twine snapped, and the paper slid away revealing a wooden chest. It was about the size of a shoebox with decorations carved into the sides and bottom. Sticking out from the top were five metal wheels, placed side by side like on a bike's combination lock. Except instead of numbers on the wheels, there were letters. They were

currently turned so that R-Y-V-E and a letter I couldn't decipher were showing.

On the left side of the wheels, a picture of a girl was engraved into the wood. On the right was a heart. Above the
wheels, the letters DODO were carved in small, neat print. I
tried opening the chest, but it was locked.

"What does D.O.D.O. stand for?" I asked.

"'Dodo,'" Tyrus said. "It was a nickname Charles Dodgson
got in school because he had a stutter and had a hard time saying his last name."

"How do you know that? You aren't even related to him."

"He's kind of a hero of mine," Tyrus said. "I've read the
Alice books probably twenty times." His face paled. "You
don't think this could actually have belonged to him, do you?
It looks old enough."

I laughed. "If it was, it would be in a museum not a moving box. It's probably a reproduction my mom bought somewhere. It's exactly the kind of souvenir she likes to pick up
when she goes to library conferences."

"What do you think's inside?" Tyrus asked.

"Paper clips or index cards." Those were the kinds of things
my mom collected. But what if it wasn't? If this chest really
was old, there could be something valuable inside. I touched
the metal wheels. "You probably have to spell something to
unlock it."

Tyrus frowned. "It would have to be a five-letter word,
since there are five wheels."

"Obviously." I pointed to the picture engraved on the
right. "How do you spell 'heart'?"

Tyrus looked at me like I was an idiot.

I balled up a fist and pointed it toward his nose. "Dyslexia, remember?"

"Oh, right. Sorry. H-e-a-r-t."

I waved at him to set the letters. Just looking at them made me feel like I was going to heave the Pop-Tarts I'd eaten for breakfast.

He turned the wheels one at a time, and when he'd finished spelling the word, I tried the box. It was still locked.

"The other one looks like a girl. But I know that word. 'Girl' only has four letters."

"What about 'Alice'?" he said. "Like from *Alice in Wonderland*? That has five letters." He set the wheels to spell "Alice," and when he finished moving the last wheel into place, a soft *click* sounded from inside the chest.

"That's it!" I yelled. I tried the chest, sure it would open, but it was still locked. I yanked harder on the lid. It wouldn't budge. "I heard something."

"Me too," Tyrus said.

I studied the wheels, trying to imagine them as a logic problem. "Alice" appeared to be part of the solution, but not the *whole* solution. What if it wasn't just one word but several? A sort of alphabetical equation. Something tugged at my brain.

"Did you say one of the Lewis Carroll books was about puzzles?"

Tyrus looked through the stack and found a book with a couple of math problems pictured on the cover. "Got it," he said, flipping through the pages. "What am I looking for?"

I searched my memories. When I was little, before my

mom realized I had dyslexia, she spent a week trying to teach me a kind of word puzzle. I could swear she'd said Charles Dodgson had invented it. For some reason looking at the wheels and the pictures on each side reminded me of what she'd been trying to show me.

"Word letters?" That was close, but not quite right. What had she said? Something about climbing from one word to another like the steps of a—

"Ladder!" I shouted. "Word Ladders. See if there's anything like that in the book."

"Yes." Tyrus turned to the right chapter and read aloud. "'Word Ladders are a type of word puzzle either invented or made popular by Charles Dodgson. The goal is to change one word to another by switching only one letter at a time. Like 'cat' to 'dog.' 'Cat' to 'cot' to 'cog' to 'dog.'" He grinned. "That's really cool. But what does it have to do with the chest?"

"It's the combination," I said. "We have to change one five-letter word to another." I looked at the pictures and saw it at once. "We have to change 'Alice' to 'heart.'"

He ran his tongue across his top lip, studying the wheels. "Is that even possible?"

"Don't ask me," I said. "You're the word expert."

"Okay, right." He spun the wheels, then reset them to "Alice." "Let's see, if I change the *c* to a *k*, we change 'Alice' to 'alike.'" He turned the wheel, but nothing happened. He looked up. "It didn't click. Does that mean I got it wrong?"

I shrugged. "What can you change 'alike' to?"

He furrowed his brow, muttering under his breath. After a few minutes, he shook his head. "I can switch 'alike' into 'alive,' but that doesn't get us anywhere since we're changing the same letter."

"Try again." I clenched my fists, feeling helpless.

Tyrus started over, this time getting much further. He changed "Alice" to "slice," "slice" to "slide," "slide" to "glide," "glide" to "glade." After a few more minutes, he shook his head. "I don't think this is getting us any closer to 'heart.'"

I tugged at my hair. "If only this was a math problem, I could solve it in no time."

Tyrus looked up. "Could we make it a math problem?" He grabbed a blank piece of paper from his backpack. I watched over his shoulder as he wrote down the alphabet and then put numbers under each letter from one to twenty-six.

A	B	C	D	E	F	G	H	I	J	K	L
1	2	3	4	5	6	7	8	9	10	11	12

M	N	O	P	Q	R	S	T	U	V	W
13	14	15	16	17	18	19	20	21	22	23

X	Y	Z
24	25	26

"See here," he said. "If we assign a number to each letter, A-L-I-C-E is 1-12-9-3-5. H-E-A-R-T is 8-5-1-18-20. We just have to figure out how to get from one to the other."

"It won't work." I sighed. "Numbers don't have to spell actual words, so there's no way of knowing if my changes would even work."

He was almost bouncing on his chair. "I know, but I can help with that part. I'll tell you the words I can make, and you tell me if I'm going in the right direction. I'll handle the spelling and you handle the logic."

Could that work? Words were his thing. Math and logic were mine. Maybe together we could figure it out. I bit the inside of my cheek then nodded. "Okay, let's go back to 'Alice' and start again."

It took us almost an hour and several restarts, but eventually we figured it out.

ALICE

SLICE

SLICK

STICK

STACK

STARK

STARS

SEARS

HEARS

"That's it!" Tyrus crowed. "All we have to do is change the *s* to a *t* and 'hears' becomes 'heart.' Do you want to turn the wheel? It was your logic that got us here."

I shook my head. "I couldn't have done it without you. Go ahead."

With one shaking finger, Tyrus turned the last wheel. As the *s* changed to a *t*, we waited, neither of us daring to breathe. For a moment there was silence. Then the chest clicked once, twice, three times, four. On the last click, the lid popped slightly open.

Tyrus yanked his hand away like he'd been burned. "You open it," he said. "I can't."

Imagining gold or gems, or an ancient treasure map—the kind of things you found in locked chests—I lifted the lid.

"Great," I muttered when I saw what was inside. "More books."

I glanced at Tyrus, expecting him to be as disappointed as I was, but his mouth was hanging so far open it looked like a doctor had told him to say "Ah."

"H-how," he stammered, then tried again. "H-how many are there?"

I counted the leather-bound books stacked one on top of the other. There were no words or pictures on the covers—just the initials CD. "Four," I said, wishing it had been treasure.

Tyrus clutched his fingers in his hair. "Charles Dodgson kept diaries his whole life. Scholars have studied them for years. But, after his death, his family discovered four of them were missing. I think we found the lost Wonderland diaries."

CHAPTER 7

The Rabbit Hole

*"Well!" thought Alice to herself. "After such a fall as this,
I shall think nothing of tumbling downstairs!"*

"Diaries, huh?"

I still didn't believe they were real, but what if they were?
When we'd sold our old house, the movers had taken a bunch
of boxes from the attic that had been there clear back when
my grandmother was a little girl. Was it possible that we'd had
Lewis Carroll's missing diaries all this time?

"What's inside them?" I asked.

"No one knows," Tyrus said, his voice filled with awe. "It's
the greatest mystery of his life."

That sounded overly dramatic, but I was intrigued. I lifted
the first book off the stack, and Tyrus gasped, but he didn't
stop me. Instead he hurried to my side as I opened the cover.

Reading gets harder for me when I'm tired or stressed, and
handwriting can be especially difficult, but this was impossible.
I scanned the page, searching for any words I could make out,
but it all looked like a mash-up of random symbols.

"What does it say?" I asked Tyrus, the excitement of opening the chest gone.

He shook his head.

I frowned. "You aren't going to tell me?"

"I . . . I can't read it," Tyrus said.

Was he making fun of me? Of my dyslexia? When I looked at his face, it was clear he wasn't.

He reached toward the book as if wanting to make sure it was real. "It's just a bunch of lines and dots."

His description of trying to read the page was so close to how I felt every time I opened a book that for a split second I felt a moment of shock. Then I looked more closely at the page.

It wasn't just that I didn't recognize any words. I didn't recognize a single letter. Not the ones I struggled with or the easy ones. He was right. The entire page was nothing but rows of lines and dots.

I turned the first page, then another, and another. Occasionally I recognized a math symbol, but the rest of it looked like someone had randomly splashed ink onto paper.

Tyrus dropped to a chair. "It's all nonsense. You were right. These can't be Charles Dodgson's diaries."

"Guess so," I said, starting to put the book back in the chest.

Then I paused. Something about the symbols looked familiar.

Because it was almost impossible for me to sound out words letter by letter, I—like many people with dyslexia—learned to read by recognizing individual words by their shapes. Patterns were key to deciphering what I was reading. I thought I recognized a pattern here too, but it wasn't like anything I'd seen before.

I flipped from page to page, growing more certain there was something there. "It looks almost like a code."

"Of course!" Tyrus grabbed another of my mom's books and turned to a picture of a rectangular card with sixteen square holes punched through it in two rows of eight. "It's called a nyctograph."

I narrowed my eyes. "Never heard of it."

"Charles Dodgson invented it to take notes in the dark," Tyrus said. "Different marks in different places represent different letters."

He pointed to the first two symbols.

$$\circ_{\boldsymbol{\cdot}} \quad \boldsymbol{\rho \colon}$$

"The circle with a dot below and to the right of it stands for the letter *A*. The next one is *B*. It's like a—"

"A code." I compared the markings in the book to the symbols on the page, recognizing them at once.

"Why go to the trouble?" Tyrus asked, leaning over my shoulder. "None of his other diaries were written in code."

For once my dyslexia seemed to help me. I'd spent my whole life trying to recognize patterns, so deciphering these was easy. Running my finger along the page, I found myself understanding the symbols faster than I ever had in my life. Was reading this easy to other people?

"Maybe he didn't want anyone to know what he was working on," I said. "Maybe that's why he hid these."

Tyrus squinted at the page as if that would help him understand it. "What was he working on?"

My eyes jumped from line to line. "These are equations. Why would a fantasy author write about math?"

"He was a college math professor," Tyrus said. "He wrote books about it."

"What kinds of books?" I asked, turning page after page.

"Let's see." He flipped through the stack on the desk. "He actually published quite a few. We have *A Syllabus of Plane and Algebraical Geometry*, 1860. Two books of Euclid, also 1860, and *The Formulae of Plane Trigonometry*, 1861."

"Planes," I repeated, nodding. "Is there anything about parallels?"

"Not that I see. Oh, wait, here we go. *Curiosia Mathematica, Part I: A New Theory of Parallels.*"

"That's it!" I slapped my palm on the desk. "It sounds crazy, but I think he was researching parallel universes."

"Like Dr. Strange," Tyrus said. "Or—"

I held up a finger. "If you say *A Wrinkle in Time*, I'm going to hit you over the head with a diary." Math equations filled my brain as I reviewed the earlier passages. The theories were way over my head, but I had a suspicion about what he was proposing. "I think he was trying to open a doorway between our world and a parallel world."

Tyrus reached into the chest. "Does it say anything about bottles?"

I looked up from the book to see him holding a green bottle no bigger than his pinky finger. "Where did you get that?"

"It was inside the chest with the other three diaries." He turned the bottle around to read the label. "'Drink in Case of Emergency.' Cool! It's like something out of one of his books."

"You aren't going to drink that, are you?" I asked as he pulled a tiny cork out of the bottle and lifted it toward his face. "It's got to be over a hundred years old."

He rolled his eyes. "I just wanted to see what was inside. It smells like bubble gum and something else. Popcorn, maybe."

"Yummy." I wrinkled my nose. "Whatever it was, I'm sure it's gone bad."

"I wasn't going to—" Tyrus raised an eyebrow and stared down at the desk. "What's that?"

The diary page I'd been reading rippled as if a breeze had blown across it. The symbols on the page blurred and began to move.

I rubbed my eyes, thinking they must have been tired from all the focusing, but Tyrus saw it too. He tilted his head. "How's it doing that?"

The center of the page bulged and then ripped neatly down the middle with a soft zipping sound. A puff of gray rose from the opening. At first, I thought it was smoke, but as more of the darkness spilled out, I realized the growing cloud was actually made up of letters floating out of the page and into the air. Not Charles Dodgson's code, but real letters.

The smoke swirled, and the letters formed words. My stomach clenched, and I tried to look away, but my head refused to move—as if the words had somehow hypnotized me.

"Are you seeing this?" I asked.

"I'd like to say no, but . . . " Tyrus nodded, his mouth open.

Sweat beaded my forehead as random words bobbed and danced in front of me. It was my worst nightmare coming to life before my eyes.

"Stop!" I gagged as the words joined into sentences I couldn't read. This couldn't be real. I raised my hands to cover my eyes. Instead, my fingers reached out to the darkness.

"What are you doing?" Tyrus yelled. "Get away from that." His voice sounded far away, like he was in another room.

I stared, transfixed by the fog of words, and one of them became clearer than the others: *CLAW.*

Instantly the smoke morphed into a curved black blade. The claw ripped the book open wider.

"Close it!" Tyrus shouted from a different building, a different city, a different . . . *world*?

The trance broken, I reached for the cover of the book to slam it shut as a huge paw burst from the page and wrapped around my wrist, gleaming claws clicking against each other.

"At last!" an inhuman voice hissed. "I've found the doorway."

Screaming, I tried to pull away, but the hand gripping my wrist was too strong.

"Help!" I yelled.

Tyrus grabbed me around the waist and pulled me back as the hole in the page grew, nearly engulfing the book. I could see an arm covered with dark, wiry fur.

The hole rippled, growing as big as a basketball. It rippled again, nearly covering the entire desk. A shadowy face with hungry green eyes and a fang-filled muzzle grinned wickedly out at me. Ice-cold claws pressed against the skin of my wrist, and I realized whatever was in that hole wasn't trying to pull me into the book. It was trying to pull itself out.

My chest tightened until I could barely breathe. My head began to spin. I was going to faint.

"Drink this," Tyrus yelled, pressing something against my lips.

I looked down to see him holding the bottle to my mouth. "Don't know what it is," I said, my tongue thick and my words slurring.

"Doesn't matter," Tyrus shouted. "This is an emergency!"

Liquid spilled over my lips, and a bubblegum taste filled my mouth. Fire burned the back of my throat.

The room tilted, and it seemed as if the world had turned inside out, as if I was now in the book, staring out at my mother's office from an impossible angle.

"No!" howled a voice somewhere below me. "Get out of the way. Let me through."

I reached for the opening, grasping at the edges of the desk, but I could feel myself slipping. My finger slid from the edge of the desk, and the pages of the diary closed around my arm. Just before the diary shut completely, I saw Tyrus put the green bottle to his lips.

I felt myself falling.

CHAPTER 8

The Surprise Entrance

*Her first idea was that she had somehow
fallen into the sea, "and in that case I can
go back by railway," she said to herself.*

Roderick Entwhistle III had an important engagement in court.

An unfortunate knave had crossed the queen, in some small way. Tripping over her footstool or misplacing her tarts was a typical offense, but with all the new rules, quarantines, and curfews, it could be anything.

Whatever the charge, that dratted Prosecutor Fury was trying to convict the lad. If the cur had his way, everyone in the kingdom would be in prison—or have their heads lopped off.

Fortunately, Roderick, like his father and his grandfather before him, was here to defend the weak and protect the poor. It wasn't a glamourous job, and it certainly didn't pay well, but it was the family business, and he would carry it on.

He pulled a gold watch from the pocket of his suit—a dapper charcoal with just a hint of pinstripe in the weaving—and held it up before his dark glasses. He tilted his head left then right, before finally coughing.

"It appears to me that it is nearly . . ."

Odo, a blubbery fellow with a full mustache, turned from the front seat of the water carriage where he was steering while simultaneously playing a game of solitaire.

"Quarter of eight, Barrister Entwhistle."

"I see that," Roderick said, putting away his watch.

Odo grinned, revealing two white tusks that curved down to well below his triple chin. "Plenty of time to make it to the trial by eleven o'clock. We could perhaps stop by that tea shop you enjoy so much for a cheese Danish—if it's still open with all this hubbub."

"Cheese." Roderick's stomach rumbled. The three carefully groomed whiskers on either side of his long aristocratic nose trembled. His glorious pink rope of a tail flicked out from the back of his suit and rubbed his belly. "A splendid idea. I'm glad I thought of it."

Removing his bowler hat, he let the sun beat down on his silver-haired head. "It appears to me that the weather is . . ."

"Clear and sunny," Odo replied.

"Quite a view. And the Arithma Sea . . ."

"Calm, and rather more purple than normal." The walrus flicked his reins, and the orange-and-yellow seahorses pulling the carriage whinnied. To their left, a blue-striped 7 leaped from the waves, flicked its fins in the sunlight, and splashed back into the water.

Roderick lifted a brass telescope from the seat beside him

and pointed it directly at Odo's back. "I observe that we are staying well away from Ornith."

"A little to the left," Odo said, and the mouse shifted his telescope until it pointed at a village on the edge of an egg-shaped bay. Nests perched high in the trees, peeked out from holes in the ground, and even crowded the sandy beach where long-legged figures patrolled the shore. "We won't travel any-where near the Bay of Avem."

"I should hope not." Roderick shivered. "Distasteful sto-ries about that lot lately." His delicate pink hands gripped the telescope. "Did I ever tell you that my grandfather, Roderick Entwhistle the First, nearly drowned in that bay?"

Odo tugged one end of his mustache with his flipper. "Once. Or perhaps two-dozen times. It's hard to keep track."

"It was before things started to change. The weather was perfect, just like today."

Overhead in the sky, which had been empty a moment be-fore, a single cloud appeared. Small and round, it swirled in an unusual way. Odo craned his thick neck to get a better look.

"The ocean was smooth as a wheel of cheddar," Roderick continued.

Odo tugged on the left rein, steering the water carriage away from the disturbance, but the cloud seemed to follow them. It was growing larger, the sky around it turning from its usual shade of pink to a disturbing greenish-gray. A stiff breeze rose from out of nowhere, and choppy waves lapped against the side of the carriage.

"Careful there," Roderick called, tucking his tail under his suit coat to keep it from getting wet.

Odo sucked his rubbery gray lips against his tusks. "Barrister, I think . . ."

"Not now," Roderick said, twitching his whiskers in annoyance. He hated to be interrupted in the middle of a tale. "As I was saying, the sky was clear and the sea was calm when, without any warning, a hole opened in the sky, and out dropped a—"

At that moment, the cloud, which had begun spinning quite violently, appeared to tear itself open. A boom like a hundred cannons shook the air, and a great wave smashed into the side of the water carriage, tilting it to one side. The seahorses spit out their bits and disappeared into the depths.

Roderick spun around, his small round ears tucking tightly to the sides of his head. His dark glasses slipped down on his nose, revealing beady eyes that had once been pink but were now a pearly white. "Do I see a . . ."

"A boy and a girl falling out of a hole in the sky," Odo said matter-of-factly before another wave hit and he was thrown from his seat into the water.

Barrister Entwhistle gripped the side of the carriage with both hands. His clawed feet scrabbled at the deck. He might have managed to hang on if a long green tentacle hadn't popped out of the dark-purple waves at that moment, wrapped itself around the water carriage, and flung the barrister—bowler hat and all—out over the sea.

"Not again!" he cried just before he disappeared under the surface.

• • •

Celia fell,
　　　and fell,
　　　　　and f
　　　　　　　e
　　　　　　　　l
　　　　　　　　　l.

At first it was terrifying! Then it was horrifying! Then it was confusing? Then it was terrifying again! Eventually it was just annoying.

She tried to scream, but the sound was sucked from her mouth in a speech bubble—like something from a comic book—and swirled away before it could reach her ears.

After making a few attempts, she realized it was pointless to scream when her voice only made an annoying

before disappearing above her head.

The tunnel she was falling through twisted and turned like the world's longest waterslide. All the colors of the rainbow—along with a few she didn't recognize—swirled along the walls like spilled paint. A smell in the air made her stomach rumble, and she recognized it as buttered popcorn. A moment later it changed to the salty tang of the beach, then freshly cut grass.

Occasionally she could see Tyrus falling above her. She tried calling out to him, hoping he could read her words as they flew by in their speech bubbles. She thought he might have tried to call to her, but she couldn't tell for sure.

With no wind racing past her face and no ground rushing to meet her, she wouldn't have known she was falling if she hadn't occasionally shot past a random object. First it was a few of the books from the library, then it was a pair of her mother's low-heeled dress shoes, followed by a handbag she didn't use anymore.

The oddest by far though was when

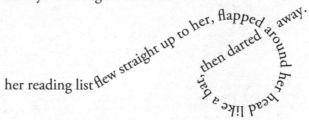

her reading list flew straight up to her, flapped away, then darted around her head like a bat.

"At least I'm not being attacked by that smoke beast," she said, the words scrolling neatly out of her mouth into another bubble. She looked down to make sure the cloud of words wasn't nearby, but other than a few grease-stained bags, a hamburger wrapper, and several french fries playing tag with each other, she didn't see anything in the area.

This couldn't be real, of course. It was all a terrible nightmare of books, her mother, and dyslexia. Wasn't there some psychologist who said you dreamed about the things that scared you most? Or was that a scene from a movie?

The question was, how long ago had the dream started? Had she and Tyrus actually opened a treasure chest containing Lewis Carroll's missing diaries? Had she been attacked by a word monster and saved by a bottle that seemed straight out of *Alice in Wonderland*? Her reading list flying like a bird seemed far more believable.

"There must have been an earthquake," she told herself. "California is known for those. I was knocked out by falling books and only thought I heard the weird voice. The chest, and diaries, and whatever that terrible creature was that climbed out of the pages were all a dream."

She should close her eyes and wait until this delusion, or dream, or manifestation faded. Eventually she would wake up or her mother would come. Or Tyrus would find her and . . .

But was *he* real? Or was he part of the dream as well? Leave it to her to have a dream where she finally made a friend only to discover her greatest fear was his greatest love.

She looked up at Tyrus and waved. He waved down, looking as weirded out as she felt.

What if it wasn't a dream? What if she really had opened a doorway to a parallel universe? That meant Tyrus was here too, and it was her fault. Didn't she owe it to him to try to get them out? She didn't see any doors or windows in the strange rainbow tunnel. She patted her pockets for her phone, but she must have left it on the desk in her mother's office.

Maybe they could get out the same way they'd come in. She tried to remember the math she'd read in the diaries, but the complex equations were already fading from her mind. She raised her head to see if Tyrus still had the bottle. Speech balloons shot out of his mouth like plumes of steam on a cold day, but his hands were empty.

She could wait for the fall to end, but generally things that plummeted through the air for an extended period of time didn't fare well when they eventually hit the ground.

She'd finally decided to grab at whatever flew past next,

even if it ripped her arm out of its socket, when she was spit out of the tunnel into a swirling red sky. She barely had time to see what looked like a walrus and a giant rat getting thrown out of a fancy boat-like vessel before she plunged feetfirst into a misty purple ocean.

A moment later, Tyrus splashed down beside her.

She kicked her feet and paddled her hands, trying to swim to the surface. Tyrus did the same. But the water held both of them in place like a giant vat of grape Jell-O. With her lungs burning from holding her breath, Celia finally gasped. She expected water to fill her mouth, but instead, she sucked in cool air with a faint taste of mint.

"I can breathe," she said, forgetting she was underwater. Her words came out sounding slightly bubbly but perfectly audible.

"Me too," Tyrus said, floating beside her.

A school of brightly colored fish swam in their direction and began bobbing curiously around them. Except the fish weren't really fish. They had fins and tails like fish. They swam like fish. But they looked like . . . *numbers*. There was a bright orange 4 with a billowing goldfish tail, a spotted 6 with glowing eyes, and clouds of tiny 2s that darted about together.

"Help!" she shouted, trying desperately to swim to the surface.

"Perhaps I can be of some assistance," a deep voice crooned from below.

Celia stared into the depths of the water. She couldn't make out anything but a bed of rhythmically swaying seaweed.

"Who's there?" Tyrus called.

Slowly, a dark shape glided out of the shadows. Celia gasped. It was a crocodile at least ten feet long, possibly even twelve. And he was wearing a golden monocle, a mortarboard, and what looked like a corduroy jacket.

Cracking open a set of jaws filled with long, sharp teeth, he cleared his throat and spoke.

> *Floating in my delta*
> *like imaginary cod,*
> *I see by your expressions*
> *that you find my figure odd.*
> *You have only seen a fraction*
> *of the grin I open wide.*
> *I am absolutely certain,*
> *we can narrow our divide*
> *Your subtraction's my addition;*
> *we can multiply our fun.*
> *Let us modify our ratio,*
> *as three turn into one.*

"This is a dream," Celia said. "A really weird, really bad dream brought on by being around too many books." She looked at Tyrus. "None of this is real. Not even you."

Tyrus took off his glasses and tried to dry them on his shirt before realizing it wasn't helping. "Unfortunately, I think it *is* real."

"How?" Celia demanded. "Where are we?"

Tyrus grimaced. "I'm pretty sure we're in Wonderland."

CHAPTER 9

The Arithma Sea

"Let me see: four times five is twelve, and four times
six is thirteen, and four times seven is—oh dear!
I shall never get to twenty at that rate!"

"Wonderland's not a real place," Celia said, shooing away a faintly glowing 3 that was nibbling on her left ear.

Tyrus held out one hand, and a sinuous 8 looped itself around his fingers like an eel. "We got sucked into Lewis Carroll's diary after drinking from a tiny bottle. We're in a purple ocean with swimming numbers while a talking alligator threatens to eat us—*in verse*. I mean, I don't remember anything like this from *Alice's Adventures in Wonderland,* but you have to admit it doesn't seem like anything that could happen in *our* world."

"Crocodile," the crocodile corrected. "It's a common misappropriation. Alligators have U-shaped snouts and prefer fresh water, while crocodiles, such as myself, have lovely V-shaped noses and congregate in salt water."

"Misidentification," Tyrus said.

The crocodile raised its head without upsetting the mortarboard. "Pardon?"

Tyrus paddled around to face the crocodile. "You said confusing crocodiles and alligators was a common misappropriation. What you meant to say was that it was a common misidentification."

"A linguist!" The crocodile chortled. "You belong in Sesquipedalian Swamp, not the Arithma Sea."

"'Sesquipedalian' is another word for 'a really long word,'" Tyrus whispered to Celia. "Which is ironic, considering 'sesquipedalian' is a really long word itself."

"I don't care what it means," Celia shouted, startling the 2s. "If this is real, we have to get out of here before that poetry-spouting reptile swims up and eats us."

The crocodile swished his tail, sending a 1 tumbling end over end. "My dearest children, I have no intention of swimming to you. It is far too much work and would be a severe breach of etiquette. There are strict rules of protocol here. If you wish to join me for supper, you must come down."

"Fat chance," Celia said.

Tyrus nudged her. "Do you see what the fish—er, numbers—are doing?"

Celia turned to see the finned numbers performing what looked like a complicated dance. A 2 and a 3 swirled through the water as the other numbers cleared away. The 2 nudged the 3 to its left, and they both floated in place directly in front of Celia and Tyrus.

Something that looked like a four-pointed starfish swam between the 2 and the 3—two of its limbs pointing up and

down, the other two left and right. Slowly it rotated until its arms pointed diagonally.

All around them, the other numbers paused what they were doing and turned to watch.

Tyrus and Celia looked at the numbers in front of them, then at each other.

"Well?" the crocodile said, tapping its claws on the seabed. "I don't have all day."

Celia narrowed her eyes. "I think he wants us to solve a math problem. The starfish looks like a multiplication sign—two times three."

"That's easy," Tyrus blurted. "I'm no math genius like you, but even I know two times three is six."

All the numbers in the bay screamed as Tyrus and Celia sank deeper in the purple water.

The crocodile grinned.

I see my little salmon,
  your eyes so filled with terror.
Come and let me comfort you.
  Your answer is in error.

"What's he talking about?" Tyrus demanded. "The answer is definitely six."

The fish screamed again as Celia and Tyrus dropped lower.

"I don't get it," Tyrus said. "Is math different here? Two times three is the same as three plus three, which equals—"

"Shh," Celia hissed, noticing the eager way the crocodile was watching them. "If you say it again, we might sink deeper."

"But I gave the right answer." Tyrus swung his fist, scattering a school of large-mouthed 9s.

"Math isn't always as easy as it looks," Celia said. "It could be a trick question."

"A trick question?" The crocodile scoffed. "I would never sink to such a thing. But *you* might."

Celia chewed the inside of her cheek. The problem seemed straightforward, but there had to be something missing. Looking closer, she noticed a tiny bubble floating just to the left of the 3.

"Could you possibly move that bubble?" she asked the 3. The 3 shook its head.

"Here, here," the crocodile called. "Questioning the participants is against the rules of the game. A clear breach of etiquette."

"Says who?" Tyrus called back. "Show us a rule book."

The crocodile burped, and a 7 with a chewed fin escaped from between his teeth. "I may have eaten it."

"Then be quiet, you bully, and let us do it our way," Celia said.

The crocodile looked wounded but closed his mouth.

Celia leaned toward the bubble. "You're a decimal, aren't you?"

The bubble bounced up and down excitedly, and Celia grinned.

"The problem isn't two times three. It's two times *point* three, which makes the correct answer point six."

Instead of sinking toward the crocodile, Celia and Tyrus floated upward. The numbers around them gave a *blurb, blurb, blurb* of approval while the crocodile roared in frustration.

The 2 and the 3 swam away as a cheerful crab and a pair of 5s took their place. The starfish rotated until it looked like a plus sign while a pair of stick-like 1s lay in parallel above each other, forming an equal sign.

"Five plus . . . *crab* equals five?" Celia read.

Tyrus wrinkled his forehead. "That doesn't make any sense. A crab isn't a number or a math symbol."

Celia thought for a moment before slowly shaking her head. "It's algebra, but instead of solving for X, we're solving for . . . *crab*, I guess. It's weird, but it doesn't make it any harder. If five plus crab equals five, crab has to be zero."

"Lucky guess!" the crocodile howled as Celia and Tyrus floated up again.

"I don't think so," Celia said. "Give us the next question."

The number fishes gave more approving *blurb*s.

"Very well," the crocodile said with a gleam in his eye that Celia didn't like at all. "But no more easy ones."

This time, the starfish floated away and a whole school of numbers spread out around the crab. Once all the fish had taken their places, they formed a series of numbers: 16, 06, 68, 88, the crab, 98.

Tyrus scratched his head. "Another algebra problem?"

"Maybe. I think we still have to solve for the crab," Celia said, "but it isn't any kind of algebra I've ever seen. It's more like pattern matching."

"I'm horrible at matching," Tyrus said. "Whenever I pick out an outfit for picture day at school, my mom always says my pants and shirt don't go together."

"It's not that kind of matching," Celia said. "I think we have to figure out what number is missing in the pattern and plug it in where the crab is. Like two, four, six, eight. Or eleven, twenty-one, thirty-one. Only I don't see any obvious pattern here."

"They all have two digits," Tyrus pointed out.

Celia nodded. "And they're all even numbers. But they don't appear to be in any specific order."

"Ten seconds," the crocodile called out cheerfully.

"Not fair," Tyrus shouted. "You didn't say anything about a time limit."

The crocodile grinned so wide Celia could see to the back of his throat. "As you said, no rule book. Nine, eight, seven, six, five . . ."

Tyrus turned to Celia. "Say something!"

"I don't know the answer," Celia cried.

"Three, two, one . . ."

"Forty-two!" she yelled, saying the first even two-digit number that popped into her head.

The numbers screeched as Celia and Tyrus dropped.

The crocodile grinned, his eyes wide.

> *You* seemed *like smart young halibuts.*
> *I fear it's not the case.*
> *The sum of your equation*
> *Is clearly quite off base.*

Celia eyed the distance between them and the crocodile's gleaming white teeth.

"Let's speed things up," the crocodile said. "I've enjoyed our little game, but all this excitement has made me quite ravenous. Get the next answer right and you go free. Get it wrong and . . ." He licked his chops. "Dinnertime."

"That's a terrible idea," Celia said.

The crocodile winked. "Not from my point of view."

Tyrus looked down. "What did you say?"

"I said it's time to eat." The crocodile thrashed his tail. "I can't wait to have the two of you for dinner."

"No," Tyrus said. "Your *point of view.*" He turned to Celia. "Grab my feet and push them up."

"You want me to help you swim away?" Celia growled.

"Never," Tyrus said. "I may not be a math genius, but sometimes you have to look at things in a new way. Push my feet up while I swing my head down."

Working together, they managed to rotate him until his head was toward the crocodile and his feet were sticking up.

"Aha!" Tyrus cried with a huge grin. "I know the answer."

Celia shook her head. "Did turning you upside down make more blood flow to your brain?"

"No," he said. "But it did let me see the problem from a different point of view." Grabbing Celia's left foot, he tugged her around until they were both floating upside down.

From that angle, the fish no longer looked like 16, 06, 68, 88, the crab, and 98. They now looked like 86, an upside-down crab, 88, 89, 90, and 91.

Seeing it that way, the answer was obvious. "Eighty-seven," they shouted together.

With a massive burble of approval from everyone except the crocodile, Celia and Tyrus bobbed toward the surface.

"I'm going to have to start reading my math books upside down," Tyrus said.

Celia grinned. If they managed to get out of this, she hoped she could bring a few of the numbers home with her. It would be amazing to have an aquarium full of math problems. She looked down at the crocodile. "Sorry—it looks like you'll have to eat alone."

A single golden tear dripped from the corner of the crocodile's eye. "I'll miss the pair of you. I feel like an empty set."

Something huge and dark started swimming toward them. It was hard to determine its exact shape in the murky purple water, but it looked like it had tentacles. As the creature drew nearer, the numbers, and even the crocodile, quickly disappeared.

"What is that?" Tyrus whispered.

"I don't know," Celia said. "And I don't think we want to find out."

They were nearly to the water's surface when the huge rat she'd seen earlier paddled by overhead. Celia quickly reached up and grabbed the end of its tail. "Hang on," she called, taking Tyrus's hand.

"What's got ahold of my tail?" the rat cried, looking down. "It's not one of those horrible creatures of the deep, is it?"

"No," Celia called back. "It's just my friend and me. Could you possibly tow us to land?"

"Absolutely not," the rat howled, still paddling its feet. "I'm a barrister, not a boat." It lashed its tail left and right, trying to shake her loose, but she clamped her fist tightly around it.

"I'm sorry," she said. "I promise I'll let go as soon as we get to shore."

"Promises are no more reliable than pancakes!" the rat shouted. "Odo, I am being assaulted by . . ."

"A bedraggled-looking boy and girl," bellowed a voice from behind them. "They appear to be the two who fell from the sky."

"It looks that way to me," the rat said.

"Keep swimming straight, and you'll reach land soon," said the voice, which apparently belonged to someone or something named Odo.

"Yes, yes, I see," the rat called, adjusting its black glasses.

After several more minutes of being towed, Celia felt her feet touch ground. When she stood, the sea came to just above her waist. Tyrus popped out of the water beside her.

"Thanks for the ride," Celia called after the rat, who had nearly reached shore. "I'm sorry for the inconvenience."

"There are laws against this sort of thing—sea-piracy, unlawful boarding, rodent-napping," the rat snarled, wrapping its tail protectively around itself. "Wait until the queen hears what you've done. She'll throw you both in the dungeon for the rest of your lives."

"The queen won't need to," said a tall gray bird with a stern-looking face. It waded through the water toward them on legs as tall as stilts. "I'm arresting you all on behalf of the Avian Constabulary Enforcement for trespassing, disturbing the peace, egg encroachment, and general nuisance-making."

CHAPTER 10

The Mathematical Defense

*"Mine is a long and a sad tale!" said
the Mouse, turning to Alice, and sighing.*

Celia pressed her face between the bars in front of her, trying to get a better view of what was happening in the village outside.

"Watch where you're stepping, you big galoot," snapped a gruff voice from below.

She looked down to see a pair of fiddler crabs, their dark eyes waving to and fro on thin stalks. "I'm so sorry," she said, moving her foot.

The smaller of the crabs brandished his right pincer, which was much larger than his left, in a menacing fashion. "You think because you have feet instead of claws you can step on whoever you want?"

"Give her a break," said the crab's companion. "Her eyes are stuck in their sockets. You can't expect her to see as well as we do."

The first crab paid no attention. "Maybe you have carapace

issues. Crabs have shells instead of skin so it's okay to tromp on us with your enormous feet, right?"

Celia glanced down at her feet, which did seem quite large compared to the crabs. "It's not either of those things. You're so small I didn't see you at first."

"Small!" the crab cried. "Did you hear that? She thinks she's better than us because she's big."

"Why do you have to take offense at everything?" the second crab asked. "Humans have it bad enough. Only two legs, dangly sausages on their hands instead of fierce weapons. Why, they don't even have antennas." She waved her own claws at Celia. "Forgive him, he can be a bit—"

"Crabby?" Tyrus suggested.

"Rude!" the crab huffed, drawing her eyestalks back into her head. "I was going to say insensitive. I suppose to you humans all crustaceans are crabby." She took her companion's large claw. "Let's go join the oysters. At least they're only a little shellfish."

"That went well," Tyrus muttered.

In the two hours since their arrest, Celia and Tyrus had been locked in a domed cell that looked suspiciously like a birdcage along with the rat, the fiddler crabs, a walrus who was playing solitaire on his large belly, and several oysters who ignored the rest of the group.

Celia wrung a stream of purple-tinted water out of the hem of her wet shirt. "We have to get out of here. I don't even know what we've been arrested for."

"Trespassing," said the walrus, looking up from his game. "It's a serious charge."

"We didn't mean to trespass," Celia said. "We were only trying to keep from drowning." If this really was Wonderland, she wanted no part of it.

The walrus moved the queen of diamonds onto the king of clubs, added a jack, then flipped through his cards—clearly cheating—until he found a ten of hearts. "You're new here."

"How did you know?" Tyrus asked.

"Your crab etiquette is lacking, you canceled your dinner engagement with Gottfried the crocodile, and your taste in swimwear is questionable at best. That, and I saw you fall out of the sky."

Celia sat beside the walrus. "It was my fault. But it was an accident. Do you have any idea how we can get home?"

The walrus studied his cards for a moment. "One of you wouldn't be The Alice, by any chance, would you?"

Tyrus shook his head. "I'm Tyrus, and she's Celia."

"Shame," the walrus said. "Before you go anywhere, you will have to deal with the charges here. The Avians have always had a strict immigration policy—no bills or beaks, no admittance. But since the attacks, things have gotten much worse."

"What attacks?" Celia asked.

The walrus studied the nearby oysters, a hungry look in his eyes, before flipping his tail. "I'm afraid you'll see for yourselves soon enough. Word is that The Alice is going to save us, but if she doesn't get here soon, there might not be anyone left to save."

Tyrus leaned toward Celia and whispered, "You think he's talking about the Alice from the books?"

"How could he be?" Celia asked. "Alice wasn't a real person."

"Well, actually, she was—she was a friend of Charles Dodgson, and—"

"Not now, Tyrus," Celia snapped. "We've got to get out of here."

Tyrus thought for a moment. "Maybe you could pretend to be her."

"And then what? Offer to save them from some mysterious attacks?" She shook her head. "Not hardly."

The walrus sorted through his cards again, twitching his bushy mustache.

"Is *this* what you're looking for?" Tyrus asked, pulling a nine of spades from between a roll of the walrus's blubber.

"Thought I felt something tickling." The walrus held out a flipper. "I'm Odo. I was taking my employer, Roderick Entwhistle the Third, to defend a client at trial when we were dumped into the drink."

Celia stared at the gray-furred figure with the dark glasses. "The rat is a lawyer?"

Roderick turned sharply in their direction, pink ears twitching beneath his hat. "*What* did you call me?"

"Here we go again," Tyrus said.

Celia stepped toward the large rodent, careful not to step on the crabs or oysters. "I'm sorry if I misspoke. If you don't mind, could you tell me which part I got wrong? People make a lot of lawyer jokes, which I promise I wasn't. On the other hand, calling a lawyer a rat could be giving lawyers a bad name."

"Lawyers give *rats* bad names," said one of the oysters. "I know a lawyer with a pet rat he named Ima Stinkface."

"Stinkface," snickered the oyster next to it. "Classic."

"You aren't helping," Celia said to them.

"Who asked you?" the oysters jeered, snapping their shells shut and turning in the other direction.

"I am neither a lawyer nor a rat," Roderick said. "I am a third-generation barrister, and a proud member of Animalia, Chordata, Mammalia, Rodentia, Muridae, Murinae, Mus, Musculus—also known as a mouse." He shook his finger in Tyrus's face. "I find you to be quite impertinent, young lady."

"I'm over here," Celia said.

"Of course, you are." The mouse turned so his dark glasses faced her.

"I don't think he can see," Tyrus whispered.

"Nonsense," Roderick snapped. "I have perfect vision just like my father before me and his father before him. The two of you look . . ."

"Familiar?" Odo suggested.

"Quite." Roderick tugged at his whiskers. "Are you . . ."

"The boy and girl who fell out of the sky and caught a ride on your tail," the walrus said.

"Precisely!" He patted his vest pockets and frowned. "Because of your irresponsible behavior, I have lost my pocket watch in the sea, and I'll likely be late for court. I'd sue the both of you for triple damages if I didn't have important business to attend to." He held out his paw. "Odo, let's be on our way."

"As soon as we are released, Barrister," the walrus said.

"Quite so."

As the mouse and the walrus headed to the other side of the cage, Tyrus leaned toward Celia. "I'm pretty sure we just got told off by one of the three blind mice."

• • •

Some time later, the large gray bird opened the cage and led everyone past rows of nests in all shapes and sizes. As the captives marched in a line, angry birds shouted insults at them.

"Flat-faced interlopers," derided a gray-and-white duck.

"Wingless refugees," snapped a snipe.

"Egg-filching foreigners," cawed a crow.

"Now, now," said their captor indulgently. "Not everyone has the advantage of being born to take to the skies."

Tyrus shook his head. "Wonderland was never like this in the books. I mean, Alice fell into a sea, but it was made of her own tears, and the birds held a race to help dry her out after. They didn't arrest anyone. And I don't remember anything about swimming numbers."

Celia looked around, wondering if she and Tyrus could make a run for it. But the streets they marched through were a maze of twists and turns. When they rounded a corner, she spotted what looked like another birdcage partially hidden behind a grove of trees.

Inside the cage was a horrifying creature. Its feathered back rose in a series of humped ridges. Two bald heads sprouted from its neck in different directions. One head had twisting horns, while the other had long, floppy ears and a single, large, unblinking eye. It raised its large wings and slobbering, orange, teeth-filled bills screamed from beneath them.

"What is that?" Tyrus asked, moving to the far side of the street.

"It used to be a duck," Odo said.

"What happened to it?" Celia asked.

"It was attacked."

Celia turned away quickly. Looking at the creature made her head ache the way some optical illusions did if you studied them for too long. "What could turn a duck into that . . . *monster*?"

The walrus sucked his tusks. "Nobody knows, but it's been happening all over Wonderland, and no one can find a way to stop it."

She hurried to catch up with the large gray bird who had arrested them. "I swear we had nothing to do with your attacks. We aren't even from here. If you let us go, we promise we'll never come back."

"You'll have to take that up with the judge," the bird said. He marched them to a stretch of open beach before coming to a halt. "All rise for the honorable Judge Dodo."

Celia looked around. Everyone was already standing except for the oysters, and they didn't have any feet.

A large, awkward-looking bird with a curly white wig balanced on his head waddled out of the trees, eating the last of a star-shaped fruit. Juice dripped down his beak onto his bright yellow feet.

"Constable Heron," said the bird in the wig. "What have you brought me today?"

"Trespassers," the constable said. "After a thorough investigation and extensive questioning, we believe at least one of them is responsible for the attacks, Your Lordship."

"What investigation?" Tyrus shouted.

Celia shook her head. "No one asked us any questions."

"Quiet in the court," shouted a fierce eagle as it swooped out of the sky and landed in a nearby tree.

Judge Dodo nodded, his wig tilting to one side. "One more outburst and I'll have Bailiff Eagle return you to your cage."

The eagle nodded.

"Did you commit the attacks, or do you know who is responsible for them?" the heron asked.

"No!" Celia said. "We only got here a few hours ago."

"Excellent questioning," said the eagle. "Quite insightful."

"Thank you," said the constable with a humble bow.

"Now then," Judge Dodo said, "having heard the evidence, it is my duty to inform you that, should you be found guilty, you are subject to swift and just punishment up to and including name-calling, hair-pulling, button-pushing, and being forced to listen to bad karaoke."

"That doesn't sound so terrible," Celia whispered to Tyrus.

"Followed by being buried completely in the sand for the rest of your natural lives, which won't be long," the judge finished.

"Okay, *that* sounds bad," Tyrus whispered back.

"Crabs, do you have anything to say for yourselves?" the judge asked.

Celia turned to see two wet depressions where the crabs

had burrowed into the beach. A single bubble rose out of the sand.

The eagle flew out of the tree and pecked at the spots. "It appears the crabs have fled our jurisdiction, Your Lordship."

"Very well," the dodo said. "Oysters?"

Where the oysters had been a moment before, only a small pile of empty shells remained.

"What's this?" the eagle asked, eying the constable suspiciously.

The heron licked his beak. "They were consumed with guilt, Bailiff."

The dodo bobbed his head. "So noted. Barrister Entwhistle, what say you?"

With a dramatic twitch of his whiskers, the mouse bowed to the judge, the bailiff, and the constable. He buttoned his still-damp suit coat and paced across the sand.

"Prepare to be amazed," the walrus whispered so loudly that everyone on the beach heard him.

Roderick Entwhistle spread his arms. "My most esteemed colleagues, allow me a moment to share a long but heartfelt tale." As he began to speak, the words leaving his mouth floated into the air, forming lines of text.

It reminded Celia of the text-filled smoke that had poured from the diary. But unlike those words, which had felt threatening from the start, these had a sense of kindness and *weight*—like a favorite poem recited by an old friend. Celia smiled as the mouse's speech formed the shape of a curving tail above his head.

A peacock may quail,
expanding its tail,
when exposed to
intruders unpleasant.
The ostrich may
duck, disparage
and cluck, while,
we've all heard
the grouse of a
pheasant. You've
offered your motion.
We've come from
the ocean,
invading
your most
sovereign
nation. I
present an
appeal. We
can work
out a deal.
Reconsider
your charged
allegation.
Pray, hear
the plea of
a mouse
from the
sea as I
lay out
a new
resolution.
Let us
end this
today.
We will
be on
our way.
Grant
a stay
of . . .

Urgle durgle, burgle and gurgle.

Celia, who had nearly been soothed to sleep by the flow of the barrister's words, blinked as the mouse abruptly spouted nonsense.

"I beg your pardon?" the dodo said.

Barrister Entwhistle removed his hat and turned it in his hands. "That is to say, *fish hop cod swap*." He swung his tail nervously. "I mean, *piggle poggle burgle boggle*."

"Something's wrong," the walrus said.

"It's my tail," the mouse moaned.

Tyrus looked down. "It has knots in it."

Everyone in the group moved closer to get a better look.

"Knots all right," the bailiff said, peering down at the mouse's long pink tail, which was tied in two complicated snaggles an inch or so above the tip.

"I'll get them," Celia said. She knelt on the beach and tugged at the twists, but they were worse than a pair of tangled shoelaces. No matter how hard she pulled and pried, she couldn't budge them.

"Allow me to cut them out," the heron said, producing a knife from beneath one wing.

"No!" the mouse wailed, clutching his tail in his hands. "That cursed Arithma Sea has given me *math knots*."

"Math knots?" Celia asked, intrigued.

"There's something written on them," Tyrus said. He leaned forward, squinting, until his nose was nearly touching the mouse's tail. "Two travelers spend from 3 o'clock until 9 o'clock walking along a level road, up a hill, and home again. Their pace on the level being 4 miles an hour, uphill 3, and downhill 6, how far did they walk?"

"It's a word problem," Celia said.

Tyrus frowned. "I don't think there's enough information to figure out the answer."

"It seems like that, but maybe . . ."

Celia used her finger to draw a line in the sand representing the road and an upside-down V representing the hill. She'd found that sometimes tricky word problems were easier for her to solve if she diagrammed them first.

"A mile takes one-fourth of an hour on the level road, one-third of an hour going uphill, and one-sixth of an hour going downhill."

She sketched ¼ over the line, $\frac{1}{3}$ on the upside of the hill, and $\frac{1}{6}$ on the downside.

"That means to go one mile out and one mile back would take a half hour. Since they were walking for six hours, and they covered four miles every hour—" She looked up with a grin. "They walked twenty-four miles."

As soon as she spoke the answer, the first knot untangled itself.

Tyrus patted her on the back. "Magic!"

"No, it's just math," she said. "Read the next one."

Tyrus scanned the knot. "A brother and sister went to a bank with no money. They borrowed nothing, sold nothing, gambled nothing, and stole nothing, but at the end of the day they had over a million dollars between them." He scratched his head. "Is that algebra or calculus?"

"Neither," Celia said. "It's impossible. It doesn't make any sense."

"Neither does most math," Tyrus said. "Those Train A and Train B problems are the worst."

"At least they use logic." Celia drew a picture of a bank with two stick figures beside it. "Are you sure you read it right?"

"My poor, poor tail," Roderick said, running his hand gently over the knot.

The dodo straightened his wig. "If that is the end of your defense, I'm afraid I must pronounce judgment."

"Wait," Celia said, holding up her hands. "There has to be an answer. If A equals the brother and B equals the sister and they have . . . how much money did you say?"

Tyrus looked down at the knot. "'A million dollars between them.'" He burst out laughing.

"What's so funny?" Celia demanded, trying to remember a math formula that might apply.

"It's a word problem," Tyrus said, giggling. "But not a *math* word problem. It doesn't say the brother and sister had a million dollars. It says there was a million dollars *between* them."

He erased one of Celia's stick figures from the sand and redrew it on the other side of the building.

"One of them stood in front of the bank, and the other stood in the back." Tyrus grinned. "Get it? There was a million dollars between them because they were standing on either side of the bank."

Celia frowned, but Roderick chirped with glee as the final knot in his tail slipped open. He faced the judge, slapping his hat back on his head.

Pray, hear
the plea of
a mouse
from the
sea as I
lay out
a new
resolution.
Let us
end this
today.
We will
be on
our way.
Grant
a stay
of our
p
l
a
n
n
e
d
execution

"An excellent summation," Judge Dodo said, clapping his wings. "Do you speak on behalf of yourself and the walrus, or for the entire group?"

Roderick ran his paws across his tail, turning in the general direction of Tyrus and Celia. "How could I not defend the children who untied my knots?"

"Very well," the judge declared. "Case dismissed!"

CHAPTER 11
The Winding Road

*She generally gave herself very good advice
(though she very seldom followed it).*

Standing at the edge of the bird village, Celia considered their options with dwindling optimism. "Are you sure we can't go with the two of you?" she asked Barrister Entwhistle, who was busy straightening his tie, and Odo, who was finishing his solitaire game.

"Out of the question," the mouse said. "We're already late, and the sun is . . ."

"Getting low in the sky," Odo finished.

"Quite." Barrister Entwhistle tugged his bowler onto his head. "The queen will be severely put out by the delay."

Celia shivered. "The Queen of Hearts?"

Odo nodded. "She's rather strict about punctuality. Shouldn't be surprised if she orders our heads lopped off."

Tyrus licked his lips. "Maybe we won't go with you after all."

"Most sensible," the mouse said. "But remember that all

of Wonderland is under quarantine. Try not to cross any more borders."

Celia looked around. "How can we tell where the borders are?"

Odo tucked his cards under one flipper. "Sometimes there is a small picket fence. Other times there is an enormous wall. Most of the time, you won't see anything."

"So we'll know we crossed one when . . . ?"

The mouse clapped his hands. "When you're arrested. In which case, you'll need someone to defend you. But don't call me. I'm far too busy. Oh, and watch out for the beast."

Without another word, he and Odo disappeared into a nearby grove of trees.

"That's a bad sign," Tyrus said.

"You mean how we could be arrested for crossing a boundary we can't see or that some terrifying beast could turn us into monsters?" Celia asked.

"Those are bad too," Tyrus said. "But I was talking about the sign."

Celia looked at where Tyrus was pointing and saw a small post with a board nailed across the front that read "BAD." She rubbed her forehead. This was exactly the kind of nonsense she hated in books. Especially the kind that Lewis Carroll had written.

"What now?" she asked Tyrus. Staying with the birds wasn't a possibility, and she wasn't about to go back into the water. That only left a cobblestone road with a set of less-than-helpful directions.

A weathered stone marker read:

HERE: **Where you are**
THERE: **Farther than Here**
ELSEWHERE: **A bit closer than There**

"Well," Tyrus said, shoving his hands in his pockets, "we're already Here. Do you want to go There or Elsewhere?"

"Like it makes any difference," Celia said. "It's all silliness anyway."

"Better silly than beheaded," Tyrus muttered under his breath.

At first, the cobblestone road was straight and well-maintained, giving Celia hope that it would lead to a town or village. But the longer they walked, the more they found sections of missing cobblestone and muddy potholes in the road. Weeds grew up through cracks, making Celia wonder how recently it had been traveled.

Even worse, the road began taking pointless turns to the left and right, occasionally making complete loops on itself, as though the path had been scribbled by a toddler with a crayon.

After walking for nearly an hour, they came to a fork in the road. The paths looked identical, but a large wooden post between them had an arrow pointing to the left. A skull and crossbones was carved into the sign along with the letters

in an ominous-looking font.

It took Celia a moment to recognize the word. When she did, she shook her head. "Not going that way."

Glancing over his shoulder, Tyrus followed her down the

right fork. The road made several more looping curves before splitting again in another fork with another sign. This time, carved into a right-pointing arrow was a crude drawing of a face with Xs for eyes. The word

TROUBLE

appeared to have been gouged out of the wood with a sharp knife—or claws.

Tyrus took a couple of steps in that direction, cupping his hands above his eyes.

"What are you doing?" Celia shouted, sure something would leap out of the grass at any moment and eat him alive.

"Aren't you even a little curious to know what sort of trouble is in this direction?" he asked.

She put her hands on her hips. "If you see a 'train crossing' sign, do you stand in the middle of the tracks to see what comes toward you? If you see a 'high voltage' sign, do you touch the wire to see what will happen?"

"No, but if there's some really amazing monster that way, I'd hate to miss seeing it."

Celia shook her head. "You are so odd."

Without waiting for him, she headed left. The road twisted and turned so many times it was impossible to keep track of which direction they were going.

They reached a third arrow that looked as if something had chewed it nearly to splinters almost obliterating the word

TROUBLE

Without waiting for Tyrus to give his opinion, Celia ran

down the safe path, only to find herself at a familiar fork with an arrow she recognized at once. It was the skull and cross-bones again.

"I can't believe this," she growled. "We're back where we started."

Tyrus looked up at the arrow, put a hand to his mouth, and laughed.

"What's so funny?" she asked, her head pounding.

Tyrus pointed at the arrow, barely able to get the words out through his laughter. "It's the first sign of trouble."

Realizing it was just a stupid riddle, Celia agreed to go left.

A few minutes later, they passed a stone monument. Tyrus grinned as he read the words inscribed on it. "'It is better to face trouble head-on than to run from where it might possibly lurk.'"

The signs only got worse from there.

"If you have come this way intentionally, turn back. Otherwise, continue."

"Behold, you shall see a sign." Followed, of course, by a sign.

Three arrows with "9:00 AM," "Noon," and "5:00 PM" carved into them, which Tyrus decided must be the "signs of the times."

They found a post with four arrows pointing in four different directions, reading "the road less traveled," "the road most traveled," "the road once traveled," and "the road never traveled (for good reason)."

Of course, Tyrus chose the last road, and it was Celia's

turn to laugh when it led to an impassible swamp, and they had to backtrack.

By the time the sun began to dip into the edge of the sea, casting everything in a deep magenta that looked too much like blood for Celia's liking, the reality that they might spend the night lost in the middle of nowhere began to sink in.

The air was growing colder, and there wasn't so much as an empty barn in sight. Even worse, the grass growing up through the road was much thicker than when they'd started and high enough that she was afraid they'd lose the road completely if they left it for any reason.

Standing at a crossroads near a post covered with arrows directing the lost traveler *this way, that way, someway, anyway, no way, low way, wrong way, long way, highway, byway,* and one arrow pointing straight up that simply read *way,* Celia wrapped her arms across her chest.

"I should never have translated that diary."

"You didn't know it would open a doorway," Tyrus said, poking a small yellow flower with a twig. Each time the stick drew near, the flower wrapped its petals around the tip, growled softly as it waved its leaves, and snipped off a bit of wood.

Celia scuffed her feet in the dust. "How did you know to drink from the bottle?"

"The label said to. It seemed like an emergency, so I did."

Celia thought about telling him it could have been poison or curdled milk or any number of nasty things, but there was no point. It hadn't killed them. In fact, it had probably saved her life. "You didn't have to drink it too. Now we're both stuck here."

"Stuck?" Tyrus looked up from the flower. "Are you kidding me? This is the coolest thing that's ever happened in my life."

She couldn't believe what she was hearing. "You *like* it here?"

"Well, I mean it's not Hogwarts or Oz, but it's definitely not Mordor either."

Celia stomped her foot and several flowers turned in her direction. "Would you stop with the book stuff?"

"This *is* book stuff," Tyrus said, spreading his arms. "We are *in* Wonderland."

She took a deep breath, trying to stop the pounding in her temples. "Wonderland is a story—one made up by an author with an overactive imagination."

"Does this look like a story?" Tyrus raised a hand to stop her from arguing. "What if *Alice's Adventures in Wonderland* wasn't something Lewis Carroll made up, but a history of what he saw when he actually came here?"

Celia shook her head. On a purely theoretical level, she could grasp the concept that they were in a different world. She'd heard the talking birds and seen the swimming numbers for herself. But the idea that they were in the actual land from the book made her feel nauseated. "If that's true, why didn't he tell people he came here himself? Why call it a story?"

"Because no one would have believed him. They would have called Carroll a fraud."

"Dodgson," Celia whispered. "They would have called *Charles Dodgson* a fraud."

That almost made sense. If Charles Dodgson had discovered a way to travel between parallel worlds, he would have been recognized as the greatest mathematician of all time. But what if he told people the world he had traveled to had talking birds and swimming numbers?

They would have laughed at him, called him a fool. That was something no serious mathematician could bear. As Lewis Carroll, though, he could tell the craziest stories in the world and everyone would smile.

"Do you realize what this means?" Tyrus asked, spreading his arms wide. "If Wonderland is real, maybe all the other fantasy worlds are too. What if Tolkien wrote about Rivendell not because it was something from his imagination, but because it was a place he'd visited? What if C. S. Lewis traveled to Narnia, not through a wardrobe but through a portal, like the one we opened?" His eyes went wide. "What if there really is a galaxy far, far away with—"

"Stop!" Celia shouted. "That's a logical fallacy. Even if Wonderland exists, it doesn't mean any of those other places do."

Tyrus set his jaw. "Fine. But we *are* in Wonderland, and any minute we could run into the Caterpillar or the March Hare." He grinned. "If we find the Mad Hatter, I am so joining his tea party."

Celia looked at the sky where strange green wisps of clouds were starting to blow in from the sea. "This isn't Lewis

Carroll's Wonderland, though. Can't you feel it? It's not just the attacks. Everything feels, I don't know, wrong, I guess."

Tyrus looked around, then slowly nodded. "Some of the things we've seen are straight out of the book—the mouse, the birds, the queen. But in the story, they were fun. Here, they feel dangerous."

Celia heard something moving in the grass, but when she turned, there was nothing there. "We could get eaten by the Jabberwocky."

"Jabberwock," Tyrus corrected. He shrugged when Celia glared at him. "'Jabberwocky' is the name of the poem; the creature is called the Jabberwock. But we don't need to worry about it because it's from *Through the Looking Glass,* which is another book entirely."

Celia heard the noise again and could swear she felt something watching them. "You know who isn't from another book? The Queen of Hearts."

Tyrus scrubbed a hand across his face. "So we stay away from the castle."

Something poked at Celia's leg. She looked down to find one of the flowers trying to nibble her pants. As she flicked it away with the back of her hand, she noticed dozens more—maybe hundreds—around them, petals snapping open and shut hungrily. She was positive there hadn't been anywhere near that many flowers a few minutes earlier.

"They must bloom at night," Tyrus said, edging toward the center of the road.

That had to be the explanation. Because the only other possibility she could think of was that the flowers had surrounded them while they were talking, and the idea of biting flowers that could pull up their roots and move terrified her. Especially because where there were small flowers that could bite the tip off a twig, there might also be big flowers that could bite—

The grass behind them rustled again, and a childlike voice called out, "You need to go."

Tyrus spun around, searching in the dim light. "Who said that?"

Peering into the grass, Celia thought she could see a brown, furry creature.

"He's coming," the creature called.

Celia recognized the voice as the same one who had called out to them in the library. "*Who's* coming? Come out where we can see you."

The creature pushed deeper into hiding as a second, dark figure stepped out of the trees on the other side of the road. Celia and Tyrus backed away as the figure bounded in their direction.

"Oh, my whiskers," the figure said. "It's late. So very, very late."

Tyrus smiled. "Is that the White Rabbit?"

"He's not right," the library voice whispered, and Celia could swear she heard whoever, or whatever, it was shivering against the blades of grass. "Don't talk to him, and definitely don't ask him about—"

The voice cut off as the figure in the trees bounded toward them.

"It *is* the White Rabbit," Tyrus said. But his grin slowly faded as the creature came closer.

This rabbit didn't look like any of the cute little white rabbits in the books and movies Celia had seen. For one thing, he was a good foot taller than either she or Tyrus. His eyes were bloodshot, and his body was so thin, she could see the outline of his ribs beneath his matted fur.

The rabbit's ears were crooked, and his wet nose loudly sniffed the two of them as he bounced to a stop. "You're not from here. My furry paws, no. Not from here at all," he said, revealing a pair of jagged front teeth that looked too long for his mouth.

Celia got a whiff of what smelled like rotting vegetables as the rabbit leaned forward and studied her with his red eyes. "Strange people in strange places at strange times. Like the other one, but different . . . *very* different."

"The other one?" Tyrus asked. "Do you mean Charles Dodgson?"

Wearing gloves that looked like they'd been stained with swamp mud, the rabbit pulled a watch from his vest. "Home, roam. Night, flight," he muttered. "My ears and eyes, but I am late."

Water dripped from the watch, and Tyrus pointed at the initials *R.e.* engraved on the back. "Is that Barrister Entwhistle's watch?"

Flashing his brownish teeth, the rabbit clutched the watch to his chest and growled. "Mine!" He narrowed his eyes and sniffed at Tyrus's shirt. "Strangers have clocks?"

"We don't have any clocks," Celia said. "We don't even know what time it is."

"No," the library voice behind them moaned.

"*Time?*" the rabbit howled, his eyes nearly popping out of his head. "You want to know what *time* it is?" Gleaming knives popped from his paws, and it took Celia a moment to realize they were his nails. Since when did rabbits have claws like a bear?

"No," Tyrus said at once. "We don't care what ti—I mean, we don't have a schedule or anything. We have plenty of, um, flexibility?"

Moving forward until his face was only inches away from Tyrus's, the white rabbit sunk his claws straight through the front of Tyrus's shirt and lifted him into the air, ripping the cloth. "Nasties at night," he hissed. His teeth, like fangs, reached past his furry chin. "Mustn't be out so late. Claws and tail, no. When night arrives, danger flies."

"Leave him alone!" Celia shouted, punching the creature in the ribs.

The rabbit only looked down at her and grinned. A string of drool dripped from his lower lip. "Time to eat. Him first. You next."

He pulled Tyrus to his mouth, and Celia yanked at his paw. A patch of mottled fur came away in her hand.

"Look out!" screamed the library voice.

The White Rabbit's head jerked up as a shadow darkened the sky above them and a scream split the air. "Too late!" the rabbit howled, dropping Tyrus to the ground. "Too la-a-a-ate." Long ears tucked against the sides of his head, he turned and bounded into the trees.

"What is that thing?" Tyrus called, looking up.

Celia grabbed his hand. "Run!"

CHAPTER 12

The Tiny Door

"And even if my head would go through," thought poor Alice, "it would be of very little use without my shoulders."

Hand in hand, they raced through the night. It was so dark, Celia could barely see where she was going. The sound of flapping wings above and behind them was getting closer, and every few seconds, an ear-shattering screech split the night, followed by a loud hacking sound. Small creatures hopped and scurried across the road, disappearing into the grass on the other side.

Trying to keep her balance, Celia ducked under a large gray branch that appeared out of nowhere. Fingerlike twigs scratched her skin and clutched at her clothes. Had they left the road or had the trees closed in around them? Evil bark faces with glowing chestnut eyes leered at them, calling out in cracked voices.

Slow down . . . come back . . . we will protect you . . . enfold you . . . devour you.

"There!" Tyrus yelled, pointing.

Straight ahead was a wall so high it seemed to block out the entire sky. A pair of old-fashioned lanterns set in the base of the wall cast pools of golden light on a wooden door. If they could reach it, they might be able to escape both the clutching trees and the terror above them. Only, the door was so far away and it looked so tiny—like something made for a doll.

"We'll never reach it!" she shouted.

Another screech that sounded like it was coming from right above their heads drowned out the last of her words, and the trees cowered as a strong wind battered the air around them.

Heads down, arms pumping, they dashed toward their only hope of escape. Celia stared into the night, hoping they were getting closer. The road sped past beneath her feet, the grass and bushes to either side were a blur, but, if anything, the wall appeared farther away, the door even smaller.

Then, as though someone had flipped a switch, the road rippled beneath her feet. She stumbled, swinging her arms to keep from tripping. The night shifted, and it felt like she was falling—not down, but forward. The wall shot toward her so fast she had to throw out her arms to keep from smashing into it. Her shoulder slammed against solid stone, and both she and Tyrus fell to the ground.

The door and the lanterns were so close she could reach out and touch them, only they were still just as small as they had appeared from a distance—the lanterns no bigger than the tip of her thumb, the door so tiny even a kitten could barely have squeezed through.

Claws in front of her ripped long gouges in the stone wall.

Hot breath bathed her face, and she turned to stare into burning gold eyes. Hovering above her, held aloft by enormous black wings, was a creature half-lion, half-eagle, and all nightmare.

"It's a gryphon," Tyrus screamed as Celia dove into the waist-high grass.

"Got that right, didn't you, mate?" the gryphon called, snapping its beak perilously close to Tyrus's face.

"You talk?" Celia asked, peeking out from behind a bush.

"What?" the monster howled. "You fink I couldn't because I'm a gryphon? That's it, ain't it?" *Hjckrrh,* it coughed, snapping its talons at her. "Come out of that grass so I can rip your ugly loaf off your neck and put it in me nest, won't I just?"

Tyrus searched the ground. "There must be another bottle around here. Like, on a table or something. That's how Alice got through the door in the book."

"Good luck with that one," the gryphon mocked, swinging around for another attack. "Queen's guards done smashed the table, and broke the bottle to smithereens just yesterday, didn't they? Wouldn't do you no good anyways. They up and nailed over the door."

The beast was right: a thick plank had been nailed across the door, and bits of glass littered the ground.

Crouched on the ground, Celia had the crazy thought that this creature sounded like it would invite you over for tea— just before ripping your head off.

Folding its wings to its sides, the gryphon plummeted toward them, its clawed legs stretched out like four sets of gleaming swords.

"Leave us alone," she screamed, rolling out of the way. "We just want to get home."

"Ain't heard that one before, have I?" the gryphon called. "Filthy dustbin lids are up to no good, I'd wager. Get rid of you right quick, I will."

It coughed again—a wet, hacking sound—and spat something into the air.

"I'm hit," Tyrus screamed, crawling to Celia's side.

At first, Celia thought the side of his face had been burned. But when she reached out to investigate, she discovered a ball of wet fur stuck to the side of his head.

"How bad is it?" he asked, squeezing his eyes shut.

Even though she was shaking, Celia couldn't help smiling. "I think you've been hit by a hairball."

"Gross," Tyrus said, scraping the gunk off his face.

"Didn't like that now, did you?" the gryphon called. "Got a lot more of it, I do. Next one'll have a bit'o spaghetti sauce in it from last night's dinner. Think on that."

"I don't know which is worse," Tyrus said. "Its attacks or its mouth."

"We need to get out of here before it stops taunting us and attacks for real," Celia said.

"This way," called the voice they had heard earlier. They turned to see a small brown rabbit in a red dress and brown boots waving them toward an opening near the base of the wall.

"Who are you?" Tyrus asked, but the rabbit was already scurrying into the hole.

It didn't look much bigger than the door had. "We won't fit," Celia shouted.

"Squeeze," the rabbit called back as she disappeared into the hole. "It gets bigger once you're inside."

Celia hesitated. She didn't want to get stuck, and she was afraid about what might be in the tunnel, but the gryphon was circling for another attack.

"Run away, nasty little pigeon droppings," the gryphon called after them with a growl. "Don't think I won't be here when you slink back."

"Go!" Tyrus shouted.

Pressing her eyes shut, Celia shoved her head into the opening and twisted her shoulders as she squirmed through. For a moment, she thought she was going to get stuck halfway in. Her right elbow was caught on something, and her feet slipped in the loose dirt behind her. Then Tyrus gave her a push, and she slid through the hole and down a dark passage.

Rubbing dirt out of her eyes, she found herself in a narrow tunnel lined with roots and crumbling dirt walls. It didn't look promising, but Tyrus was already shoving in behind her.

"Follow me," the rabbit called, her booted feet disappearing around a corner.

Celia squirmed down the passage and discovered the rabbit was right. The farther she crawled, the wider the passage became. Several times, she passed rooms filled with baskets of vegetables and neatly made beds.

As the tunnel widened, the rooms appeared to grow as well. The beds that had appeared doll-sized at first were now big enough to sleep five. The carrots went from finger-sized to so big it would have taken a week to eat just one.

Her limbs felt weak and rubbery, and her fingers seemed to be shrinking. "I feel strange," she called back to Tyrus.

"Me too," he answered, his voice sounding muffled and . . . *slobbery*?

The tunnel tilted upward, the roof high enough that she could have walked. But when Celia tried to stand, she couldn't feel her legs. Her heart pounding, she crawled over the crumbling earth and came out of the ground into what looked like an enormous garden.

Tomatoes the size of cars hung from vines as tall as skyscrapers. Craning her neck to look up at a tree, she realized it was actually a gigantic head of lettuce. Off to the right, green beans as big as canoes swayed slowly in the breeze.

A long, slimy creature with greenish skin crawled out of the opening behind her. It waggled a pair of stubby antennas that hung from either side of its face like a mustache and an even longer set that rose from the top of its head. "Something's weird."

Celia stared at the creature. It sounded like Tyrus's voice, but . . .

"What happened to you?" she asked, trying not to shudder.

The antennas on its head waggled as its wet lips curved into a frown. "Celia? Is that you?"

Celia realized she had changed as well. Her legs were gone, and her body was bright yellow and covered with some sort of mucus. Poking out from either side of her mouth were two of the stubby mustache antennas.

How could she be looking down at her own mouth?

Somehow, she managed to look left and right at the same

time and found herself staring into her own bulbous eyes, which were attached to long stalks high above her head.

"What are these things?" she cried, waggling the feelers on the sides of her mouth.

"I think they're called tentacles," Tyrus said. "The ones on top are used for seeing and smelling, and the ones by your mouth are used for tasting." His humped body gave what might have been a slug shrug. "I read a book about it."

"Of course, you did," Celia said, trying not to gag.

"That was *not* what I was expecting to happen," a voice echoed from far above them. It was the rabbit's voice, as it might have been sounded if it had been spoken into a microphone, amplified hundreds of times, and broadcast through a stadium's speakers.

Celia looked up at a gigantic hairy monster. The ground shook as the rabbit stepped past the tomato vine and looked down at the two of them. It wriggled its pink nose, and Celia realized the small, brown rabbit they'd followed into the hole was now at least five stories tall.

"Whoa," Tyrus shouted. "You're huge!"

The rabbit blinked her enormous eyes. "Um, actually, you are just very small."

"What did you do to us?" Celia cried.

"I'm not quite sure," the huge creature's voice boomed. "I've never taken a human through a rabbit hole before. I guess it had unexpected, um, consequences?"

Tyrus crawled to a sign outside the entrance they'd come through.

"What does it say?" Celia asked.

He raised his eyestalks to get a better view. "'Enter at your own risk. Possible side effects may include happy feet, jazz hands, food allergies, psychological rash, strained imagination, bad voice impressions, increased appetite, and sluggishness.'"

"Increased appetite," he said, eying the giant lettuce. "I could really go for a salad."

"Sluggishness?" Celia yelled at the rabbit. "You turned us into *slugs*."

"Oh, gosh," the giant rabbit said. She reached down and scooped up Tyrus and Celia in her furry paw so they were roughly on the same level. "At least you don't have to worry about getting jazz hands, right?"

"Is that supposed to be some kind of joke?" Celia's thick body shuddered.

Tyrus wriggled his slug mustache. "You're the one who called us here. I recognize your voice from the library."

"I'm Sylvan," the rabbit said with a grin. "I'm so glad you heard me. I wasn't sure you would. See, there was this horn thing back where they store the clocks, but it hadn't been used in a while, and I wasn't quite sure how it worked—or even if it *did* work—only, it had a spiderweb in it, and I know rabbits aren't supposed to be afraid of spiders, but—"

"Stop," Celia said. "I don't care about the horn, or the spiders, or the clocks."

"Sorry," Sylvan said. "I get carried away."

Celia sighed. "It's okay. Change us back to humans, and we can go our own ways."

Sylvan flapped her ears. "I don't know how to do that. I'm sort of new to this whole thing."

"We can just go back through the tunnel," Tyrus said, starting to crawl off the rabbit's paw. But Sylvan was already shaking her giant head.

"That might not be the best idea."

Celia seethed. "Why not?"

"It *could* change you back. But it could also change you into something worse, like a toadstool or a drop of owl spit. Besides, the gryphon's probably still back there. It takes him a while to work up to it, but once he runs out of hairballs, he's been known to rip to pieces anyone who invades his territory."

"What are we supposed to do?" Celia asked.

Sylvan shrugged her enormous rabbit shoulders. "Great-Great-Great-Grandfather Gotland said you'd, you know, save Wonderland."

"Save it from what?" Tyrus asked.

"Not sure." The rabbit flapped her ears again, creating a gust that nearly knocked them both off her paw. "I probably should have paid more attention in the meeting." She tilted her head. "Can you still save us when you're, you know, small?"

Celia had had enough. "Put us down!" she shouted.

When they were back on the ground, she gave the rabbit her fiercest glare. "We aren't saving anything."

"You have to," Sylvan said with all the sincerity of a kid explaining that the sun rises in the morning. "The great cheese clock said you would. Or was it the clock with all the gears?" She scratched behind her right ear. "Which one of you is The Alice?"

Celia shook her head. "Neither of us."

Sylvan laughed. "That's funny."

"She's not joking," Tyrus said. "I'm Tyrus, and she's Celia."

Sylvan stopped laughing, and her eyes grew wide. "Are you sure?"

"Don't you think we'd know our own names?" Celia snapped.

"Oh, no." The brown rabbit's mouth trembled, and her eyes glistened. "I've made a terrible mistake." A tear the size of a basketball plopped from her furry face to the ground. A couple of drops hit Celia's skin and sizzled like acid.

"Watch where you're crying," Celia said. "The salt in your tears burns slugs."

But Tyrus was crawling up to Sylvan's giant boot. "It's okay," he crooned. "Everyone makes mistakes." He wagged the feelers on his face sympathetically. "I'd hug you, but I don't have any arms."

Celia's eyestalks drooped. Leave it to Tyrus to make her go from righteous anger to guilt in less than thirty seconds.

"How old are you?" Tyrus asked.

"Six months." Sylvan sniffed.

Tyrus nodded. "You're just a kid. Tell your Great-Great-Great-Grandfather What's-his-name that you called the wrong people. I'm sure he'll understand."

"All right." The rabbit wiped her eyes. She thumped the ground with one foot.

It was like an earthquake had hit the garden. Tyrus and Celia bounced into the air and back down, tumbling tail over tentacles.

"N-n-n-not s-s-s-so cl-l-l-lose," Celia yelled.

Sylvan stopped thumping. "Sorry, I'll go talk to them in person." With a few quick hops, she was out of the garden.

"What are we supposed to do until you get back?" Celia yelled as the giant rabbit hopped away.

"Try looking for an annnnn-tiiii-doooote," Sylvan's voice echoed back, and then she was gone.

CHAPTER 13

The Missing Antidote

Everything is so out-of-the-way down here,
that I should think very likely it can talk:
at any rate, there's no harm in trying.

"Look for an antidote?" Celia asked. "That's her advice?"

"It'll be okay," Tyrus said, leaving a glistening trail in the dirt behind him as he crawled next to her.

Celia waved her front tentacles, trying not to think of them as a mustache. "How is it going to be okay? We're slugs."

"Things always worked out in the book."

Celia tried to glare at him but wasn't sure if slugs were capable of glaring. "Would that be the book about the psycho white rabbit and the hairball-spitting gryphon? Because I think I must have missed that one."

Tyrus curled his body in a protective circle. "Sure, things are different, but this is still Wonderland."

"More like Wonder-what's-wrong-with-this-land," Celia said. "Alice never got turned into a slug."

"But it's still kind of cool. I mean, who else can say they've seen a real gryphon or swam in a sea full of numbers?"

"I don't want to think about it," Celia said. Her body ached. It felt like her brain had been stretched, folded, and bent into a pretzel. "This world doesn't make sense. There's no logic to it."

"Does everything have to be logical?" Tyrus asked.

"Yes," she said, more harshly than she intended. "Life is like a puzzle. Logic is what holds the pieces together."

"I guess." Tyrus nibbled on a stalk of grass. "The thing is, in real life the pieces don't seem to fit each other most of the time. Here, even with everything that's happened, I feel like it's all going to work out."

"That's because you read too many books," Celia said. "Authors make their own rules. They change things around and switch things up. They invent words that never existed, make up names no one can pronounce, and create crazy lands no one can understand. It's all nonsense."

"Sometimes I need nonsense," Tyrus murmured with a shrug.

Celia paused, feeling the truth of what he'd said. "I guess the real world can be pretty boring sometimes."

Tyrus laughed. "None of the bullies back home ever spat a hairball on me. Although, they probably would have if they could."

Celia stared up at the stars. At least *they* looked normal. She didn't recognize any of the constellations, but she hadn't been much into astronomy anyway. She could pretend she was in her own backyard looking at the night sky.

"Until we figure out why a gryphon that once shared poems with a mock turtle is trying to kill people and why a rabbit whose biggest worry was clean gloves has now grown fangs and claws, we need to be careful."

Tyrus grinned.

"What?" Celia asked.

"You're quoting from the book," he said. "You've read it."

She gritted her teeth. "I saw the movie."

"No, you can always tell the difference between people who have read the books and people who've only seen the movie."

Of course, she'd read the books. There hadn't been any choice in her house. Growing up, her mother had read them to her not once but over and over again until she loathed even the sight of the little girl with the long blonde hair and the pinafore dress.

Tyrus crawled through one of the rabbit's huge footprints. "Do you think maybe we could, you know, save Wonderland from whatever has messed it up?"

"No," Celia said, her voice firm. "That is exactly the kind of thinking we have to avoid. If we start viewing this as a story where a couple of kids come to the rescue, we're going to end up getting killed. This isn't our world. Let the creatures who live here deal with Wonderland while we figure out how to get home—if that's even possible."

"It is," Tyrus said, without a trace of doubt.

"How can you be so sure?"

"Because *he* did."

"*He?*"

Tyrus looked at her with the glow in his eyes he always got

when discussing books. "Lewis Carroll, or Charles Dodgson, if you prefer. If he found a way back, so can we."

"He's the one who discovered the formula," Celia said. "Without his diary, I could never remember the math to open the door."

"Then we find someone who knows the math. Someone he talked to. Or someone who saw what he did. First, though, we have to find a cure for our sluggishness." He looked around and pointed to a group of creatures coming in their direction. "Maybe they can help."

Celia raised her eyestalks to their full height. Twenty pale insects with large brown heads, pincers, and spindly antennas rode on six-legged beetles with shiny backs. The beetles all had giant, pointed jaws that looked like horns on the front of their heads. All the riders wore armor and carried shields and sharpened sticks that Celia feared could do a lot of damage to a slug's body.

"I think those are soldier termites," Tyrus said.

"Were *they* in the book?"

"No," he said. "But they're probably friendly."

Celia didn't have a lot of experience with giant insects, but since when did friendly creatures carry spears and wear armor?

As the insects rode up, Tyrus nodded his blunt head. "Greetings, fellow pests. Could you help us?"

"*Help* you?" spat the leader of the group, a fierce-looking insect with a red face. The beetle he was sitting on snapped its jaws open and shut with a loud clacking. "We will tease you mercilessly, pelt you with unripe rutabagas, spin you about

until you become helplessly dizzy, then send you off on annoying errands with poor directions."

"Poor directions! Poor directions!" the rest of the termites
chanted, banging their spears and shields together.

Celia backed away, wondering whether a couple of slugs
could outrun the terrifying beetles. But Tyrus curved his lips
into a smile that didn't quite work on his slug mouth.

"We're terribly sorry to bother you. You look like you're
out on a hunt or something. Cool armor, by the way. You see,
we accidentally got changed into slugs."

"We *hate* slugs," the leader said. "Disgusting slimy things
with mucus-secreting bodies, external breathing pores, and no
fashion sense."

"No fashion sense," the others roared, plugging their
noses.

"Wow, you really know your biology," Tyrus said. "But we
aren't really slugs. We just crawled through the wrong tunnel.
If you could tell us how to change back, we'd appreciate it."

A termite with a brown abdomen and a haughty expression moved its beetle alongside the leader. "We will never tell
you where the antidote is."

"So, there *is* an antidote?" Celia asked, her curiosity temporarily overriding her fear.

The lead termite glared at the second-in-command. "We
will reveal nothing to these pernicious slugs."

"We're actually humans," Tyrus said.

"Humans!" The termite stuck out its tongue and blew a
wet raspberry. The rest of the group did the same. "We hate
humans even more than we hate slugs. Loud voices, opposable

thumbs, and terrible table manners. We will stab your over-sized feet, beat you until you tell bad jokes—"

"You hate slugs *and* humans?" Celia interrupted.

The second termite sneered. "We are Antipathies. We hate everything."

The leader glared. "Stop talking. It's my turn to be leader today."

"Sor-ry," the second mocked, drawing out the word and rolling his eyes. "See if I let you help when it's my turn."

Celia shook her thick head. "I don't think an antipathy is a creature."

"She's right," Tyrus said. "It's an intense dislike. For example, I have an antipathy for cauliflower."

"You dare disrespect the mighty cauliflower?" the lead termite shouted, his eyes bulging. "It is high in fiber, an excellent source of phytonutrients, and has a delightful snowball-like appearance." He raised his spear above his head. "For this insult, I will feed your stinking human-slug corpses to my trusty mount."

The beetle flashed its sharp jaws in the moonlight.

Tyrus laughed. "I don't think so."

"Tyrus," Celia hissed, wishing she had a hand to pull him back with. "This might be a good time to remember we aren't in a story."

"They won't eat us," Tyrus said. "Those are stag beetles. They don't eat anything—just decaying wood—and they only drink tree sap and fruit juice."

"Enough of your lies, you cauliflower-hating slugs!" the leader howled.

The second termite scratched his nose. "He might be right. I've never actually seen my beetle eat anything since it was a grub."

"I thought I told you to let me do the talking," the leader said, poking the second termite's shield.

"Don't push me," the second said, smacking the first over the head with his spear.

The two of them leaped off their beetles and began pulling each other's antennas and poking their eyes.

"Fight! Fight! Fight!" the crowd yelled, joining the battle. Even the beetles took part, snapping at one another with their humungous jaws.

Celia watched the melee for a moment before turning away. "I don't think we're going to get any help from them."

"Maybe they really are Antipathies," Tyrus said as the two of them slimed their way off through the grass.

"How did you know about stag beetles?" Celia asked.

Tyrus slid his slug body over a twig and beneath a bush covered with fragrant white blossoms. "Is that really a question you need to ask a book nerd?" He turned his eyestalks left and right. "There has to be someone around here who can help us find the antidote."

"Could you keep it down?" a voice asked from above.

Celia and Tyrus looked up to see a group of long white silkworms resting in hammocks hanging from the branches over their heads.

"Good evening," Celia said.

"Is it?" asked a worm wearing a pair of stylish red sunglasses.

"It's not *bad*," said the worm next to it, sipping a drink through a straw.

"No," agreed the first. "But not especially good either."

"Quiet." A third worm yawned. "I'm trying to sleep. I mean, I'm not actually *trying*. But if it happens, it happens." It adjusted a white blossom hat over its eyes.

"Sorry," Celia whispered. "Could one of you possibly tell us where we could find the antidote to change us from slugs back into humans?"

"We could," said a worm, half-heartedly dabbing red nail polish on its feet, although Celia wasn't sure the silkworm even had toes. "But we probably won't."

If Celia had arms, she would have climbed up and knocked the lazy things out of their hammocks. As it was, she could only give them a stern expression. "Why not?"

"Too much effort," said the worm with the drink.

"Not really any point," agreed the worm in the sunglasses.

Tyrus narrowed his eyes. "You wouldn't, by any chance, be Apathies, would you?"

The worm with the nail polish splashed a little half-heartedly on one foot before setting it aside. "The boy thinks too much."

The sleepy worm started to roll over, sighed, and flopped back onto its stomach. "And he talks too much."

"I'll take that as a yes," Tyrus said. He leaned toward Celia. "Apathy is a lack of feeling or emotion."

Celia snorted. "I have a hard time reading words, not understanding their meaning." She shouted up at the worms.

"How much effort would it be to tell us where we can find the antidote? You don't even have to get out of your hammocks."

"It's not the getting up part," the worm in the sunglasses said. "It's the deciding part. Should we? Shouldn't we?"

The worm with the drink nodded slowly. "It makes my head spin."

"I don't think they're going to help us either," Tyrus said. "They can't commit to anything."

Celia thought for a moment, then grinned. "That's okay," she said, loudly enough that all the worms could hear. "They shouldn't tell us if they feel strongly about keeping the antidote's location a secret."

The sleepy worm lifted its hat. "I wouldn't say we feel *strongly* about it."

"No, no," Celia said, sliding away. "A secret is a secret. You absolutely can't tell us the location of the antidote. It would be against your ethics."

"We have ethics?" the worm with the sunglasses asked, lowering its shades.

"*I* don't have ethics," said the worm with the drink.

Celia winked at Tyrus. "Prove it."

"The antidote is just over that hill," called all the worms at once.

"I guess you *don't* have ethics," Celia said.

"Certainly not," the worm with the half-painted nails said.

"*Certainly* seems a little strong," said the worm with the drink.

"I'm too tried to be certain about anything," said the sleepy worm.

Tyrus and Celia exchanged a look, then climbed slowly toward the hill, leaving the Apathies behind.

"Nice work," Tyrus said.

Celia laughed. "Logic has its uses."

When they reached the top of the hill, Tyrus pointed to a small stone table in a circular clearing below. "Watch this," he called. Laying down a thick trail of shiny mucus, he slid to the bottom of the hill like a kid on a sled.

"Slow down," Celia called. "You'll break your neck."

"Not possible." Tyrus laughed. "Slugs don't have any bones."

Wondering how she had gone from a girl whose biggest worry was attending a new school to a spineless mollusk in less than twenty-four hours, Celia laid down her own mucus trail and slid after him. By the time she caught up with Tyrus, he was leaning over one of nine small cakes arranged in a square on the table.

"Stop!" she shouted, as Tyrus opened his mouth and prepared to take a bite.

"What?" Tyrus asked, turning his eyestalks toward her.

"You're just going to randomly eat one of these?"

Tyrus pursed his lips. "The worms said the antidote was on this side of the hill, and in the book—"

"Alice eats a cake," Celia finished. "I know. But how many times do I have to remind you that *this*—"

"Isn't a story," Tyrus said. "I get it. But we can't just sit around waiting for someone to rescue us. We're going to have to take a few risks."

They stared at each other, caught in a standoff, until Celia nodded. "Okay, we take risks, but only when we have to. And we think them through carefully first."

Tyrus nodded. "Deal."

Together, they studied the nine cakes on the table. It was hard to see in the dark, but Celia noticed one thing right away. "They're different colors. See, the first row is yellow. The second row is red, I think, and the third row is . . . purple?"

"More of a mauve," Tyrus murmured. "The patterns are different too."

He was right. The ones on the left were striped, the ones in the middle had zigzags, and the ones on the right had polka dots.

"I wonder what the difference means?" she asked.

"We could try a tiny taste of each to see what happens," Tyrus suggested.

A soft green light appeared in the trees to their left, illuminating the clearing. "That might not be the best idea," said a musical voice.

A creature with beautiful black wings, a striped body, and a glowing green tail emerged.

"You're a firefly," Tyrus said.

The creature flew over their heads, flitting from spot to spot before landing on the grass beside them. "Maybe yes, maybe no."

"Please tell me you're not another Apathy," Celia said.

The firefly turned in a circle and blinked her tail on and off four times. "I can see why you might think that."

"So, you are?" Tyrus asked.

"I didn't say that."

Celia frowned. "But you didn't say you weren't either."

The firefly fluttered her wings and smiled mysteriously.

"I don't care what you are," Celia said, "as long as you can help us."

"We crawled through a rabbit hole and turned into slugs," Tyrus added. "The Apathies on the other side of the hill said we could find the antidote here, but we don't know which of these cakes will change us back."

"I've heard rumors of such transformations," the firefly said. "People with conditions not unlike your own ate cakes, which may or may not have been like these, and experienced a rather startling metamorphosis."

Celia scrunched her rubbery body together until she felt as if she might explode. "Could you possibly be any more vague?" Then it hit her. "You're a Vagary, aren't you?"

The firefly blinked her eyes and danced a short jig.

"Inexplicable, unpredictable, and erratic," Tyrus said. "How can we trust anything she tells us?"

"Are you saying you *don't* want my help?" the firefly demanded, her tail burning blindingly bright.

"No," Celia said at once. "We'll take all the help we can get."

"Very well." Returning her tail to its normal brightness, the firefly plucked several stalks of grass. Muttering strange words, she held the blades in the air, then dropped them slowly to the ground before studying the patterns they made. At last she nodded. "Be careful. Choose the right cake and you will become human again. Choose the wrong one and not only will you remain slugs forever, but you will also be struck with a horrible curse. I will answer . . . *five* questions."

"Why only five?" Tyrus asked, examining the fallen blades of grass.

"It's my favorite number," the Vagary said. "Now you have four questions."

Tyrus looked up. "What do you mean? I thought you said we had five."

"You did, but you used one of them to ask why you only got five. That was your first answer. This is your second. Now you have three."

"Wha—" Tyrus started to say, but Celia cut him off.

"Stop asking questions. Don't you see she's trying to get you to use them all up before we learn anything?"

"I don't think he does." The firefly chirped and made shadow figures with her back legs. "Now you have two."

"We still have three," Celia said. "I asked Tyrus the last question. Not you."

The firefly lowered her glow until everything was in shadows. "That issss againsssst the rulesssss," she whispered in a creepy voice. "Then again, I'm not sure I have any rules. So I'll give you three. But as punishment, they may only be yes or no questions."

"I almost prefer the Apathies," Tyrus whispered. "At least they told you where they stood."

"I know," Celia whispered back. "But she's the only help we have. Let's make our questions count."

"I can hear-r-r-r you," the firefly said in a singsong voice, circling above their heads. "Actually, I can't. Fireflies don't have ears. Do you want to know how we can hear with no ears?"

"No," Celia said at once. She studied the cakes, trying to figure out the best way to narrow it down.

"We could ask which color the antidote is," Tyrus suggested.

"Sorry," the firefly said. "You can only ask yes or no questions."

"Fine," Celia said. "Is the correct cake purple?"

"Mauve," Tyrus corrected.

"The cake that will change you back is neither purple nor mauve," the firefly said. "I will count that as one question, because of exception 1.2.88 in the Manual of Asking."

That narrowed it down to six cakes.

It was Tyrus's turn. "Is the correct cake yellow?"

The firefly blinked her tail on and off enthusiastically. "Yes!"

Celia studied the table carefully. "If we ask if the correct cake has circles on it and the answer is yes, that will mean it's the one with the polka dots. But if the answer is no, it could be either the zigzags or the stripes. Even if we turn the question around and ask if the correct cake has straight lines, a yes answer will only rule out the polka dots."

Tyrus shook his head. "That's the problem with yes or no questions. No matter what we ask, it's impossible to narrow down from three to one for sure."

"Unless . . ." Celia grinned. Maybe she could use the firefly's own vagary against her. "Since you know which of the cakes is the antidote," she said to the firefly, "if Tyrus were to point at each of the three yellow cakes, and ask you, one by one, 'Will this cake turn me into a human?' which cake would you say yes to?"

"Sorry," the firefly said, shaking her front leg reproachfully. "I told you only yes or no questions. Since your question did not have a yes or no response, I cannot answer it, and you have lost your last question."

"No," Tyrus moaned.

Celia only smiled wider. "You didn't say anything about the questions needing a yes or no *answer*. You only said they had to be yes or no questions. And since you didn't spell that out exactly, my question, which included the word *yes* and *no*—k-n-o-w—qualifies. Please answer the question."

The firefly gaped at Celia, her tail buzzing on and off with a sharp electrical hiss. "Very tricky. I should disqualify you. But since that seems exactly like something I would have done, I will answer your question. The cake that will change you back is the yellow one with the zigzags."

CHAPTER 14
The Terrible Creature

*"If you're going to turn into a pig, my dear," said Alice,
seriously, "I'll have nothing more to do with you."*

"How did you know that would work?" Tyrus asked, when
they had eaten the cake with the zigzag pattern and returned to
their human forms.

"Is that really a question you need to ask a logic nerd?"
Celia asked.

Tyrus bowed. "Touché."

Back on their feet, they could see they were in the middle
of a deep wood. The branches overhead were so thick only a
little moonlight showed through. The cold air raised goose
bumps on Celia's arms, and the occasional fluttering of wings
and random squeaks and chirps made it clear there were creatures nearby, but she hadn't seen any.

"Where to now?" she asked, shivering. "We can't spend
the night here."

Tyrus shrugged. "Like you said, this is a lot different

from—" He stopped speaking and pulled her behind a large tree.

"What is it?" she asked.

He shook his head, peering into the darkness. "I thought I heard . . ."

A branch cracked, and they both ducked.

A bush rustled nearby. Slowly, they peered around the tree. Celia gripped Tyrus's arm, ready to pull him away at the first sign of danger. When would he get it through his head that they were *not* heroes?

The branches of a scrubby pine rattled, and they both tensed, until a small brown head peeked out at them.

"Sylvan?" Tyrus said.

The rabbit beamed. "You aren't slugs anymore."

"No thanks to you," Celia said.

Tyrus knelt. "Did you talk to your grandparents?"

The rabbit bounced excitedly. "Yes, and you were right. They weren't mad at all."

"They understood about your mistake?"

Sylvan grinned up at them, clutching a piece of old paper to her chest. "That's the best part. I didn't make a mistake."

"You didn't?" Celia asked, her stomach tightening.

"No. Grandmother and Grandfather explained everything. Before Mr. Dodgson left, he said that when Wonderland was in danger, someone from his world would return to save it." She held out the paper.

The last thing Celia wanted to do was open the paper, but Tyrus and Sylvan were staring at her. Her hand shook as she reached down and took the page. It definitely seemed old, like it would fall apart at the first touch.

Carefully, she unfolded it, telling herself that Charles Dodgson couldn't possibly have known that she and Tyrus would come here. Even if he had, he would never tell anyone that a couple of kids who could barely look out for themselves would save an entire world.

Still, as she peeled the last fold open, a part of her was convinced she would see her name printed there. So, when she saw what was inside, her stomach unclenched, and she let out a huge sigh. Feeling like a blade had been pulled away from her throat, she turned the paper so Tyrus could see it.

"Alice," she giggled. "It says 'Alice.'"

Tyrus seemed disappointed, but Celia was almost giddy as she turned to the little rabbit. "You see, it *is* a mistake. Neither of us is named Alice."

The little rabbit only smiled wider. "But you *are*."

Tyrus tilted his head. "I don't understand."

Sylvan clutched her little paws to her chest. "Grandfather says that the Clock of Action is never wrong. It says Wonderland is in terrible danger and that The Alice will save us. He said that the Horn of Beckoning can only call the one Mr. Dodgson spoke of." She looked happily from Tyrus to Celia. "That means one of you has to be The Alice."

• • •

Twenty minutes later, after much arguing and more than a little pleading, Celia still hadn't convinced Sylvan that the rabbits had called the wrong people. Even worse, the bunny refused to return home, saying that her grandparents had told her to help The Alice any way she could.

"Help with *what*?" Celia asked.

"Saving Wonderland, of course," Sylvan responded pertly.

Tyrus was intrigued. "How do we save it?"

The brown rabbit shrugged. "No idea. Grandfather said you would know."

"But we don't," Celia said. "Doesn't that fact make it obvious that neither of us is The Alice?"

Sylvan only wrinkled her annoyingly cute little nose and shook her annoyingly cute little head.

"Did you find out what we're supposed to save it from?" Tyrus asked, hunching beside her.

The rabbit tucked her ears down and lowered her voice. "A hauntstrosity."

Tyrus wrinkled his forehead. "What's a *hauntstrosity*? I've never heard of that word."

"I don't know," Sylvan whispered. "But it could be a kind of monster. Or a demon. Or possibly a fiend. Some people say it has horns. Others say it has claws." She put her paws to her mouth. "The twins think it breathes fire, but Cousin Velveteen says you can't see it at all."

Celia snorted, but Sylvan didn't appear to notice.

"It attacks at night, and anyone it bites goes mad."

Tyrus jumped up. "That's why the gryphon attacked us. And the birds in the cage. And the White Rabbit. The creatures of Wonderland aren't bad, they're infected."

"Great," Celia said. "Let me know when you figure out how to fix that. Also, how to stop a creature that might have

claws or breathe fire or be invisible. I'll be over here, freezing."
As she turned to walk away, she realized the woods had gone silent.

Peering into the darkness, she saw something dart from one tree to another.

"Is it the creature?" Tyrus asked, easing in beside her.

"I don't think so," Celia whispered.

As they watched, a boy slipped out of the shadows. He didn't look much older than they were. His arms were filled with loaves of bread, cheese wheels, and a basket of apples. What appeared to be a string of linked sausages hung over his shoulders and looped around his waist like a belt. He shifted the basket of apples and shoved a pastry into his mouth, his cheeks bulging.

"Finally, another human," Celia said. "Maybe he can tell us how to get out of here."

Before she could ask him, a breeze came out of nowhere, spinning the leaves and pine needles like a mini tornado.

Clutching his food to his chest, the boy backed away.

The darkness thickened into a cloud of smoke. Celia's stomach clenched as the smoke formed letters, then words, then entire sentences. She narrowed her eyes, trying to understand what the spinning sentences said, when Tyrus gripped her arm.

"It's a werewolf."

As soon as he spoke, the words formed into a skulking creature with a doglike snout and thick fur. But—unlike a dog—it walked on two legs. Shoulders sloped and back bent, it sniffed the air, then started toward the boy.

Tyrus stepped forward, and Celia grabbed his arm.

"Where are you going?" Celia demanded.

"We have to help him," Tyrus said.

Before Celia could tell Tyrus what a crazy idea that was, the boy spun around and spotted the creature. His stubby nose wrinkled, his piggish eyes widened, and he squealed with fright. Still holding the food, he darted into the trees.

Flashing its fangs, the werewolf snarled and loped after him.

Tyrus shook off Celia's hand and raced into the woods, screaming, "Leave him alone!"

Looking back at Sylvan, Celia threw her hands in the air. "I can't believe this." But she wasn't about to lose Tyrus, so she sprinted into the woods as well.

Together the two of them chased after the boy and the werewolf. Trying not to run into any trees or poke her eye out on a branch, Celia didn't know where they were going let alone what she would do if Tyrus caught the werewolf.

The boy was surprisingly fast for someone carrying what looked like a week's worth of groceries. He darted in and out of the woods, ducked behind bushes, and doubled back on his trail with an almost animal-like speed. Each time the beast got close, the boy squealed and scurried away.

A few yards ahead of Celia, Tyrus skidded to a stop so quickly that she crashed into him, knocking them both to the ground.

"Where did he go?" Tyrus cried, leaping to his feet.

Celia looked around. There was no sign of the boy or the werewolf. From the other side of a tall hedge, a scream burst the silence, sending shivers up her spine. She and Tyrus pushed their way through the woods to find the boy lying on the ground only a few steps in front of a small house with a white fence.

The werewolf was nowhere to be seen.

"Are you all right?" Celia asked, turning the boy over.

He didn't appear to be wounded, but he was clearly in pain. "Tell her," he said, writhing on the ground.

"Tell *who*?" Tyrus asked. "Where are you hurt?"

"My . . . mother," the boy grunted.

Something was happening to him. His mouth twisted as long, curved tusks pushed out from his lips.

"It's the same thing that happened to White," Sylvan whimpered, covering her eyes with her paws.

The boy's pug nose grew wide and flat, and short, spiky hair sprouted from his face. His clenched hands twisted with a crackling sound as if his bones were breaking. A pair of wide leathery wings rose from his shoulders.

As Celia and Tyrus backed away, the creature that now looked like a mix between a pig and a bat turned its red eyes on them and opened its mouth. With its tusks jutting from its jaw, it was hard to understand him, but Celia thought he might have said, "She'll help you if you get on her good side," before he spread his wings and flapped into the night sky.

CHAPTER 15

The Unusual Duchess

*"If everybody minded their own business,"
the Duchess said, in a hoarse growl, "the world
would go round a deal faster than it does."*

"That creature," Tyrus said, still panting from the run. "It's the same thing that tried to come out of Charles Dodgson's diary back in the library, isn't it?"

Celia licked her lips.

"At first, it looked like smoke," Tyrus said. "But then, it turned into words and sentences—like a jumbled-up story. I saw the word 'werewolf' in the smoke right before it turned into one."

Celia rubbed her eyes, trying not to think about it. What could be more terrifying for a girl with dyslexia than a creature made out of words? Did the monster somehow know that about her, or was it simply a horrible coincidence?

"What were you thinking, running after them?" she demanded. "If the werewolf had turned around, it could have been *you* sprouting tusks and flying away."

Tyrus lowered his head. "I only wanted to help."

"I think you were quite heroic," Sylvan said. She hopped over to him. "Maybe *you're* The Alice."

Tyrus opened his mouth, but Celia stopped him. "No. You are not *The Alice*, whatever that means. Neither am I. We are two kids who accidentally got sucked into this crazy world. Whatever's going on here is their problem, not ours. We need to find a way to get home before something kills us."

Tyrus rubbed the back of his hand across his mouth but didn't disagree. Instead, he studied the well-lit two-story house with neatly trimmed shrubs, blooming flower gardens, and a white picket fence that looked like it could have fit into any suburban neighborhood.

"I guess we should tell whoever lives here what happened to her son."

For once, Celia agreed. If the creature that attacked the boy was the same thing that had come out of the diary, it could be looking for them.

The house didn't seem dangerous, but then again, many of the creatures that had tried to kill them didn't appear to be a threat at first either. She cupped her hands to her mouth. "Hello! Is anyone home?"

"I guess we can knock on the door," Tyrus suggested when no one responded.

"I guess." The home looked perfectly normal. So why did she keep thinking of the witch's candy house in the story of Hansel and Gretel?

"I'd rather spend the night out here," Sylvan said, curling up under a bush.

Celia cautiously approached the door. Beside the porch

was a large stone statue of a frog in a wig, wearing short pants with long socks and a jacket with fancy embroidery running up its sleeves.

"And I thought garden gnomes were creepy," Tyrus said, keeping well away from the statue.

Celia tilted her head. "I think I hear voices inside."

On the door was a metal knocker shaped like a gargoyle. Celia didn't want to touch it, and when she stretched out her hand, the gargoyle flicked its tongue and slurped her fingers.

"Gross!" she said, snatching her hand away. "It licked me."

"That wasn't in the book either," Tyrus said. "But it's kind of awesome."

"You taste like annoyance mixed with a healthy dose of exasperation," the door knocker pronounced.

"That's disgusting," Celia said, wiping her hand on her pants. "You don't randomly lick people without their permission. You shouldn't even lick them *with* their permission."

"What does annoyance taste like?" Tyrus asked.

The gargoyle winked one metal eye. "Saltier than discontent, but not quite as full-bodied as vexation."

Tyrus held out his hand. "What do *I* taste like?"

"Are you crazy?" Celia asked. She tried to pull back his arm, but the gargoyle was too quick.

It smacked its full lips. "Ah, jubilation laced with maple syrup. One of my favorite combinations."

Tyrus grinned. "I had waffles for breakfast."

"This place is driving me nuts," Celia said, running her fingers through her hair.

"You are being driven nuts by this place."

She scowled at Tyrus. "Why are you repeating me?"

Tyrus shook his head. "I didn't say anything. It was the frog."

The stone statue rolled its bulbous eyes in their direction. "Nothing was said by the boy who tastes like syrup. The frog was the one doing the speaking."

After everything they'd been through, Celia found the idea of a talking frog statue relatively normal. At least it wasn't trying to lick her. "We're lost, and we need a place to spend the night."

The statue rubbed its face with the backs of its webbed hands. "You need a place to spend the night, since you seem to be lost."

She wrinkled her nose. "Yes. So, can we stay here? Will you let us in?"

The statue nodded, its wig tilting to one side. "If I were to let you in, you could quite likely stay here."

Celia balled her fists. "That's annoying. You're just repeating what I'm saying in a different order."

The frog gave her a knowing smile. "The order in which I'm repeating what you have said is most likely annoying you."

Tyrus stepped forward. "Let me try." He furrowed his brow. "Your permission . . . given to us of . . . the house being entered, would . . . please us both."

The statue clapped its hands. "Please, both of you, enter the house. With my permission."

With that, the door swung open.

Tyrus smirked, and Celia narrowed her eyes.

As they stepped cautiously inside, the gargoyle licked the tip of Tyrus's ear. "Yum, vindication."

The voices Celia had heard from the outside grew louder as they entered the house. Unfortunately, the voices didn't sound happy.

"This is disgusting!" a woman shouted from behind a doorway across the room. "Absolutely inedible."

"It's your confundant recipe!" yelled a man with a snooty accent that sounded vaguely European. "If you don't like it, find a new one."

"I'll find a new cook!" the woman howled. A moment later, a dish flew through the doorway and shattered against the wall to their left.

Tyrus gasped. "I know where we are. This is the Duchess's house."

"Isn't she the one with the baby who turned into—"

"A pig? In the book," Tyrus agreed. "That must have been her son who turned into a half-pig, half-bat . . . thing."

Celia looked around the room. The walls were covered with designs so bright they made her eyes hurt. Mismatched pieces of furniture in garish fabrics and gold leaf trim fought for space with hideously ugly statues and swarms of knick-knacks.

In the center of the room was a large painting of a beaver driving a tractor and planting ice-cream sundaes in the middle of a cemetery. Beneath it, printed in fancy letters, was written "Better late than Tuesday."

"She has interesting taste."

"More like *no* taste," Tyrus said.

Something smashed in the other room, and the man's voice shouted, "Get someone else to cook your putrancious food. I quit."

Celia pressed her lips together. "The boy said to get on her good side. How do we do that while also telling her that her son turned into a pig-bat and flew away?"

Tyrus poked his shoe at a pile of metal parts and wires jumbled in the corner. "If she's anything like the Duchess in the book, she may not have a good side. That woman was psycho."

An extremely thin man stomped into the room. His dark hair was combed into elaborate swirls that rose at least a foot above his head. "Too much spice on this. Not enough spice on that. I throw my pots and pans into the sea and you taste my vexignation."

A tiny old woman with watery eyes and a sharp chin charged after him. "It would undoubtedly taste better than your soup." She rounded on Celia and Tyrus. "Who are you, and what are you doing in my house?" she yelled.

Celia had been planning out what she would say, but at the woman's sharp gaze, every word fled her brain. "We, um . . . I mean . . . we wanted to tell you . . . ?" She turned to Tyrus.

Tyrus stepped forward. "Your son got attacked by a werewolf, turned into a pig-bat, and flew away. But I really like your painting."

Celia gaped at him. He shrugged and mouthed, "Trying to get on her good side."

"My painting?" the Duchess snarled, her face twisting. "Is that what you're here for—to steal my art?"

"We aren't going to steal anything," Celia managed to say. "We're just trying to tell you that your son—"

"Thieves!" the woman shouted, drops of spit flying from her lips. "That's what you are. What will you take next? My food, my cook, my toad?" She shook her finger in Celia's face. "One who steals from a thief robs not only their trust but their punctuality."

Celia looked at Tyrus. "I'm not sure what that means."

"Thank you for your wise advice," Tyrus said. "I'm sure it will make more sense after we've slept on it." He swallowed. "You seem like a very smart woman and *kind.*"

"I'll tell you what kind of woman I am," the Duchess said, jabbing him in the chest with a sharp finger. "The kind who will call the cards on you. He who dances with noodles wakes up with back warts."

Had she just said she would call the *cards*? And what did warts have to do with noodles? How did you get on the good side of a woman screaming nonsense in your face?

Celia noticed an ornate mirror hanging on the wall. Reflected in its surface, she could see herself and Tyrus standing in front of a little old woman. The woman in the mirror looked familiar. Her hair was the same color as the Duchess's, her clothes identical. But unlike the distorted shrew screaming at them, her eyes seemed kind. Her cheeks were pink and full, and she gave them a welcoming smile.

Celia turned, looking for the woman in the mirror, but there was no one there.

"Get out now, you treacherous trespassers! It is a truth universally acknowledged that a platypus in possession of a cello must be in want of a haircut." The Duchess raised her arms above her head, hands clenched in fists. At the same time, the woman in the mirror raised her arms, opening them in a welcoming embrace.

Her good *side.* Celia looked from the woman screaming at them to the reflection in the mirror. Moving quickly, she stepped around the Duchess. Turning toward what should have been the woman's back, she found herself looking at the face from the mirror.

Instantly, the Duchess stopped shouting. The kind-looking woman reached out to squeeze Celia's hands. "Poor dears. You look exhausted. Let me get you some dinner and soft beds. After all, home is where your spleen is."

CHAPTER 16

The Dead C.A.T.

*"Please would you tell me," said Alice, a little
timidly . . . "why your cat grins like that?"*

Celia woke to the smell of breakfast cooking, and for a moment, she was sure she was home and this had all been a stress dream brought on by attending a new school.

Even before she opened her eyes, she knew it wasn't true. She seldom remembered her dreams, and when she did, they were usually about losing her locker combination or forgetting to study for a test. She didn't possess the imagination to come up with the things that had happened to her in the last twenty-four hours.

After washing her hands and face in a basin near her bed, she opened the door and stepped into the hallway.

Tyrus stood at the top of the stairs, leaning over the hand-rail.

"What is it?" Celia asked. "Are the Duchess and the cook fighting again?"

Tyrus put his finger to his lips. "It's the Duchess. But she isn't fighting."

Leaning next to Tyrus, Celia could clearly hear two voices. "Who is she talking to?"

"I think herself." He shoved his glasses up on his nose. "Only she isn't talking. She's . . . *singing*."

As they listened, a melodious alto voice floated to them.

> *I love to see the daffodils*
> *that spring up from the ground*

"That's nice," Celia said.

Tyrus shook his head. "Wait."

A second voice—this one a flat tenor—joined in.

> *I take my little shovel out*
> *and give their heads a pound*

The alto sang again.

> *How sweetly sings the mockingbird*
> *that flutters through the sky*

The second voice responded.

> *I pluck each nasty feather out*
> *and bake him in a pie*

Celia shuddered. "That's not creepy at all."

"There you are, you sleepyheads," the Duchess said, appearing at the foot of the stairs.

Celia tensed until she was sure they were looking at the woman's good side.

The Duchess waved. "Gaté has made breakfast for you. Follow me into the kitchen."

"No!" Celia and Tyrus shouted together, racing down the stairs as the woman began to turn around.

"We'll walk next to you," Tyrus said.

"So we can see your beautiful face," Celia added.

"Beauty is only skin deep," the Duchess said. "But gall bladders are more trouble than they are worth. That's the moral of that."

"I'll try to remember it," Tyrus said.

Careful to stay one step ahead of the woman, they entered the kitchen to find the chef expertly flipping pancakes from a griddle onto a platter. Neither he nor the Duchess showed any lingering effects from the previous night's quarrel.

"Help yourself," he warbled, handing them each a plate. "My creations are fantabulous, as always. If I do say so myself. Which I do."

"They look great," Tyrus said.

The Duchess covered her mouth with one hand. "His pancakes are as bland as paper, but a healthy dollop of hot sauce perks them right up."

Careful never to let the woman turn her back on them, Tyrus and Celia joined her at the table.

"Is your son joining us, by any chance?" Celia asked, noticing an empty place setting.

The Duchess snorted. "Sus made a pig of himself last night. He'll sleep the rest of the day."

Celia whispered to Tyrus. "Does that mean she knows what happened to him or . . . ?"

Tyrus shrugged.

The Duchess dumped a bottle of hot sauce onto her food. "Spice is the spice of life."

"I think I'll stick with syrup," Celia said, her eyes watering from the smell.

Tyrus nodded. "Same."

"Suit yourself." The Duchess shoved a forkful into her mouth and grunted with satisfaction.

Celia cut a square of pancake and nearly choked when she put it in her mouth. It tasted like the cook had put an entire bottle of pepper into the batter.

"Where will you go now?" the Duchess asked.

"We're trying to find our way back home," Celia said, attempting to wash the pepper taste away with a cup of juice.

"The moral of that is always carry a map. That's what I told him the first time we met."

"Him?" Tyrus asked, smothering his pancakes with syrup and taking a huge bite. Celia hid a smile behind her hand as his eyes began to water.

"Mr. Dodgson," the Duchess said. "Charles, as he preferred to be called."

Tyrus leaned forward. "You met Charles Dodgson?"

"Several times," the Duchess said. "I assume you come from the same place. The two of you speak like him." She nodded at Celia. "If you don't mind me saying, you have a striking resemblance to the man. Something about the lips."

146

"He's a distant relative," Celia said, moving her pancakes around. "You don't happen to know how he got home?"

The Duchess chewed thoughtfully. "You'd want to speak with the queen. He spent a great deal of time with her when he was here."

Tyrus shook his head and subtly drew a finger across his throat.

"Is there anyone else we could talk to?" Celia asked.

"The Hatter," the Duchess said, but then shook her head. "I'm afraid he wouldn't be much help these days."

Tyrus dropped his fork. "The *Mad Hatter?*"

"*Quite* mad. His decline began right around the time Mr. Dodgson left. So sad. I used to visit his millinery shop quite often before he . . ." She tapped a finger to the side of her head.

"That's a hat shop," Tyrus said.

"Hmm, yes. Such lovely bonnets he made—with teapots and flowers."

"And teeth and claws," cackled a voice from the back of her head.

Celia shared a worried glance with Tyrus. This might be a good time to leave. "Could you take us to his shop?"

"Heavens no, child. I've a dozen things to do, including teaching my cook how to properly season his meals."

"What did you say?" Gaté asked, his eyes narrowing.

"Ask not why your food goes uneaten," the Duchess said. "Ask what you can do to make it taste better."

She rubbed her sharp chin. "It's a shame the cat isn't available to guide you. He went everywhere with Mr. Dodgson."

Tyrus leaped from his seat. "The *Cheshire cat?* Is he here?"

"I'm afraid not," the Duchess said, patting her mouth with her napkin. "He's dead."

Tyrus collapsed into his chair.

"Poor thing got slower and slower until . . . kaput." She held her wrinkled hands in front of her and mimed breaking a stick in half. "Nothing is certain but death and yard care."

"No," Tyrus whispered.

"Such a shame to see his body lying around the house. I tried to put him together again, but I'm no good at that sort of thing. So messy. And all those bits and pieces sticking out."

Tyrus gagged, and Celia was afraid he might throw up. "You tried to put a . . . *dead cat* back together?"

"Now it's only a pile of rotting parts," the Duchess said, waving her hand toward the living room. "Poor Sus poked his toe on one of the loose wires just the other day."

"Wires?" Tyrus asked. "You mean that pile of junk in your living room—?"

"—is the Cheshire cat?" Celia finished. She pushed her plate away and exchanged a glance with Tyrus. "It's a mechanical cat?"

"Of course." The Duchess finished her food and burped. "Been meaning to throw the pieces away for months. Are either of you any good with that sort of thing? If you can get him working again, he's all yours."

• • •

"I can't believe the Cheshire cat is a robot," Tyrus said as Celia sorted pieces in the front room of the Duchess's house.

Celia held up a mechanical cat head. Its eyes were shut,

148

but—even unplugged—its mouth curved up in a wide grin. She studied the wires hanging out of the bottom and tried plugging them into matching connections in what she hoped was the cat's body.

Tyrus tilted his head. "Have you ever worked on anything like this?"

"All the time," she snapped. "I have a complete robotics lab at my house."

"Glad you're back to your snarky self," he said. "Guess that's what happens when you get a good night's sleep."

"Sorry." She picked up one leg and shoved it into a socket, tightening a nut until the gears meshed. "It's just nice to see something here that makes sense. It's not even that complicated. I've seen IKEA bookshelves that were trickier to assemble."

Not that she expected to get the robot working. A smart third grader could fit the pieces together and connect the wires. Diagnosing why a complicated piece of electrical equipment failed was way beyond her skill.

But there was something satisfying about creating order out of disorder. With no instructions to decipher or manuals to read, she let her fingers sort each piece, twisting and turning them until her brain showed her where it went. She would never admit it to anyone else, but sometimes she was afraid her brain was only good for embarrassing her and making her look stupid. It was a relief to know she was capable of something useful.

"You did it," Tyrus shouted.

Celia looked down to see that she had assembled all the pieces. Now that it was put together, it did look more catlike.

A switch on its collar was set to OFF. Tyrus pushed it to ON, and the two of them waited.

When nothing happened, Celia shrugged. "Sorry. I didn't see any kind of power source or cord, so . . ."

"That's all right," Tyrus said. "At least it's not jumbled on the floor in pieces anymore. Maybe we could find somewhere to keep it safe in case, you know, we find batteries or something."

"That would be nice." As Celia patted the top of the robot's head, a spark of static electricity jumped between her fingertip and the metal. Gears spun, and motors powered up. The tail spun around, and something inside clunked.

"What did you do?" Tyrus asked.

Celia shook her head.

After a few boops and beeps, the two large green eyes flickered open. The robot turned its head toward Celia and Tyrus.

"Where am I? And who am I?"

"You don't know?" Celia asked.

The robot blinked. "I seem to be having difficulty downloading my long-term memory."

Celia looked at a rusted metal plate on its collar. One glimpse of the long, unfamiliar words told her she would never be able to read them.

Tyrus rubbed the dirt and grime off the metal. "'Clandestine Automaton Tabby,'" he read. "What does that mean?"

"I'm not sure. I think Mr. Dodgson chose it because it abbreviates as C.A.T."

"So you *did* know Charles Dodgson," Celia said.

"I believe so. He and another fellow built me this mechanical body when mine was starting to fade away after an unfortunate incident with a . . . a firefly, I think. My memory seems to be coming back." The grin on its mechanical face grew wider and wider until it was a little frightening.

"Could you turn that down?" Celia asked. "It's kind of freaky."

"Certainly." Blue sparks shot out from a vent near its front left leg. "Is that better?"

"Not really," she said. "But don't try it again. I'm afraid you might hurt yourself. Do you know how Mr. Dodgson got back to his world? We were brought here by mistake by a rabbit who thinks one of us is Alice."

"There are no mistakes," said the cat. "Only opportunities waiting to be discovered. Except for whoever thought calf's-foot jelly should be eaten. That was undoubtedly a mistake of the worst kind."

Celia had no idea what calf's-foot jelly was, but it sounded disgusting. "Mistake or not, we need to get home. Can you help us?"

"I don't . . . I don't . . . I don't . . ." the cat repeated, its tail spinning wildly.

Tyrus slapped it on the back, and the cat's eyes blinked. "Thank you. I don't remember anything about Mr. Dodgson leaving, I'm afraid. Perhaps I will when all my memories finish downloading."

"Could you at least point us in the right direction?" Celia asked.

"Certainly," the cat said. "Where would you like to go?"

She pinched her lower lip. "I'm not really sure."

"In that case, you may go any direction you want. If you walk long enough, you are sure to end up somewhere."

Tyrus grinned. "Finally, something that sounds like the book. Do you know anyone who might be able to help us?"

The robot buzzed and beeped for a moment before saying, "You might ask the other fellow who helped build me. Quite an ingenious chap. Had a penchant for hats, I think."

"The Hatter!" Tyrus blurted. "Do you know where he is?"

"I seem to recall the March Hare living to the east of here and the Hatter living to the west."

"Can you take us to him?" Tyrus asked.

"East it is," the cat said.

Celia frowned. "I thought you said the Hatter lived to the west."

"He does. But it's quite unlikely he would be home."

Celia sighed. "Can you please take us to wherever the Hatter is, Mr. Cat?"

"Directly and correctly," the robot said. "I believe that I prefer to be called Cheshire, though I have no idea why."

It stepped forward with its front right leg, but when it tried to move its left leg, smoke drifted out of the back of its head. Its tail spun, and its eyes snapped open and shut. It turned toward Celia. "Perhaps you could give me a push."

CHAPTER 17

The Mad Hatter

*"In that direction," the Cat said, waving its
right paw round, "lives a Hatter: and in that
direction," waving the other paw, "lives a March
Hare. Visit either you like: they're both mad."*

"Did you figure out how to save Wonderland yet?" asked
Sylvan as she bounced along beside them.

Celia didn't bother responding. After she'd readjusted
Cheshire's legs several times, the cat managed to walk fairly
well except for an occasional annoying squeak.

"It's good to be out and—*squeak*—about again," Cheshire
said.

"How long were you . . . *off*?" Tyrus asked.

"According to my internal—*squeak*—clock, seven years.
Not that I have any—*squeak*—recollection of that time."

"Seven years," Celia murmured, wishing she had a can of
oil. "So you just fell apart, and they left you on the floor?"

"It would appear so," Cheshire said. "The last thing I remember is hearing a whispering sound behind me and a dark
cloud swirling through the front door while the Duchess and I
were discussing the merits of gingersnaps."

Sylvan gasped. "The hauntstrosity."

Tyrus nodded. "There's a monster attacking creatures all over Wonderland. We saw it turn the Duchess's son into a pig-bat."

"Many children eat like—*squeak*—pigs. And pigs, for the most part, eat like children," Cheshire said in a lecturing tone. "While children have been known to eat pig on occasion, most would consider it a breach of etiquette for a pig to eat a—*squeak*—child."

"That's not what we mean," Celia tried to explain, but the cat wasn't about to be interrupted.

"Were a pig to change into a child, it would be frightfully awkward for everyone involved. Would one leave the pig in the sty with its friends or invite it into the house to—*squeak*—run wild? On the other hand, I've known many boys and girls who would make much better pigs than they do children."

"Look out!" Tyrus shouted as Cheshire walked straight into a tree with a loud *clang*.

"Are you all right?" Celia asked, checking his head for cracks.

"Not in the least," Cheshire said, twirling his tail. "I am half right. And half left. Not to mention half front and—*squeak*—half back. Top and bottom is another matter, because—"

Assured that the robot was no worse off than before, Celia folded her arms. "Do you even know where you're going?"

"I know where I've—*squeak*—been," Cheshire said, giving her a meaningful look. "Which is often the most overlooked part of determining where one is going."

"I almost never remember where I've been," Sylvan said, thoughtfully. "I should probably pay more attention."

"But you *do* know how to take us to the Hatter, right?" Tyrus asked, waving a hand at the deep wood surrounding them. There were no signs of a trail or any markings. "Because it looks like we're lost. Do you—"

He looked around, but the cat was gone.

"Where did he go?" Tyrus asked. "It's like he disappeared the way the cat in the book did."

Celia scowled. "I think I'm going to regret putting him together."

After searching for the cat for nearly an hour, they gave up and continued to look for the Hatter. Though they found several houses and buildings in various states of disrepair, they didn't see a single person. They did come across a patch of insolent pumpkins, but the only responses they got when they asked for directions were insults and rude suggestions.

"I hope Cheshire is okay," Tyrus said.

Celia snorted. "He's probably busy explaining to a squirrel why nuts aren't squirrels, but squirrels can be nuts. Except it's rude to call squirrels nuts and even more rude to call nuts squirrels."

"What's that?" Tyrus asked, pointing to a tall brown spire rising above the trees ahead of them.

Celia squinted at the structure. "It looks almost furry."

"It looks like a rabbit ear to me," Sylvan said. "But maybe a little longer." She tilted one of her own ears to demonstrate.

Tyrus grinned. "I know where we are. Come on!"

Together they ran through the trees until they emerged in

a clearing at the back of a large house. At least Celia thought it was a house. Instead of being covered with shingles or tiles, the roof was made of thick brown fur. The tiny hairs rippling in the breeze looked soft enough to sleep on. The spire they'd seen from the woods was a chimney. An identical chimney tilted to one side, forming a pair of rabbit ears. She was almost positive the orange-hued walls were made of carrots.

But this house looked run-down and deserted. Several sections of the roof had caved in, and the windows were all broken or covered with thick layers of dirt. The carrot walls had large patches of brown rot, and one entire corner looked like it had been eaten away by insects.

Faded pennants fluttered briefly in the breeze next to dozens of ragged strings. It took Celia a moment to realize the colorful, shriveled blobs at the end of the strings were deflated balloons.

"I don't think anyone lives here," she whispered.

"No," Tyrus said. "I hear voices."

As they walked around the side of the house, an enormous tree came into view. Beneath the tree was a long table, surrounded by at least twenty seats, ranging from kitchen chairs to folding chairs, rocking chairs, recliners, a bar stool, and even a love seat.

A rabbit in a tattered gray suit looked up from his tall wingback chair and frowned. "I wish you had told me you were coming. I would have provided more seating."

A brown-and-white mouse, who appeared to be sleeping with his face buried in a large book, looked up blearily. "Did I ever tell you the story of the unexpected guests?"

"Have some tea," the rabbit told the mouse, filling a cup nearly the size of a mixing bowl. "It will perk you up."

"Indubitably." The mouse flopped forward—its face now planted firmly in the cup—and snored bubbles in the dark brown liquid.

"I'm sorry, Mr. Rabbit," Celia said. "We didn't know we were coming ourselves until we got here."

Sylvan shook her head rapidly. "He's not a—" she started to whisper to Celia.

"Do these magnificent appendages look like *rabbit* ears?" The creature snorted. He opened his gray jacket. "Do I wear white year-round like a fashion-addled simpleton? My house is not a dank hole in the ground." He scowled at Sylvan.

When it was clear Tyrus and Celia had no response, he wrinkled his nose. "I am a hare. The March Hare to be precise."

"I'm a dormouse," the mouse burbled, his face still buried in the massive teacup.

"And you are late," the March Hare said. "We expected you . . ."

The dormouse yawned. "Twenty years ago."

"We weren't even born yet," Tyrus said.

"A poor excuse." The March Hare took a biscuit from the table, which was overflowing with platters, plates, and bowls of all sizes—none of them matching. "We finished our party hours ago. It's nearly time to start."

That was exactly the kind of nonsense that made Celia's head ache. The tablecloth was so stained and worn it was almost impossible to tell what the original color had been. Beneath the table and chairs was at least six inches of broken crockery. Something was clearly very wrong here, and yet Tyrus barely appeared to notice.

"I've dreamed about coming here," he said. "Can we join your tea party?"

Seated at the head of the table was a striking man in a high-collared shirt and a full-length green cloak. A matching scarf hung from his neck, and his black top hat adorned with a silver band was tilted at a debonair angle. Dark hair covered one eye, stopping just short of his high cheekbones.

Unlike the house and the table, the man had a vibrancy Celia had never seen before—as though the air around him was clearer somehow, magnified. Every color, from his clothes to his cheeks, seemed to leap out in an extra dimension.

Leaning back, pointed boots crossed on the table before him, he studied Tyrus and Celia with an eye the exact same shade of green as his cloak. The intensity coming from his body was multiplied ten times in his eyes. Celia knew she had never met him before, and yet he seemed to recognize her. His lips rose into a wry grin as he spread his arms wide.

"The three of you are most welcome."

CHAPTER 18
The Tea Party

"I've had nothing yet," Alice replied in an
offended tone: "so I ca'n't take more."

"You mean you ca'n't take less," said the Hatter;
"it's very easy to take more than nothing."

Celia looked at the chairs, trying to decide where to sit.

"Don't stand on ceremony," the hare said, waving his hands.

"I'm sorry, I . . ." Celia swallowed. It was hard enough to meet new people, but when the new people included a pushy hare, a sleepy mouse, and an unnervingly handsome man, it only made things worse.

"Don't stand on ceremony," the hare repeated.

Something wriggled under Celia's foot, and she looked down to see a snail in a tuxedo crawl out of the grass under her shoe. "I'm so sorry," she said, moving her foot. "I hope I didn't hurt you."

"Sure, sure—step on the hired help," the snail squeaked. "What do we matter?"

"I really am sorry," Celia said, but the snail only grunted, carrying away a tiny shard of broken plate on the back of its shell. At that rate, it would take it a couple of centuries to clean up the trash under the table.

"Fetch us more sugar cubes," the March Hare called after the snail. "And try not to slime the pantry this time."

As Tyrus climbed into an overstuffed purple chair with a matching ottoman, a deep voice laughed. "He picked me because I'm the most comfortable."

Tyrus looked down at his chair. "You talk?"

"I can't dance or sing," the chair said through a mouth set between its back and cushion. Two large purple eyes set into the armrests blinked.

Tyrus rubbed his glasses with the sleeve of his shirt. "Is it okay if I sit on you?"

"Just don't spill the jam." The chair grinned.

"He'll be bragging for a month about getting picked first," the hare said.

Not sure she liked the idea of sitting on living chairs that could talk, Celia finally selected a rocking chair whose seat and arms were worn by years of use.

"Thank you, child," the chair said in a grandmotherly voice.

Sylvan hopped onto a bright yellow beach chair that leaned back comfortably and murmured, "Excellent choice, bunny-meister," in a surfer accent.

"Excellent decision," the Hatter said. He waved a hand at the goodies on the table. "Choose wisely."

Celia's stomach rumbled. Other than the peppery pancakes, this was the first food she'd had since entering Wonderland. She studied the plates of fancy frosted cookies, delicate little cakes shaped like roses, and a tureen of steaming green broth filled with vegetables and chunks of meat.

As Tyrus reached for a cookie, the March Hare threw a jam-covered scone at his head. "Mind your manners."

"Manners?" Tyrus asked, pulling back his hand.

Celia's mother had never cared much for formality at the dinner table—especially since most of the time their food came from a paper bag filled with ketchup packets. She vaguely remembered something about different-sized forks for different parts of the meal.

"They don't know the rules," the Hatter said. As he brushed back his hair, Celia noticed dark bruise-like circles under his eyes. They were especially noticeable against the pale white of his skin.

"Read them the rules of etiquette," the hare said.

The Dormouse looked up, wiped his whiskers, and opened the book he'd been sleeping on when they first arrived. "*The Etiquette and Policies of Tea: A Quintessential List of Manners for the Proper Lady and Gentleman Regarding Noon Tea, High Tea, Low Tea, and Frivoli-tea.* 'First and thusly, whenever possible, one must greet one's hostess with a gift of loose hardware, a secret handshake, or a swift slap to the back of the head.'"

"What?" Celia asked, sure she must have misunderstood.

"'Second, and of much greater consequence than the first,'" the Dormouse continued, "'when selecting items of palatal significance—'"

"Food," the March Hare clarified.

The Dormouse gave him an irritated glare. "'One must

never overfill one's plate. Rather, one should overfill one's neighbor's plate while borrowing liberally from it. Placing cookies on one's head, shoulder, knee, or in one's pocket, lap, or neighbor's pocket is also acceptable.'"

Sylvan giggled, and the Dormouse appeared to lose his place.

"Get to the best part," the hare said.

"Crumpet tossing . . . spoon juggling . . . saucer switching . . ." the Dormouse muttered, running his paw down the page. "Ah, yes, here we are. 'Lastly, and of greatest import, under penalty of belittlement, befuddlement, beratement, and bereavement, tea party guests must never under any circumstances select food with their fingers, hands, serving utensils, or napkins.'"

"That's the silliest thing ever," Celia snapped. "How are we supposed to put food on our plates if we can't use our hands or utensils?"

"I favor my ears," the hare said, flipping a cake to himself with one floppy ear.

"I use my tail," the Dormouse said, wrapping himself a cookie.

The Hatter tilted a saucer with one boot, somehow managing to roll an entire pile of cakes to a spot directly in front of him without knocking any on the floor.

"I could use my toes," Tyrus said, starting to untie his shoe.

"Don't you dare," Celia said. She studied a plate of star-shaped Danishes, before rolling up her sleeve and clumsily knocking the pastries off the tray with her elbow.

A small green head popped out of the tureen and shouted, "Unimaginative!" before disappearing back into the liquid.

"Mocking turtle soup," the Dormouse muttered through a yawn.

"Are there rules about pouring tea?" Tyrus asked, dragging a plate of cookies across the table with his teeth.

"Rules for tea?" the hare scoffed. "Absurd!"

As Celia bit into her first Danish, the Hatter stood. "I'm afraid the party is over."

"What?" Tyrus asked. "We just started."

"Just finished you mean," the March Hare said. He nudged the Dormouse. "Shove left."

The Dormouse sat up, blinked, and moved from his stool to a deep recliner, where he instantly fell back asleep. The hare moved to the stool the Dormouse had been sitting on, while the Hatter took the hare's spot.

"Well?" the hare asked, looking at Celia and Tyrus.

"I think they want us to rotate seats," Tyrus said.

Picking up her cup and saucer, Celia moved to Tyrus's spot.

"Nice knowing you," the purple chair called as Tyrus took an uncomfortable-looking wooden seat.

"Thanks for hanging ten, little dudette—or in your case, eight," the beach chair told Sylvan as she hopped off him. "It was gnarly. Come back soon."

"Let the party begin," the March Hare said, taking a hearty gulp from the cup the Dormouse had been sleeping in.

"The reason we came here," Celia said, "is that we're trying to find our way home. You see—"

"First things first," the Hatter said.

"Entertainment before business," the March Hare agreed. He nudged the Dormouse. "Tell us a story."

The Dormouse climbed to the top of his recliner. "Ahem, I share with you now a story of friendship, adventure, adversity, noble goals, and ultimate tragedy."

Celia heaved a sigh, but Tyrus leaned forward, his eyes glowing.

Clasping his hands behind his back, the Dormouse cleared his throat and began to recite.

> *Jack and Jill*
> *Climbed up the hill*
> *Because their throats had dried.*
> *Jill fell back*
> *And so did Jack*
> *And that is how they died.*

"That's not how it goes," Celia said.

Tyrus put down the cake he was eating. "What a terrible story."

"Ingrates," the Dormouse said peevishly. He hopped into his seat, curled up, and went back to sleep.

"A wonderful tale," the March Hare shouted, climbing up on the table. "Now, we dance."

Clapping his hands above his head, he began to do a jig, kicking plates and cups everywhere as the Hatter clapped along.

"Yes!" Tyrus called, swaying back and forth in his seat.

Sylvan thumped her furry feet in rhythm, but Celia ducked her head, afraid of getting hit with pieces of broken crockery.

"Bravo!" the Hatter said as the hare collapsed into his chair again. He turned to Celia and Tyrus. "Now it's your turn."

"I could tell you the story of *The Little Prince*," Tyrus suggested. "I know it by heart."

"It sounds noble," the March Hare said. "And short. I like it."

"No!" Celia slammed her hand on the table, making her cup jump. "We didn't come for parties or cookies or stories. We're here because we accidentally came through a door from our world and we need to find a way home."

"You mean, you need to find a way to save Wonderland," Sylvan said.

Celia scowled. "No. I don't."

The Hatter leaned forward, resting his elbows on the table. His posture was casual, but something in his eyes made her feel like he was giving her his full attention.

"I see. How can I help you?"

Now they were getting somewhere.

"The Duchess told us you knew Charles Dodgson," she said, concentrating on keeping her words in the right order. "He would have come here a long time ago, although I don't know if time works here the same way it does in our world. Do you remember him?"

The Hatter nodded. "Yes."

Celia sighed. "We think he might have come here on purpose, but we came on accident. We found his book, and I accidentally opened a doorway." She noticed Sylvan's disappointed gaze and tried not to feel guilty, then turned back to the Hatter. "The rabbits think one of us is Alice, but we're not. They want us to save Wonderland, but we can't. We just want to go home. It's time we go back."

The Hatter's jaw trembled, and, for a moment, she thought he was going to argue with her, but he simply nodded. "Return time."

"Exactly," Celia said. "Did Mr. Dodgson ever talk to you about how he got here and how he hoped to get back?"

"Yes."

With that single word, Celia felt like a weight had been lifted from her shoulders.

The Hatter picked up his cup, his hand shaking, spilling tea on the table in front of him. "How can I help you?"

"We're hoping he might have told someone about the math he used."

The Hatter traced a circle in the spilled liquid. "I see."

"He went home and—"

"Now it's your turn."

"I'm so glad you understand." She turned to Sylvan. "I really am sorry we can't help you, but we aren't the people you think we are. After all the crazy things we've seen, I'm terrified." She turned back to the Hatter. "The Duchess thought you might be able to help, so we found our way here."

"With a little help," said a familiar voice.

Celia turned to see a pair of green eyes staring at her from the rocking chair to her right.

"Cheshire," the March Hare said. "So good to see you."

The Dormouse woke, squeaked at the sight of the cat, then disappeared under his chair.

"Don't worry," Cheshire said. "I never—*squeak*—eat mice. At least I haven't so far. But I could use a bit of—*squeak*—oil."

"I've got something much better," the March Hare said. Before Celia could stop him, the hare hopped over the table and jabbed a spoonful of butter into the cat's gears.

"No!" Celia said, afraid the Cheshire cat would start smoking or burst into flame.

But the cat only stretched its legs and grinned. "Thank you, old hare. That is much better."

"Bravo," said the Hatter, clapping his hands.

"How did you find us here?" Tyrus asked. "And how did you leave without us seeing you?"

Cheshire winked. "A good friend always manages to appear when they are needed and disappear when they are not. Therefore, I must be needed. Or possibly I'm in need of something myself. At the moment, I believe I need a scone—with honey."

"Glad to oblige, old boy," the March Hare said, dolloping a spoonful of sticky honey onto a scone.

"Can we get back to talking about how to get us home?" Celia asked.

"First things first." The Hatter reached under the table and pulled out two hats. He tossed the first—a derby topped with a unicorn horn. Tyrus caught it in midair.

The hare nodded. "Imaginative and unique. Well played."

The Hatter's lips quirked in a wry grin as he pulled out a white top hat adorned with gold numbers and math symbols.

With a flick of his wrist, he sent it spinning through the air. It bounced off the table in front of Tyrus's cup, and Celia barely managed to grab it before it rolled off the table.

"A logical choice," Cheshire said.

"Thank you." It was a little large for Celia's head, but the Hatter couldn't have been expected to know her size. Then again, how had he prepared these hats for them at all when he hadn't known who they were or that they were coming?

"I don't wear hats," Sylvan said as the Hatter reached under the table again.

"Wise decision," the March Hare said. "They'll give you hat ears."

As Celia took off her hat, the sound of running boots came from all around them.

The Dormouse squeaked from beneath his chair, "The cards are here!"

The Hatter stood, the skin across his cheeks pulled so tight it looked like it might tear. His smile disappeared. "I'm afraid the party is over."

Celia spun around. For a moment, she saw nothing. Then, as though materializing out of thin air, six soldiers appeared. Each of them wore a red or black uniform over a starched white shirt. Stenciled on each jacket was a number or letter followed by either a diamond, a heart, a spade, or a club.

Tyrus turned to run, knocking over his chair, but the leader of the group—the jack of hearts—drew a gleaming sword. "Halt! By order of the queen."

"What do you want?" Celia shouted. "Leave us alone."

The jack turned again, and for a moment became invisible.

They were *real* cards—so thin they disappeared when viewed from the side.

"The queen has been searching for you," the card said.

"You're making a mistake," Celia said, holding her hat in front of her. "I'm not who she thinks I am."

She started to say more, but the Hatter gave her a sharp look. In three lightning-quick steps, he bounded between the soldier and Celia and Tyrus, positioning himself so he could see both groups. "They don't know the rules," he said, green eyes glinting dangerously.

"Are you interfering with the queen's business?" the card asked, shifting his blade toward the Hatter.

Like a snake deciding whether or not to strike, the Hatter fixed his eyes on the soldier's. His right hand disappeared inside his cloak. "Choose wisely."

For a moment, Celia was sure the jack was going to attack the Hatter. Instead, he slid his sword back into his scabbard and turned to his men. "Get those children out of here. The stink of this place makes me sick."

"Excellent decision," the Hatter said, slipping his hand back out from under his cloak.

Sylvan curled into a frightened ball as two more soldiers pulled up behind the house in a black carriage adorned with red hearts.

Celia scooped the rabbit up, pressing Sylvan's trembling body to her chest as the cards pulled them away. "You didn't answer our questions," she called to the Hatter. But he had already dropped back into his original seat, lifting his boots onto the table. She looked for the Cheshire cat, but, once again, he had disappeared.

"Thank you for your party," Tyrus said as the soldiers pushed them through the carriage door. "And the hats."

Sylvan peeked over Celia's shoulder. "Thank you for the scones."

Celia glanced back at the Hatter. She could see the tension in his body, and she could swear he wanted to say something to them, but he simply tipped his hat and nodded. "The three of you are most welcome."

CHAPTER 19

The Queen of Hearts

*"Get to your places!" shouted the
Queen in a voice of thunder.*

"That is so not how I imagined the Queen of Hearts's castle would look," Tyrus whispered as the cards drove the carriage through a set of red gates.

Leaning out the window, Celia studied the building in front of them.

After all the stories she'd heard about how terrible the queen was, Celia had expected dark forbidding walls, vines with poisonous thorns, high turrets with sharp points and isolated towers, and gallows everywhere.

This looked more like an office building—straight lines, practical windows, and neatly trimmed rectangular bushes. Everything appeared organized and straightforward with individual cards moving smartly about their business.

"I don't think I'm allowed to be here," Sylvan whispered, her whiskers twitching.

"I'll take care of you," Celia said, patting her head.

"What now?" Tyrus asked the jack of hearts as he escorted them out of the carriage and onto the cobblestone drive. "Are you going to throw us in prison? Or cut off our heads?"

"Do you *want* to be thrown in prison?" the card asked.

"No," Celia said.

"Then I will have my men escort you to your rooms where you may bathe, change into clean clothes, and enjoy light refreshments until the queen sends for you."

"What about our rabbit friend?" Celia asked.

The card looked at Sylvan. "Does she need a change of clothes too?"

"No, your royalness," Sylvan said.

The jack of hearts almost smiled. "Stick together, and you will be fine."

That sounded far too reasonable. The Queen of Hearts in Lewis Carroll's books was fearsome and unpredictable. "Are we going to be put on trial?"

The soldier, who had started to walk away, turned back, and Celia was once again shocked that he and the rest of the cards only had two dimensions. From the front and back, they looked completely normal. When they turned, it was like seeing a hologram disappear before her eyes.

"What would you be tried for?" the soldier asked when he reappeared. He faced Celia, his expression hard.

"I'm not sure," she admitted. "Trespassing, or stealing tarts, or painting the roses?"

His face softened as one side of his mouth pulled up. "Have you been stealing tarts, young lady?"

She shrugged. "I haven't seen any tarts to steal."

"If you do, don't." He waved to his men. "See them to their rooms and make sure they have everything they need."

"I don't trust them," Tyrus whispered to Celia as they were marched along a walkway that ran in a straight line from one building to the next. "This whole place is too . . . organized."

Celia didn't trust the cards either, but unlike Tyrus, she looked at the organization with a hint of optimism. Outside the castle walls, she'd come close to despairing. What hope was there of finding a way home when no one knew what was going on? Where the weed-covered roads twisted and turned with nonsensical signs? Or when there weren't any roads at all? Maybe the queen was just as tyrannical as the book said, but this looked like the kind of place where things got done.

The room she and Sylvan were taken to was as utilitarian as the rest of the castle. Not in a "welcome to your prison cell" kind of way, but more like an "everything is exactly where you need it to be" way. Tossing her top hat onto a dresser, Celia poked her head into the bathroom. It was well organized, with a toothbrush for her and another for Sylvan, hairbrushes, soaps, and scented candles. The tub was perfectly round and filled with water that was warm but not too hot.

Lying across one of the beds were several outfits which looked both stylish and functional. Trying them on in the bathroom, she was shocked to discover they fit better than the clothes her mom bought her. Some were a little froufrou for her tastes, and she could have done with fewer embroidered hearts, but after changing into fresh pants, a shirt, and a jacket with plenty of pockets, she felt almost normal.

There was a platter of berries, some freshly baked bread, and even tarts. No wonder the soldier had smiled.

"It has to be a trick," she said to Sylvan. Was it possible the food had been drugged?

But why go to all the trouble of making everything look normal if the queen was only going to chop off their heads? Maybe this room wasn't the kind of place where you'd put an honored guest—after all, there were guards outside the door. But it might be the kind of room you'd offer to someone before making a deal with them. The question was, what kind of deal?

Sylvan sniffed the bread and nibbled a few of the berries. "They're fresh." So much for the theory of drugged food.

Once she was clean and dressed, Celia opened the door and looked out into the empty hall. Then two cards appeared, stationed on either side of the door.

"Can we leave?" she asked them.

The card to the right—a four of spades—nodded. "Where would you like to go?"

"I'm not sure," she admitted. "Maybe Tyrus's room?"

"Of course." The card led Sylvan and her across the hall, two doors down, and bowed. "Would you like me to announce you?"

She couldn't help grinning. "I think I can do that myself." She knocked on the door.

"Who is it?" Tyrus demanded.

"The three bears," she said. "Let us in, Goldilocks."

Tyrus opened the door, clearly not amused. He didn't

appear to have bathed, and the clean clothes from his bed were crumpled on the floor.

"You didn't have to make a mess," Celia said.

Tyrus watched the guards distrustfully. Once the door was closed, he grabbed her hand and pulled her to the balcony. "Have you seen what's outside?"

"Is it the hauntstrosity?" Sylvan asked, hopping up onto the railing.

By the tone of his voice, Celia expected to see recently beheaded bodies. Instead, she looked out at a green lawn mown in a perfect checkerboard pattern with a border of perfectly manicured red roses in alternating squares, triangles, and octagons.

"What am I missing?" she asked.

Tyrus narrowed his eyes. "Give it a minute. It'll come to you."

She looked again, noticing the way the stone benches, white gravel pathways, and two evenly spaced fountains gave the gardens a sense of balance and symmetry. "It's, um, too green?"

He leaned toward her until his mouth was nearly touching her ear. "Too neat, too straight, too perfect."

Sylvan looked up at him. "How can something be too perfect?"

Tyrus jutted out his jaw. "How do you get such straight lines? Not a pebble out of place?"

Genuinely confused, Celia shook her head. "Good gardeners?"

"Dark magic," Tyrus whispered, glancing over his shoulder

as though someone might be watching. "Trust me, I know evil when I see it. If we wait long enough, we'll see some uniform-wearing children bouncing balls to the same rhythm until they get called in for lunch."

"You're worried this is a playground?" Celia said, trying not to laugh.

Tyrus glared at her. "Are you telling me you don't sense a dark foreboding about this place? A cloud of gloom seeping into the marrow of your bones?"

Now she did laugh. "We've been threatened by crocodiles, birds, a gryphon, and a woman with literally two sides. We've seen swimming numbers, talking oysters, a boy turned into a flying pig, and hundreds of other things that shouldn't even be possible."

"Don't forget being turned into slugs," Sylvan added. "Although, that was mostly my fault."

Celia rubbed the bunny's head and stared at Tyrus. "After all that, you're terrified of a neatly mowed lawn?"

"It's not just that." Tyrus walked back inside. "Look around. What's missing?"

Celia studied the furnishings. They looked so similar to hers they could have been matching hotel rooms. There wasn't much to see—a bed, some furniture, a closet. "I give up," she said, rubbing her forehead. "What am I missing?"

"No books," Tyrus said at once. Before she could respond, he continued. "No art, no paintings, no photographs, no statues."

Tyrus paced across the room. "I've read *Alice's Adventures in Wonderland* over and over and not once does Lewis Carroll mention this building."

"I don't think he mentions the queen's palace at all."

"But don't you think he would have, considering this boxy building is nothing like the rest of Wonderland?"

Celia ran her hands down the side of her pants, enjoying the feeling of being freshly bathed and wearing clean clothes. "Maybe he didn't mention it because it was so *boring*. Maybe he didn't think anyone would care about a building that didn't stand out, or benches and walkways that were clean and neat."

"Or maybe its boringness is a trap. You've heard what everyone said about the queen. She's crazy. She cuts off people's heads."

Sylvan shuddered. "I've never even met her, and she terrifies me."

"I'm scared too," Celia said. "But so far, almost nothing has been like it was in the book. What if this is the same? What if the creatures outside the castle are the horrible ones and the queen is actually, I don't know, *normal?*"

Tyrus's mouth dropped open. "You're saying Lewis Carroll lied about everything?"

"No." Celia held up her hands. "I'm saying it's been over a hundred and fifty years since he was here, and maybe things have changed. Maybe the queen has mellowed. Maybe she's willing to listen to reason. Barrister Entwhistle seemed to be alright with coming here. Maybe we should see what the queen has to say before deciding she's going to feed us a poison apple or prick our fingers with a cursed spinning wheel."

Tyrus's mouth snapped shut. "This isn't a fairy tale."

Celia bit the inside of her cheek to keep herself from pointing out how hypocritical his statement was.

Someone knocked on the door, and they both turned.

A card stepped inside and declared, "Her Majesty, the Queen of Hearts, requests your presence in the garden."

Tyrus grabbed the unicorn hat the Hatter had given him from his bed and shoved it on his head.

"You're not going to wear that to see the queen, are you?" Celia asked, glad she had left her hat in her room. "It doesn't even fit right."

He grimaced. "I want to look good when she cuts off our heads."

Following the guards along a series of brightly lit hallways, Celia felt her shoulders tense. What she'd told Tyrus and Sylvan was true. She didn't see anything sinister in neat gardens or a lack of books—in fact, she found it kind of refreshing.

But that didn't change the fact that everything they'd seen of Wonderland so far was as bad or worse than what Charles Dodgson had written about. The queen in his books was a raving lunatic with a serial killer's mentality. What if she was worse as well and she really had been fattening them up before the slaughter?

As they left the castle and stepped outside, Celia was so sure she'd see a psychotic killer with an ax-wielding executioner that she looked right past the smiling, middle-aged model in a red tennis dress. But then she noticed the woman's small gold tiara adorned with red heart-shaped gems, and a heart-shaped pendant on a tasteful gold chain.

"Your Majesty," the card said. "I present your guests from the world Earth."

Celia dropped to her knees, eyes locked on the ground, trembling. "Y-y-your M-m-m," she stuttered, unable to get the words out.

"Oh, you poor dear," the queen said, hurrying toward them. "You must be Alice."

Celia glanced at Tyrus, but before she could answer, the queen grabbed her hand and pulled her to her feet.

"Has it been the most terrible thing?" the queen asked. "Lost and alone with all those horrible creatures and . . . *unusual* people?" She knelt to look at Sylvan, who was hiding behind Celia's back. "And who's this?"

"Sylvan Rabbit," the creature said timidly.

The Queen of Hearts opened her mouth. "Not White's daughter?"

"Great-great-great-great-great-something-daughter actually."

Giggling like a child, the queen put her hand to her chest. "My, I *am* getting old." She turned to Tyrus. "And you would be?"

Tyrus stared at the ground, hands clenched, as though bracing for an attack. "Here to save Wonderland from whatever curse you've put on it. We demand to know any information you have about the creature that's attacking everyone."

Celia glared at him. "We came here on accident, and we're just trying to figure out how to get home."

Looking from Tyrus to Celia, the queen bit her lip and shook her head. "I can't imagine how frightened you must be.

I will do everything within my power to help you return to your world." She turned to Tyrus and raised one hand. "As far as whatever is happening outside my gates, I swear I have my top cards looking into it. I will not rest until the creature is found and stopped, no matter what it takes."

CHAPTER 20

The Greatest Power

*"What do you know about this business?"
the King said to Alice. . . .*

"Nothing whatever," said Alice.

"The cooks won't be serving dinner for an hour yet," the queen said. "That will give us time to talk."

Tyrus snorted. "About what?"

What was he doing? If he was so sure the queen would order both of them beheaded, then he should stop provoking her. But the queen simply patted him on the shoulder.

"About getting the two of you home, of course." She touched the rim of Tyrus's unicorn derby. "The Hatter's work?"

"That's right," Tyrus said, yanking it away from her fingers.

"It's . . . *unusual*," the queen said. "It seems a little small though. I'll have one of my tailors look at it for you."

Tyrus grunted and tugged the front down over his eyes, making the back stick up. "I like it the way it is."

"He's kind of nervous around you," Celia said to the queen

as they walked past cards sparring in a courtyard and toward a beautiful stable. "We *both* are. We've heard, uh, stories."

The queen chuckled. "'Off with their heads. Paint the roses. Execute the slackers.' That sort of thing?"

"Yes," Celia said, surprised at how open the queen seemed to be about everything.

"I suppose it's to be expected," the queen said. "I *am* demanding. I simply want things done in a certain way, and I don't put up with nonsense. I suppose I can have a temper. If that makes me a monster, then aren't we all at times?"

"You don't have any books or artwork," Tyrus said

The queen stopped so abruptly Tyrus nearly ran into her back. "We have both a wonderful library and a large arts program. I'm afraid I don't have time for them, myself. Someone has to keep the kingdom running. I'm sure my husband would be happy to show them to you after dinner."

"Your husband?" Celia asked. She remembered the King of Hearts from the book, but not a lot of details.

"There he is now," the queen said, pointing to a man nearly half her height wearing a large gold crown.

"Darling," the king said, kissing her on the hand. "You look ravishing, as always. And these must be our guests."

Celia's first thought as the king shook their hands was that he had seriously married up. While the queen was tall and regal, he was short and dumpy with a slightly unsure expression on his face.

"I've prepared the croquet courts," he said, leading them to a smooth green lawn. "The gardeners painted fresh boundary lines this morning, and I had them measure the wicket spacing three times."

"This court has been in place since Mr. Dodgson designed it over a hundred and fifty years ago," the queen told Celia. "But it doesn't hurt to make sure things are kept neat now and again, does it?"

"No," Celia said, thinking of the fast-food wrappers scattered around her house.

"Did we find the mallets and balls?" the queen asked.

The king dropped his head. "They've disappeared again. I've got a dozen of our best people working to discover who keeps taking them."

"This is unacceptable," she snapped, her jaw tight. "Someone will—" She took a deep breath and smiled. "Someone will need to fetch the flamingos and hedgehogs."

"Already here." The king hurried to a polished wooden rack that held six pink flamingos and six hedgehogs—each a different color. He rubbed his hands down the front of his jacket. "Each flamingo is exactly the same size, and the hedgehogs have been groomed to roll perfectly straight."

"It will have to do," the queen said.

"Do we have to play croquet?" Celia asked, remembering how that had turned out in the book. "It might distract us from our discussion."

"Nonsense," the queen said, selecting a flamingo and a hedgehog. "Croquet is the perfect thinking sport. It involves physics and geometry. The precise calculations of billiards combined with the strategy and planning of chess."

"Not to mention animal cruelty," Tyrus said, glancing at Sylvan.

The queen's lips narrowed before she forced them into a smile. "On the contrary, every precaution is taken to protect all of our living equipment. The flamingos' feathers provide more than adequate cushioning, and the hedgehogs are protected by a thick layer of fur. If it bothers you, you don't have to play."

"I won't," Tyrus snapped.

"I'm afraid you're a little small to hold a mallet," she told Sylvan. "But feel free to explore. I believe there's a vegetable garden by the stables if you're hungry."

"Thank you," the rabbit said with a quick curtsey.

The queen turned to Celia. "Are you the kind of person who enjoys combining mental acuity with physical precision? Your friend, Mr. Dodgson, was quite the fan."

"I've never played, Your Majesty," Celia said.

"The first thing to know is that hoops are called wickets. Please do not refer to them as rings or goals," she said, glaring at her husband. "The wooden poles are called stakes."

Carefully pointing out each shot, the ideal strategies, and the proper angle to take, the queen walked Celia from wicket to wicket. Celia was delighted to discover that the queen was right. It was exciting to apply the concepts of math to a sport that was slow-paced but competitive. After a few minutes of playing, she completely forgot that Tyrus and the king were behind them.

Celia took careful aim and sent her blue hedgehog sailing

through a wicket. "It's surprising to find something like this when the rest of Wonderland is so . . ."

"Uncivilized?" the queen finished, making an even better shot with her red hedgehog.

"Yes," Celia nodded, thinking of how to word her next question. "Isn't there something you can do to make it more . . . ?"

"Like this?" They walked down the court to line up their next shots. "I suppose I could force everyone to do things my way. Straighten their roads, clean their houses, mow their lawns. I could force them to take croquet lessons." She raised an eyebrow. "Is that what you were thinking?"

Celia shook her head. "I guess not."

"Wonderland is an odd place," the queen said, hitting a perfect shot. "Frankly, I don't understand most of the creatures in my kingdom, and I suspect they feel the same way about me." She brushed a stray lock of hair from her eyes. "Have you ever felt like you don't fit in?"

Celia nodded, doing her best to replicate the queen's shot. Her hedgehog didn't roll quite as straight as she had hoped, but she thought with practice she could be good at the game. "P-pardon me for needing rosy." She felt her face heat up and tried again. "I mean, being nosy. But if you're so concerned about your citizens, why have you placed them under quarantine? And why are they locked out of the castle? It seems like this would be the safest place for them."

"I'd like to invite them all for tea and crumpets—there'd certainly be enough space to house them—but I fear they'd make such a terrible mess of the place. Can you imagine what they'd do to this venerable court?"

Remembering what kind of shape the March Hare's house had been in, Celia shook her head. "I guess not."

"And then there's the creature itself," the queen said, giving her hedgehog a nudge to make it curl back into a ball. "Until we can figure out what it is and why it's attacking, we must keep our headquarters secure. A quarantine is the best way to keep the sickness from spreading. But enough of our world, tell me about where you come from. I've seen a bit of it in my magic mirror. Is it really as wonderful as it seems?"

"Some parts," Celia said. "But other parts are almost as strange as here."

For the rest of the game, the two of them shared stories, laughing and comparing notes on what they liked and disliked about their worlds. Celia was surprised—maybe even shocked—to discover how much they had in common. The queen won the croquet game, but Celia didn't care. She was already looking forward to the rematch.

As they walked back into the castle, Tyrus and Sylvan hurried to Celia's side. "Have you figured out what she's up to?" Tyrus asked. "I'm positive she is behind what's happening to Wonderland."

Celia felt her face heat up. "I'm, um, working on it."

"That was some act you put on," Tyrus whispered. "Listening to the two of you laugh, I almost thought you liked the witch."

Celia frowned. "It doesn't hurt to be polite. She's doing the best she can."

"You really believe that?" Tyrus asked.

She wasn't sure what she believed.

They were soon seated at a long table covered with a pristine white cloth. Servants hurried in and out with platters of roasted meats and steaming vegetables, hot breads, and enough desserts to make Celia's stomach ache. Every dish was perfectly seasoned, and no one danced on the table or told outlandish stories.

Sylvan was served a salad of lettuce topped with fresh clover and an entire bowl of raw carrots.

All in all, it was one of the best nights of Celia's life, and she felt disappointed when the queen ordered the last of the plates cleared and said, "I suppose it's time to get the two of you home."

"We can't go home until we save Wonderland," Tyrus whispered to Celia.

She nudged him with her knee while addressing the queen. "Thank you so much for your hospitality. We won't forget it."

The queen nodded demurely. "It was our pleasure." She turned to her husband. "Dear?"

"Oh, yes." The king smiled nervously and hurried out of the room. A moment later he returned with a chest roughly the same size as the one Celia and Tyrus had found in the box of Charles Dodgson's belongings. Unlike that box, which had been hand-carved and looked like an antique, this one belonged in a museum. It was a work of art covered in jewels and gold engravings.

Holding it carefully in his arms, the king scurried to the

table and set it before Tyrus and Celia. "I believe you are familiar with this?"

Sylvan sniffed the box as Celia turned it, looking for some clue of what it might be. "Um, maybe you could remind me?"

The king laughed nervously, glancing toward his wife. "Mr. Dodgson left it before he returned to his home."

"Oh, sure," Celia said. "I must have forgotten."

The queen leaned forward. "You know what it is, of course."

Celia turned to Tyrus, but he was glowering at his plate. She was on her own. Her tongue stuck to the roof of her mouth, and she took a long drink of water to buy herself time to think. "It's the box that Mr. Dodgson left so that you could, um . . . help us get home?"

"Obviously," the queen said with a slight frown. "He traveled Wonderland from one side to the other, taking notes and drawing pictures. He came back from one of his last trips with this."

"He called it the source of all power in Wonderland," the king blurted.

"Be quiet!" the queen snarled, glaring at him.

"Sorry, my dear." He rushed to her side and pulled a ring from his coat pocket. It had a large ruby heart in the center encircled by small diamonds that sparkled as if each contained a light of their own. "I had this made for you today."

"More trinkets?" She took it from him with a yawn and held it up to the light. "It's pretty enough, I suppose," she said, slipping it onto her only ringless finger.

"What kind of power is it?" Tyrus asked. "In the box, I mean."

The king looked at his wife before answering. "We don't know, exactly. Only that it's strong enough to—"

"To open a door from our world to yours," the queen said, her eyes dreamy.

Tyrus clenched his fists. "If it's so powerful, why not use it to save your kingdom?"

Sylvan pushed aside the last of her carrots and nodded.

The queen frowned. "Perhaps we could. But if we did, the two of you would never get home." She looked at Celia. "Is that what you want?"

"No," Celia said before Tyrus could answer. "We want to go home. Which means, I guess, we need to open the box."

"Why else would I have brought you here?" The queen tilted her head, studying Celia closely. "Are you feeling all right, Alice? You seem a little dull-witted this evening."

Sylvan's eyes widened as she looked from the queen to Celia.

Tyrus frowned and whispered, "You didn't tell her you're not Alice?"

Celia touched the gold box. She'd explain everything once they were home. Taking the lid carefully in her hands, she tried to lift it. It wouldn't budge. She pushed harder, but it seemed stuck.

"Let me try," Tyrus said. He tugged at the box, trying to pry it open with his fingers. When that didn't work, he turned it over, looking for a latch of some kind. "It's locked."

"Of course it is," the queen said, rising halfway from her throne. "Are you sure the two of you know what you're doing?"

Celia's heart raced. The queen had been nice to her, but she was still a queen. "It's just a little different from the other boxes he left for us." She searched for wheels or another type of combination, but other than the gems and gold, the box was completely smooth. There had to be a hidden lever or a switch, but she couldn't even see a line where the top met the bottom. "Have you tried . . . prying it open?"

"What kind of a question is that?" the queen snapped, her face beginning to grow red.

The king hurried to her side and placed a hand on her shoulder. He glanced at Celia. "We've had every craftsman in the kingdom try cutting it, smashing it, burning it. Nothing. We assumed since Mr. Dodgson left it for the one who would follow him . . ." He held out his hands, eyes darting between the box and his wife.

"Are you saying you *can't* open it?" the queen demanded, her voice cold. "Mr. Dodgson was quite specific that the next person who came from his world would be able to use it."

Celia cringed.

The king licked his lips. "We've been waiting a long time, you see."

"Let me try again," Tyrus said, taking the box from Celia. As both their hands touched the box at the same time, there was an audible click, and one of the gems slid aside.

"What's that?" the queen demanded.

The king grabbed the box and turned it over, revealing a small opening. "A keyhole!"

"Finally." The queen turned to Tyrus and Celia. "Which of you has the key?"

"Neither of us," Tyrus said. "We didn't even know there was a box until you showed it to us."

The queen's face went red. "What are you saying?"

Tyrus looked from Celia to the queen. "Are you going to tell her, or should I?"

Celia put her hands over her face. "The thing is . . . I'm not Alice."

"*What?*" the queen shouted.

"There's been a mistake. My Celia is name." She could feel her brain reacting to the stress, causing her to stumble over words and leave things out. "Tyrus and I were here by we . . . The library. Smoke. A barble. I mean bottle."

"A *mistake*." The queen stood, her eyes icy with rage. Her face turned red, then to an even darker shade. Her cheeks lengthened, and her mouth grew until it was as big around as a cantaloupe. Her beautiful golden hair turned into a nest of snakes, hissing and snapping. Her fingers grew and curved, the nails turning from red to black.

"No!" the king shouted, struggling to hold her back. "They are only children. They didn't know."

"They lied to me!" the creature in the tiara howled. "If they can't open the box, I have no more use for them. Off with their heads!"

CHAPTER 21

The Daring Escape

"Either you or your head must be off."

"I told you," Tyrus said, pacing their prison cell.

Sitting on the floor in the corner, Celia pressed her face against her knees, wishing he would be quiet and leave her alone with her misery.

"I knew she was bad from the start," he repeated for at least the sixth time since the queen's cards had locked them up. "I felt it as soon as I entered the castle. I told you she was using black magic, but you wouldn't listen."

"You said kids in uniforms were going to bounce balls," Celia said, without bothering to look up.

"I was wrong about that, but I was right about the croquet balls and those bright white lines and perfectly measured wickets. I knew the queen was evil. But you wanted to be best buddies with her because she gave us nice rooms and liked math. And now it turns out she's the beast."

"We don't know that for sure," she muttered.

"Are you kidding?" he asked, grabbing the metal cup from their water bucket and slamming it against the bars. The ringing pierced all the way to the center of Celia's brain. "Did you see the way her hair turned into snakes and her nails turned into claws? She can probably turn into whatever kind of monster she wants."

"Fine," Celia snarled, pressing her hands against her ears. "You were right and I was wrong—about everything. I was wrong about becoming your friend. I was wrong about opening the doorway. I was wrong about trusting the queen. I was wrong about all of it! And now we're going to be executed because of my wrongness. Is that what you want me to say?" She squeezed her eyes shut, determined not to cry.

"Don't worry, Alice," Sylvan said, patting her hand. "You can't die until you save Wonderland."

Celia was too tired to bother arguing.

A moment later, the springs on the cot next to her squeaked. "I'm sorry for saying those things," Tyrus said softly. "For what it's worth, I'm glad you opened the door, and I'm really glad we became friends."

She cracked open one eye and looked up at him. "If we hadn't, you wouldn't be stuck here, waiting to have your head cut off."

"Yeah," he said. "That part's pretty bad. But up until that happened, this was the best trip of my life."

She snorted. "You need to get out more."

"That's true," he said. "But even if it wasn't, I still can't imagine a better one. Unless it was that tour where they take you to New Zealand and show you all the places where they filmed *Lord of the Rings* and *The Hobbit,* because—"

"Stop," she said, laughing despite her misery.

Tyrus laughed with her. "I also wouldn't mind going to London and seeing the Harry Potter museum."

Celia raised a finger. "So help me, I am not going to spend the last night of my life talking about fantasy books."

"Fair enough." Tyrus fiddled with the unicorn horn on his hat. "You're also the best friend I've ever had."

"Let me guess," Celia said, standing up and walking to the bars. "I'm also the *only* friend you've ever had."

"Well . . ."

She turned around, leaning against the cold metal. "The thing I don't understand is how the queen went from wanting to help us to wanting to kill us so fast."

"It's logic," said a voice from across the hall.

Celia peered out to see a familiar figure in a gray suit and dark glasses locked up in a cell one down from theirs. "Barrister Entwhistle?"

"The Third," the mouse said. "You and your friends are looking well."

Celia started to ask him how he could possibly say that considering he couldn't see when Tyrus spoke up instead.

"What are you doing here?" he asked, peeking through the bars.

"The same as you," the mouse said. "I crossed the queen, and she condemned me to death."

"I'm so sorry," Celia said. Only a few hours before she'd

been playing croquet with the queen; now they were on death row.

"Not to worry," the barrister said. "I've been here before, and no doubt I'll be here again. It's the cost of protecting the innocent."

Tyrus frowned. "You've been here before?"

"Many times," the mouse said, swinging his tail. "I defend someone the queen is angry at, she orders my beheading, the king pardons me, and a month or two later, we do it all over again. Odo will be waiting to take me home once I'm released."

Celia collapsed against the bars, relief taking all the strength out of her legs. "No one really gets beheaded, then? It's all an act?"

The barrister wriggled his nose. "Well, the queen orders executions daily, but there are only two or three beheadings every month. Her Majesty prefers logic, and this is just logic carried to the extreme. If something gets in your way, remove it. But if the cards lopped off heads every time she commanded them to, there'd be no one left for her to rule. Therefore, logic also demands that she allow her husband to pardon those she needs. As long as you are of use to her, she lets you live."

"She wanted us to open a box," Tyrus said.

The mouse nodded. "The queen has a magic looking glass she uses to spy on her kingdom. After Mr. Dodgson visited us, she discovered she could view other worlds through her mirror as well. Those worlds draw her like a Rhinopotamus to flozz-berry jam. Shortly after that, Mr. Dodgson disappeared, leaving only the box and a piece of parchment with a name on it."

"Alice," Sylvan said from under the cot. "The queen was so angry when Mr. Dodgson left that she ripped up the parchment and threw the box on the floor."

The mouse nodded. "So I've heard."

"That's the paper you gave me," Celia said, turning to Sylvan. "But if the queen shredded the parchment, how did the rabbits get it?"

Sylvan climbed out from beneath the cot. "White gathered the pieces when she wasn't looking and pasted them back together. The Rabbit family has been protecting it ever since."

"An admirable gesture," the mouse said. "Since you are here, I assume you were not able to open the box?"

Tyrus scratched his head. "We don't have the key."

Barrister Entwhistle's whiskers drooped. "I'm sorry to hear that. For both of you as well as for Wonderland. Now that the queen knows you are unable to help her, your chances of being pardoned are slim indeed. I fear she will do something drastic."

"How do you know all this?" Tyrus asked.

"Mr. Dodgson was a friend of the family," the mouse said. "It is because of him that we became who we are."

Celia crinkled her forehead. "How so?"

The barrister polished his glasses on his suit jacket while Tyrus unconsciously did the same with his shirt. "Before Mr. Dodgson opened a doorway to our world, my family were simple country mice. We had no name, no title, no purpose in life other than foraging for food and avoiding being eaten by predators. After my grandfather pulled him out of the sea, Mr. Dodgson rewarded him with a lovely engraved gold pocket watch.

"It seemed a small thing at the time, but because of that one small change, my grandfather reexamined his life. As the new owner of such a fine timepiece, he knew he had to make something of himself. He took on the name Roderick Entwhistle—because of the watch—trained to become a barrister, and committed his life to protecting the rights of others." The mouse patted his vest pocket and frowned. "Alas, it appears I will be the last Entwhistle to see my grandfather's treasure. I lost it in the Arithma Sea."

Celia was about to tell the mouse she knew what had happened to his watch when someone came scurrying down the hallway.

"Hurry," whispered a little man in a dark cloak. "We don't have much time. The guards are changing shifts, and they will be back in a few minutes."

As the man slid a key into the door of their cell, his cloak slipped back, revealing the side of his face. "Your Majesty?" Celia blurted.

"Hush," the king hissed, throwing a sack over his shoulder. "If the queen knew what I was doing, I'd be the next one sent to the executioners." He looked both directions, then whispered, "Follow me."

Celia scooped up Sylvan, and she and Tyrus hurried to keep up with the king as he raced through several hallways and up a flight of winding stairs. Pausing on the landing, the king held up one finger, then hurried down a narrow corridor and through a heavy wooden door.

"Whew," he said, throwing back his cloak. "That was close."

"Where are we?" Celia asked. Unlike the rest of the castle, this room looked more like the overflowing warehouse of an antique store than a hotel room. Inventions, gadgets, and devices were shoved so closely together it was nearly impossible to tell where one stopped and the next began.

Something that looked like a four-wheeled bicycle with an elephant's trunk fought for space with an elaborate dollhouse on legs that rested on a giant metal glove with gears that was gripping a glowing green crystal ball.

"My hiding space," the king said, wiping sweat from his forehead. "It's where I keep all the things the queen has ordered destroyed over the years. Things that don't make sense—at least to her."

"This is amazing," Tyrus said, reaching toward a rocking horse that had what looked like a pair of flamethrowers attached to its sides.

"Don't," the king said, pulling him back. "I'm afraid many of these things *don't* make sense. My wife is right about that. Some are quite dangerous. I should probably have let her destroy them. Only each of them represents someone's hard work, their imagination. How can that be tossed in the incinerator like so much garbage?"

This man, so filled with passion and idealism, was nothing like the groveler who had catered to the queen's every whim at dinner and, before that, during the croquet game.

Sylvan sniffed the musty air. "Where did it all come from?"

"Gifts from our subjects," the king said, looking over his collection. "There was a time when craftsmen came from far and wide to bring us the most exceptional creations you can imagine. The problem was, unless the queen felt they were practical—logical—she had them destroyed and ordered that the people who made them be executed."

"Why hide everything?" Tyrus asked. "Why not just tell her 'This is my stuff, and I'm keeping it?' I mean, you are the king."

The king shuddered, and Celia once again saw the frightened little man she'd observed before. "That wouldn't go well."

Celia tilted her head. "You're the one who's been stealing the croquet equipment, aren't you?"

"There were some unfortunate accidents with the wooden mallets and balls in the past. It's better if she plays with something a little softer." He licked his lips. "Out of all the gifts we've received, there are only two she kept—a mirror that lets her see wherever she wants . . . and this."

He pulled a purple cloth off a wooden desk, revealing Charles Dodgson's box.

"You took it from the queen?" Sylvan asked.

"Borrowed," the king said. "If she discovered it was missing, the next croquet game she played would use heads for balls instead of hedgehogs." Grasping their shoulders, he pulled the four of them into a tight circle. "I understand why you wouldn't want my wife to open this box. I wouldn't want her to come to my world either if I were you—Charles Dodgson certainly didn't."

Tyrus touched the box, then looked up. "She's the one who's been attacking the creatures of Wonderland, isn't she?"

The king hesitated, then nodded. "I'm afraid so. I tried to convince myself it couldn't be her. She can be a wonderful person, despite her temper—though you might not believe that after what you just saw. But I've lied to myself long enough. Because of my inaction, Wonderland is in incredible danger."

Sylvan wrinkled her nose. "Why would the queen want to destroy our world?"

The king fidgeted with the buttons of his coat. "I have a theory. Really little more than an idea, but I think she's been stealing power from Wonderland to try to force open the box."

Celia frowned. "What kind of power?"

"Pure logic. She sucks it out of them like blood, until they become—"

"Monsters," Sylvan finished, shuddering.

The king nodded. "To be honest, I don't know how it works. Only that she can wield it as a weapon, and the more logic she steals, the more powerful she becomes. The problem is that, whether she realizes it or not, she is being changed by her own weapon. Every day she becomes worse. I'm afraid that soon she'll be strong enough that she can syphon it off without even leaving the castle. When that happens, Wonderland is doomed."

Tyrus grabbed the king's sleeve. "How can we help?"

"The two of you need to leave now, while you still can," the king said. "Return to the world you came from, and never come back."

Sylvan thumped her back feet. "That's not what the clock said."

Celia patted the rabbit's head and asked the king, "If Tyrus and I leave, what happens to the rest of you?"

The king sighed. "I hope that once the queen sees that the box has been opened, she'll give up her insane plan of traveling to other worlds. If she releases the logic she's built up, over time, things should return to normal."

"And if she doesn't?" Tyrus asked.

The king took a deep breath and once more became a man of action. "Then at least only one world will be destroyed. No matter what happens here, you cannot let her enter your world. I've seen glimpses of your technology in her mirror. With that kind of power to feed on, she could open so many doors to so many worlds . . . She would never be stopped."

He reached for a sack and handed it to Tyrus. "I had your belongings collected. After you open the box and leave, I'll place it in her room. She'll assume you escaped and took the power with you."

"Won't she just follow us through the door?" Tyrus asked.

"Mr. Dodgson said that it closes once someone goes through," the king said.

Trying not to look at Sylvan's disappointed face, Celia nodded. "I understand. Where's the key?"

The king blinked. "You don't have it?"

"Of course not," she said. "We told you that at dinner."

He stared at Celia. "Then you *aren't* Alice?"

Sylvan's whiskers quivered. "The cheese clock said—"

"No, it didn't," Celia cut her off. Hadn't the king been listening at all?

"Oh my. My, my, my, my, my." The king drummed his fingers on the desk. "I assumed that was just a story to keep my wife from opening the box." Outside, bells began to chime.

His face turned white. "I have to get this back now, before she discovers it's missing."

"What about us?" Tyrus asked.

"Escape, before she has you executed," the king said, pointing to the window. He wrapped the box back in the purple cloth. "If you find the key, return and I'll try to help you. But watch out for the cards. As soon as my wife discovers you're gone, she'll send them after you. If the ace of clubs discovers your trail . . ." He wiped his forehead again and opened the door.

Celia looked out the window. "It's three stories straight down. How are we supposed to get out?"

"Take the writing desk," the king said, before hurrying through the doorway and slamming it shut behind him.

CHAPTER 22

The Writing Desk Raven

"They're dreadfully fond of beheading people here:
the great wonder is, that there's anyone left alive!"

"How are we supposed to take this thing with us?" Celia asked, staring at the writing desk. "It must weigh two-hundred pounds. And what would be the point?"

Shoving her way through the king's strange collection, she searched for something they could use as a rope or ladder.

"Look at this," Tyrus said, wiping dust off the top of the desk. "There's a hat engraved into the wood."

"Nice," Celia said, without stopping her search. "Let me know if it has a parachute inside. Better yet, a rocket." She studied the rocking horse, wondering if they could use it as a weapon if the cards discovered them.

Tyrus continued studying the desk. "This hat looks almost exactly like the one the Hatter was wearing at the tea party. It even has an *H* in the middle, like a logo. Do you think he built this? Cheshire said the Hatter helped build his mechanical body."

"I don't care if the queen herself made it. Unless you plan on writing us out of here, help me look for some way to escape."

Sylvan pushed open a box filled with tiny wind-up frogs. It took Celia a minute to figure out the sign inside read *Extreme Danger,* and she quickly shut the lid.

"Come look at this!" Tyrus called.

He had managed to unfold the sides and front of the desk until it filled nearly the entire space in front of the door. "What does this look like to you?" he asked.

She shrugged. "An unfolded writing desk?"

"Sure, but imagine these sides as wings and the front as a head. What would it look like then?"

"A bird," Sylvan said, hopping up and down excitedly.

Celia sniffed. "Maybe. But that doesn't make it one." Why did he pick the worst times to go off on these fantasy binges?

Ducking under the desk, Tyrus yanked on something. With a whir and a click, the desk began to change. The sides expanded and curved until they really did look like wings. Drawers popped out, and shelves formed a head and tail. The four legs combined into two and talons emerged.

"I knew it," Tyrus yelled, clapping his hands. "In the book, the Hatter asks why a raven is like a writing desk, and it's because they both fly."

Outside, a loud clanging began to sound. People started shouting.

Tyrus grabbed the bag containing their belongings and hopped onto the desk.

"I hope I'm not going to regret this," Celia said, tucking

Sylvan into a drawer and climbing behind Tyrus. She couldn't believe they were about to try piloting a writing desk, but she couldn't believe anything else that had happened, so why should this be any different?

"Do you know how to control this?" Sylvan asked, bouncing in her drawer.

"I think so," Tyrus said, with a nervous grin. "See this drawer with the *A* on it? I'll bet that controls the altitude. And this inkwell has a *D*. That could be for direction."

"Could be?" Celia asked, not sure whether it would be worse if they discovered the desk didn't fly or if Tyrus managed to get it into the air and it did.

Tyrus eased open the drawer marked with the *A*. The desk shuddered, then rose several feet above the floor. Pressing his hat down on his head, he turned the inkwell like a joystick. Slowly, the desk floated toward the window.

"Here we go!" He shoved the inkwell all the way forward, and they were both thrown backward as the writing desk-turned-raven shot out the window and over the stables.

• • •

Two hours later, they were still aloft and far away from the castle grounds. Celia was wondering how much longer the writing desk could fly without stopping to rest or refuel—or whatever flying writing desks needed—when she heard a noise in the distance. She listened more closely.

"Do you hear that?" she asked.

Tyrus tilted his head. "It sounds like . . . music."

"There," Celia said, pointing to a nearby valley.

As Tyrus guided the writing desk over the trees, a dozen large bonfires came into view. Around the fires, figures moved in a synchronized pattern while a group of musicians played instruments on a small stage.

"They're dancing," Tyrus said. "I'm pretty sure the orchestra is playing a waltz. Let's go down."

"How do you know it's safe?" Celia asked as Tyrus steered the desk toward the music.

"When was the last time you heard of a bunch of dancers attacking anyone?"

Celia was going to say she'd seen a lot of things for the first time since coming to Wonderland but she was done flying and wanted to stretch her legs. She pointed to a grove of trees. "Let's land over there so we can sneak in and get a better look."

Tyrus guided the desk into position and landed with only a couple of bumps. A few minutes later, they crept close enough to see the fires.

Figures in beautiful gowns and formal suits moved to the rhythm of the music. Several of the dresses had dirt stains and a few of the men's suits were threadbare, but dancing on a dirt floor in the middle of the woods probably had that effect.

A woman in a fox mask turned in the arms of a man with the face of a turtle. It wasn't just humans dancing either. There was a bear, a boar, a goat, a large lobster, and even a lion. The animals were in costume as well. Some wore masks to make themselves look human, others wore masks of different animals, and a few even peeked out of carved pumpkins.

"It's a masquerade ball," Celia said, swaying to the music.

Although Celia had never been to a single school dance,

watching the couples spin and twirl around the dance floor nearly made her wish she could be out there with them. Not that she ever would. She was as graceless as a cow. Even more graceless, since a cow with a bear mask was doing a surprisingly good job of dancing with a turtle in a flamingo mask.

As she, Tyrus, and Sylvan edged closer, the song ended. The dancers stepped away from their partners and, in unison, placed a hand behind their backs and bowed. As their torsos bent forward, each of their masks fell to the ground. Only it wasn't just their masks that fell, it was their heads. Suddenly the floor was littered with rolling heads, and every dancer straightened, revealing a severed neck.

Unable to stop herself, Celia screamed. Something moved behind her, and she turned to find a woman in a puffy pink dress. Like the others, the woman's neck ended in a stump. She clutched a walrus head under one arm.

The walrus head grinned, its tusks gleaming, and said, "Welcome to the Headless Ball."

• • •

Celia's heart was still pounding an hour later as she and Tyrus sat around a fire with a group of creatures who called themselves "The Headless."

"Have a drink," said an owl wearing the head of an old woman.

Celia accepted the cup, trying to keep her hand from shaking, and took a long swallow. The liquid tasted like pumpkin, chestnuts, burning leaves, and cranberry sauce—a combination that sounded terrible but was actually quite good.

"Autumn juice," the owl-woman said with a gentle smile. "Quite relaxing after the excitement of a busy summer."

She did feel a bit better. Taking another sip, Celia examined the rest of the group over the top of her cup. An otter with a chicken head, a turtle with a fox head, a well-dressed man with a turtle head, and a lobster with a pumpkin head all smiled back at her. They looked like something from a horror movie, but they seemed very nice.

Tyrus set his empty cup on one of the logs they used as benches. "You were all . . . ?"

"Part of a traveling circus?" asked the turtle-fox.

"He wants to know if we were beheaded," said the otter-chicken, "but he's too polite to say it."

"Ignore Vulpes," the owl-woman said. "His sense of humor gets out of hand after a night of dancing. Yes, my dears, we were all beheaded by the queen for one imagined offense or another. In the olden days, the king pardoned everyone she condemned. But things have . . . *changed*."

"After Mr. Dodgson left," Tyrus said, and all the creatures nodded.

Another thing that wasn't in the book. Celia took another drink to steady her nerves. "How did you end up here? I would have thought that after . . . you know." She gestured vaguely to her neck, and the owl-woman nodded wisely.

"We don't know ourselves, dear. Having your head lopped off is disorienting to say the least. When it happens, you expect to find yourself, well, dead. Instead, we each woke up here."

Tyrus rubbed his glasses on his shirt, obviously intrigued. "How did your heads get mixed up?"

"They're not mixed up," said the man-turtle. "We take turns."

"It's the only fair way," the otter-chicken explained. "Not everyone who arrives here has a head. We assume a few get lost along the way, or maybe they were damaged in the . . . *removal*. And then there is the occasional accident. We lost an excellent boar head in a flash flood just last month."

The turtle-fox chuckled. "This is the only place where you can literally lose your head."

"Don't start with the puns," the owl-woman said, winking at Celia and Tyrus. "They can get quite out of hand if we don't stop them from the beginning. Since we're short on noggins, we rotate every day. Everyone gets a chance to try all the heads that fit them. Those without use whatever is available."

Unable to talk, the lobster-pumpkin shrugged and nodded.

"Around here, we're all trying to get ahead," the turtle-fox said.

Everyone around the fire booed him to silence.

"And you all get together and dance?" Celia asked.

"It cheers us up," the owl-woman said. "My favorite is the quadrille."

The man-turtle licked his beak. "If you don't mind me asking, are you two from the other world? You remind me very much of Mr. Dodgson."

"Yes," Tyrus said. "Did you know him?"

Everyone in the group nodded excitedly.

"He was a delight," said the otter-chicken.

"A true gentleman," the turtle-fox said. "Had his head on straight, that one. No pun intended."

The owl-woman adjusted her hair. "Of course, that was before we were beheaded."

"I'm so sorry," Celia said. "You don't by any chance know about a key he might have left here?"

There was a collective gasp from the creatures around the fire. "The key to the Box of Power," said the man-turtle. "Are you Alice?"

"She is," Sylvan said.

Celia rolled her eyes. "I'm not."

The owl-woman flapped her wings. "Are you going to save Wonderland?"

"Yes, we are," Tyrus said.

The lobster-pumpkin raised his claws above his head in a silent cheer.

The otter-chicken clucked. "About time. The beast has been especially hard on our group. We've lost almost a third of our dancers, and our band has gone from an octet to a quartet. If this goes on much longer, we'll have to hum our own music while we dance."

Celia chewed the inside of her cheek and leaned toward Tyrus. "Didn't you hear anything the king said? The best chance we have of helping Wonderland is to get the key, open the box, and go home."

Tyrus sniffed. "Of course, that's what he *said*. Because he's a good man, and he blames himself for what the queen has done. But it was clearly a lie."

"And how would you know that?"

"The same way I knew the queen was bad. I have a sense for these things. Didn't you see the way his eyes kept fluttering when he was telling us how everything would go back to normal after we left? The queen said the box is the most powerful thing in Wonderland. When I find the key, I'm using the power to defeat her."

"Good on you," the turtle-fox said. "I hope you find it."

Celia glared. "Well, when *I* find the key, I'm using the power to take us home and seal the doorway, so the queen has no choice but to return the logic and set things back to normal."

The otter-chicken clucked. "Sounds reasonable. I'm in your corner."

Tyrus folded his arms across his chest. "Who says I'll go with you?"

"You won't have any choice," Celia snarled. "Since I'll have the power, I can control who goes and who stays, and *you're* going."

"Huh. If you find the key first, I'll fly away on my desk."

"I'll bring you back."

Sylvan hopped onto the log. "If you want to know what I think—"

"We don't!" they both yelled together.

The owl-woman flapped her wings at the group. "I think they need some privacy."

As Celia opened her mouth to respond, a familiar shape marched out of the trees into the clearing.

"Sounds like I've arrived in the middle of high-level negotiations," Cheshire said.

"Chessy, old friend," the otter-chicken said. "So good to see you. Things were getting a little tense."

The man-turtle looked like he would have pulled his head into his shell if he'd had one. "I've seen friendlier interactions at a jousting match."

"You can't cook a proper stew without turning up the heat," Cheshire said with his usual grin.

The turtle-fox laughed. "We'd heard you'd gone to pieces, Cheshire."

"The rumor of my demise was quite accurate," Cheshire said. "But my friends here pulled me together." He turned to Celia and Tyrus. "Perhaps the two of you can put off your bickering for the night. I have someone I'd like you to meet in the morning who might be able to provide some insights."

CHAPTER 23

The Amazing Metamorphosis

"Who are you?" said the Caterpillar.

The next morning, the sky had turned a frightening greenish-yellow. Odd snakelike clouds slithered through the sky, and the humidity made it feel like walking through a slow warm rain. Once, they spotted a gryphon flying in the distance. The air had an electrical charge to it that even the plants seemed to feel, curling their leaves and crouching toward the ground.

"Why can't you tell us who we're meeting?" Celia asked Cheshire, slapping at the bugs buzzing around her face.

"It's not the Duchess again, is it?" Sylvan asked. "I've heard her cook makes rabbit stew."

"Some things are better discovered than told," the robotic cat said.

"And some creatures are more annoying than helpful," Celia snapped. They'd been hiking up and down hills for nearly three hours, and she was tired and cranky. "Are you sure you even know where you're going?"

Cheshire barely gave her a glance as he said, "The more one is sure of where they are going, the less likely they are to get there."

It was like talking to a fortune cookie. "I don't know why we can't fly," she muttered. Sylvan looked as perky as ever, but Celia's feet were killing her.

Tyrus studied the sky. "I think it's a good idea to stay out of sight."

Celia snorted. After their argument the night before, Tyrus had refused to speak to her—which was fine, because she didn't want to talk to him anyway. She just wished she could make him understand that as much as he loved novels, real life wasn't like that.

Authors told stories of kids doing amazing things—slaying dragons, solving mysteries, defeating villains. No one wanted to read about a kid who locked his door and hid under his covers. In real life, kids went to their parents or called the police.

If books told things the way they really happened, the dragon would have eaten the main character by chapter two, the bad guys would get away, and the detectives would tell the kids to stop meddling in their police work.

Tyrus peeked at her out of the corner of his eye. "Do you ever wonder if you make a difference?"

"Are you finally talking to me?" she asked, then shrugged. "A difference in what?"

"In anything. I mean . . ." He exhaled slowly. "I told you how books saved my life. But for what? If all I do is spend my life hiding in them, what's the point? Have you ever felt that way?"

Sylvan nodded. "I didn't want to be the one to call The Alice at first. But now I'm glad I did, because I got to meet both of you."

Celia wiped sweat from her forehead. "I guess everyone wants to make a difference. But how can we? We aren't rich. We aren't powerful. We're a couple of kids who get bad grades and don't make friends."

Tyrus picked up a twig and snapped it in half. "Maybe it doesn't have to be that way. We could fight back."

"Did you ever try standing up to one of the bullies at your old school?"

Tyrus didn't say anything, but she could see the answer in his eyes.

"What happened?" she asked.

"He punched me in the face and threw my library books down a sewer grate. I spent three months paying the replacement fees."

"No!" Sylvan said with a gasp.

That was the way it usually worked out. In the movies, the kid learns karate and teaches the bully a valuable lesson. Then they all go out for milkshakes and become best friends. In real life, you get chocolate milk dumped on your head and the other kids call you *stain* for the rest of the year.

"I just don't want to see you get hurt," Celia said. "The queen has an entire army. If we tried to fight her, we'd end up with the rest of the Headless."

"Probably," Tyrus muttered, but she wasn't sure he was

convinced. She could see him charging into battle against the cards and getting himself killed. She wasn't going to let that happen.

"It doesn't make any sense," she said as they followed Cheshire on a winding path that seemed to crisscross itself more than once. "If Charles Dodgson had wanted us to save Wonderland, he would have called his book *Celia's* Adventures in Wonderland or written about Tyrus going through a mirror."

"He used the name Alice because he knew a girl named Alice Liddel," Tyrus said. "His stories weren't about what's happening now. They were a way for him to tell everyone about the things he'd seen back then. And maybe even a way to help us now."

"Help us how?"

Tyrus rubbed the back of his neck. "If it wasn't for the story, we wouldn't know that Wonderland was a place worth saving. We'd never have heard of the Hatter or the March Hare or the Cheshire cat."

"That alone makes the story quite helpful, in my humble opinion," Cheshire said.

Overhead, the sky grew unnaturally dark.

"Look out!" Sylvan yelled as a black tornado appeared. The four of them pressed against the trunk of a large pine as the tornado moved slowly back and forth, blowing Celia's hair around her face and making her ears pop. At last, it rose back into the air and disappeared over a nearby hill.

"I've never heard of a tornado acting like that," Celia said.

Tyrus shook his head. "It's looking for something, or someone."

That was impossible. A tornado wasn't alive. And yet, Celia breathed a sigh of relief when the sun came back into the sky.

A few minutes later, Cheshire stopped near a large bush covered with large berries.

"Finally, we get to rest," Celia said, leaning against a pile of rocks.

Tyrus examined the berries. "Are these edible?"

"Quite," the cat said. "Help yourself."

Celia's stomach rumbled. They hadn't had any breakfast, and they'd been walking for hours.

Tyrus popped a berry in his mouth. "Delicious!"

Celia filled her hands and mouth with berries, eating some, giving some to Sylvan, and putting the rest in her jacket for later.

As she licked the juice from her fingers, Tyrus gaped at her.

"What?" she asked. "Do I have seeds in my teeth?"

Tyrus winced. "You're, um, shrinking."

"I'm what?" She looked at the pile of rocks, which was rapidly growing to the size of a hill, then a mountain. Blades of grass shot up to the size of trees.

Tyrus was getting smaller too. And Sylvan.

"How?" she demanded, her voice as tiny and high-pitched as a mouse's.

"The berries," Tyrus said, shrinking alongside her.

"You said they were safe," she shouted, shaking her tiny fist at the Cheshire cat towering above them.

"No, I said they were edible," Cheshire's voice boomed. "They also make you small. You'll be back to normal in no time. Until then, I suggest you explore the opening to your right. There's someone inside I'd like you to meet."

Celia turned to see a hole at the base of the rocks. It had been too small to see when they arrived but was now the size of a cave. "Oh no," she muttered, her voice sounding like she'd breathed in helium. "Not another tunnel."

• • •

"I don't like this," Celia said as they trudged into the hole. The damp cold of the tunnel chilled her sweaty skin.

Tyrus rubbed his hands over his arms. "I think it's kind of exciting."

"If I turn into a slug again, I'll never forgive that cat," Celia said.

Sylvan wrinkled her nose, hopping alongside them. "This isn't a rabbit hole."

If this wasn't a rabbit hole, what kind of hole was it? Celia imagined all the many things that lived in holes under rocks, and none of them were good.

At least there was enough light coming from the opening behind them to see where they were going. But how long would that last? And what if whatever was in there had a taste for small things? Would it even ask why they had come before eating them?

"Look," Tyrus said, pointing to a narrow thread crossing the passage above their heads. It resembled an electrical wire or a phone line except it gave off a dim gold glow. Every few seconds, what looked like a glowing drop of water raced along it. "What do you think it is?" he asked, reaching toward it.

Celia tugged his hand back. "I think it might be better not to touch it until we know."

A little farther, they came across another of the strange threads, then two more. The deeper they walked, the more threads they saw until the entire tunnel glowed with them and the walls appeared to be in constant motion from the drops racing back and forth. There were so many of them it looked almost like . . .

"A web." Celia's throat tightened, and her skin turned to ice. "Tell me it's not a spider."

Tyrus clasped her hand in his, staring at the glowing tunnel with awe. "It's not a spider," he said. "We're walking through a cocoon. And I think I know where we are."

"Who. Are. You?" called a voice from around the corner.

"I knew it," Tyrus said, squeezing Celia's hand. "It's the caterpillar."

"I'm afraid you're a little late for that," the voice said with more than a trace of humor.

Tyrus led Celia and Sylvan around the corner and into a huge cavern where they both stopped, frozen with wonder.

At first, Celia thought she was looking at an angel. Its majestic wings glowed with every color of the rainbow, like a glorious, living, stained-glass window that changed with every flutter. It wasn't an angel, though; it was the most beautiful butterfly she'd ever laid eyes on.

The butterfly's body was a glistening ebony with long

graceful legs, two feelers so delicate they looked like the least breeze would snap them in half, and a face that was both kind and wise.

"Cheshire cat got your tongue?" The butterfly's laugh sounded like wind chimes. "I assume that's who brought you here. No one else knows my hiding place."

"Your Majesty," Celia said, thinking the glorious creature had to be royalty.

"Oh, no," the butterfly said. "I'm no monarch. I merely facilitate communication. I gather information from one part of the world and pass it along to another, monitoring it as it travels by."

"It's a pleasure to meet you, sir," Tyrus said.

Wind chimes filled the air again as the butterfly laughed. "'Ma'am' would be more appropriate."

"Oh!" Tyrus's face turned red. "It's just that when he wrote about you . . ."

"Mr. Dodgson called me a boy?"

Celia nodded. "I'm afraid he did."

"As it so happens, caterpillars are neither boys nor girls. At least not until we become pupae. I, of course, emerged from my cocoon as a female, so, your friend, Mr. Dodgson, can be excused for his mistake."

"What should we call you?" Celia asked.

"My name is Kat—with a K," the butterfly said.

Tyrus waved at the thousands of cables overhead. "So, this is like a computer network? Is that stuff fiber optics?"

"I'm not sure what that is," the butterfly said. "Our world has little of what you call technology. Cheshire is one of the few exceptions, and even he wasn't always that way. Think of this more like a central nervous system. Every world is a living thing with a mind, thoughts, feelings, and dreams. This is part of Wonderland's subconscious. My job is to help keep things in order."

Tyrus rubbed his jaw. "We know Wonderland is in danger."

"Very much so." The butterfly studied the network of threads above her. A few were gold like the ones in the tunnel, while several others were green or blue. But more than three-quarters were red. "Things are seriously out of balance in our world. If something doesn't change soon, it will be too late to recover," the butterfly continued. "I'm sure Mr. Dodgson didn't mean to start it, but his presence here all those years ago seems to have set things off."

"Can you stop it?" Celia asked.

"*I* can't," the butterfly said meaningfully.

Tyrus's eyes lit up. "I knew it."

Celia's shoulders slumped, dreading what was coming. This was just another person telling her what she had to do. She should have known. "I'm not Alice."

"You most certainly are not," Kat said.

Sylvan's eyes grew wide.

Celia felt the rabbit's folded paper crackle in her pocket. "But you're going to tell me I have to save your world anyway, aren't you?"

The butterfly's laughter rang through the chamber again. "Good heavens, no! You are small children, and this is a much bigger world than you know. It's not remotely possible for the two of you to save Wonderland. At this point, I don't believe even Mr. Dodgson himself could save it."

"But the prophecy," Sylvan squeaked. "The cheese clock said The Alice would come and save us."

"Did it?" the butterfly asked. "Or did you decide that's what it said? Prophecies are slippery things. One person's prediction is another's nonsense. At best, omens are signs of what might come given the exact right circumstances and the best of luck. At worst, they put undue pressure on the shoulders of those who feel obligated to fulfill them."

The weight Celia had been feeling almost since they arrived lifted, but with it came an unexpected sense of disappointment. She knew she wasn't powerful enough or smart enough to save anything, but it stung to hear the words anyway. "I told everyone it was a mistake. I'm no hero."

Tyrus stared at his feet. "I thought we could make a change."

Kat's eyes glowed. "What kind of change did you have in mind?"

"I don't know." Tyrus shrugged. "Something."

The butterfly fluttered her wings, and the room grew brighter. "That might be possible."

Celia looked up. "But you said . . ."

"I said the two of you can't save the world. I didn't say you couldn't *change* it."

Celia stared up at the glowing red threads that seemed to expand even as she watched. "How? We don't have the box or the key."

"But you do have ideas," the butterfly said. "Ideas are like seeds. They start out as tiny things, so small only you know they exist. But once you plant them, they can grow, spread, change."

"Tell us what to do," Tyrus said.

Kat looked down at him with a sad smile. "I can't do that. I'm afraid you'll have to come up with the ideas on your own."

"But I don't have any ideas," Celia said, her frustration boiling over. "Even when I do, they're almost always stupid."

The butterfly's face grew stern. "There is no such thing as a stupid idea. You are capable of much more than you know. The most important thing is to keep your temper."

Shame clamped a tight fist around Celia's heart as she remembered all the times she'd blown up since coming to Wonderland. Had this glorious creature seen it all? "I am so sorry," she said, staring at the ground. "I have a hard time controlling my anger."

"Anger isn't necessarily bad," the butterfly said. "Especially if you use it as a force for good. But that's not the kind of temper I'm talking about."

"You mean balance?" Tyrus asked. "Like tempering justice with mercy?"

"An excellent definition," the butterfly said. "Tempering can also mean to strengthen. A blacksmith tempers a blade so it won't break in battle."

Celia looked up into the butterfly's eyes. She knew she could be strong at times. She had to be to deal with her dyslexia. But she also felt brittle. Some days the smallest setbacks could make her crack.

"I don't think I'd make a very good blade," she said. "You should find someone else to fight your battle."

"There are times we can choose our battles," the butterfly said. "But, far more often, the battle chooses us." She gently reached out to take each of their hands. "I asked 'Who are you?' when you first arrived. Perhaps if the two of you spent less time trying to be someone else, you would discover who you are."

The back of Celia's throat burned. She wanted to know who she was, but she was also terrified to find out.

"Ask your questions quickly," the butterfly said. "Our time is short."

"What do you mean?" Celia asked. "Is something going to happen?"

"Something has already happened," the butterfly said. "It started long before you arrived. I've been preparing for it, but you must leave soon."

"Where should we go?" Tyrus asked. "What should we do?"

The butterfly released their hands and looked up as the wires overhead began to buzz. Black threads slipped into one of the red wires, turning it a murky purple.

"You must find a way to free the Hatter," she said. "He has been trapped, but he might be able to help if you find a way to release him."

"How do we do that?" Celia asked.

Sparks exploded from the cavern ceiling. The dark wire snapped, and a stream of letters began to pour out like a cloud of smoke.

"The hauntstrosity!" Sylvan cried. "It's here."

The letters swirled into words, which then formed sentences.

"No one read the letters," Celia screamed. But it was too late. A pattern she recognized flashed in front of her and the word 'wasp' filled her brain before she could stop it.

"Leave now!" the butterfly commanded Celia, Tyrus, and Sylvan as the smoke sentences formed dangling legs, broad wings, and a yellow-and-black body with a terrifyingly long stinger on the back. The nightmarish wasp buzzed around the room, before flying straight at the butterfly.

Tyrus picked up a rock and charged forward, but Kat flapped her magnificent wings, knocking the three of them backwards.

The giant wasp plunged its stinger into the butterfly's thorax, and Kat began to writhe, her body twisting and shrinking, the color draining from her wings.

"No!" Celia screamed. Heat baked her face as all around them the wires glowed red and burst into flames. A hand grabbed her arm.

"We need to go," Tyrus shouted, yanking her backward.

"No. We have to save her." Celia tried to pull out of his grasp, to find some way to put out the flames that filled the room, but the smoke was too thick, the fire too strong.

"There's nothing we can do," Sylvan said.

Allowing herself to be pulled, Celia stumbled after Tyrus as the cocoon sparked and sizzled, dropping flaming pieces of thread all around them. Fire licked at their skin, and smoke singed their lungs until, at last, they burst out of the tunnel and into the fresh air. The Cheshire cat was waiting for them.

"The hauntstrosity attacked Kat," Celia screamed as her body began to grow back to its normal size. "We have to save her."

The Cheshire cat shook his head, his tail hanging straight down. "It's too late."

"No!" Celia cried again, burying her face in her hands.

Beside her, tears left dark trails down Tyrus's cheeks, and Sylvan wept openly.

"I know," the Cheshire cat said gently. "I know." Even though his eyes were mechanical, they appeared to glisten. "We must leave, before the creature comes for us as well."

CHAPTER 24

The Exciting Discovery

"Have you guessed the riddle yet?"
the Hatter said, turning to Alice again.

Celia looked at the glowing clouds that slithered through
the night sky. Every few minutes, a bolt of electricity shot from
one of the clouds, shattering trees or lighting bushes on fire.
The earth rumbled back, shaking everything above it as though
it was at war with the sky.

After the attack on Kat, the four of them had returned
to the desk and flown around, looking for some place to take
cover. They found an abandoned barn and had been hiding
inside it ever since. In that time, they'd seen two packs of cards
march by, another black tornado, and several giant creatures
that looked like a mix between a spider and an ostrich. Two
gryphons had flown past—their glowing eyes searching for
prey—along with something that looked like a beaked jellyfish.
The normal birds seemed to be hiding until the storm passed.

The world felt like a lit fuse. Celia was afraid to think what
would happen when the fuse reached its end.

"Whatever's happening out there is getting much, much worse," she said.

Sylvan glanced up from the hay bale where she'd been resting while Cheshire studied the mice that scurried through the shadows.

"What does it matter?" Tyrus asked, sitting on the splintered wood floor with his knees against his chest.

Celia walked back into the barn's dim interior and stared down at him. "You're giving up?"

He looked at her through the smudged lenses of his glasses. "It's not giving up when you never had a hope of success in the first place."

"Is this about what Kat said?" Celia asked, kneeling beside him.

He looked away. "I knew our chances of saving Wonderland were small, but at least there *was* a chance. Now that we know there isn't, what's the point?"

Celia thought for a moment. "Kat told us we couldn't save Wonderland."

Tyrus curled his hands into fists. "Thanks for rubbing it in."

Celia shook her head. "But technically that was a prophecy too, and she said herself that prophecies are slippery things."

"Are you saying you *want* to save Wonderland now?"

Celia stood. "I'm not saying anything. Only . . ." She rubbed her forehead. "When we first got here, I hated Wonderland. There are almost no rules, and what rules there are don't make sense. It's like playing a game where the pieces change, the score doesn't matter, players take turns out of order, and you're not even sure there's an actual objective. But the longer we've been here . . . I don't know."

"It's growing on you," Tyrus said.

She flapped her hands. "Maybe it is. The more I think about it, the more I realize this might be exactly the kind of place I've been searching for. Where else could so many misfits live together without anyone judging them? They don't even try to hide their differences. It's like they're proud of being strange."

The corner of Tyrus's mouth rose ever so slightly. "So now that I've decided to quit, you want to fight. You're just saying that to disagree with me, aren't you?"

Celia rolled her eyes. "Why change now?"

Sylvan hopped closer, her ears perking up. "Did you say something about saving Wonderland?"

Celia's smile faded. "No. I mean, not really." She bent down to look the rabbit in the eye. "You have to realize that even though we might seem big to you, we're still kids. Even if we wanted to help, there's not much we can do. I know your clock told you we were the ones, but it's time for you to go back to your family and tell them the clock made a mistake." She reached into her pocket and took out the parchment. "Take this with you."

As she held the paper out to the rabbit, she noticed the letters were slightly uneven. As she examined the parchment more closely, she could see where it had once been torn into three distinct pieces—probably during the queen's tantrum—and then glued back together.

An idea popped into Celia's head. She held the paper up to the light of the barn's entrance. The left and right edges of the parchment looked like they had been ripped while the glued pieces attached to the middle section had straight edges.

Feeling a cold sweat on her back, Celia gently tugged where the parchment had been glued together so many years before. She was left holding three distinct pieces.

A

LI

CE

"What are you doing?" Tyrus asked.

Studying the pieces in her hands, she felt dizzy. "The left side of the *A* and the right side of the *CE* should be smooth because they were the original edges of the page. But they're not. I think whoever pasted these put them together wrong."

Carefully, she laid the pieces on the ground so the flat edges of the parchment were on the outside.

CE   LI   A

With trembling hands, she pushed the pieces together. They fit perfectly.

Watching over her shoulder, Tyrus pulled his glasses from his face, rubbed them furiously, then put them back on.

"The paper doesn't spell Alice," he said. "It spells Celia. Your name was the one Charles Dodgson wrote all along."

• • •

"Okay, okay," Tyrus said, circling the barn's interior and clutching the three pieces of parchment in his hands. "First, we open the box. Next, we make the queen return the stolen logic. Then—"

"Stop." Celia felt hopelessness once again wash over her. Before, when she'd been sure Sylvan had called the wrong person, it had been easy to convince herself there was nothing she could do. Now she knew she was supposed to save Wonderland, but she still didn't have any answers. "We don't even have the key."

"Then we start with that," Tyrus said. "Let's get the Hatter out of whatever trap he's in and see what he can tell us."

"And how exactly do we go about that?" Celia asked.

"We could start with the tea party. Maybe we missed something there."

Celia pinched her lower lip. "I honestly don't remember all that much about it. I was pretty overwhelmed."

"Me too," Tyrus admitted, tugging down his unicorn hat. "Except for the cookies—the amazing double-layer ones with yellow filling. I remember those."

Celia raised an eyebrow. "You think the cookies are a clue?"

Tyrus shrugged. "Probably not."

Cheshire spun his tail. "Which part of the party are you interested in?"

"Any of it," Celia said. "All of it. Can you help with that?"

"Certainly. I can play the recorded conversation forward, backward, or sideways. I can play it in one of seventeen dialects, thirteen accents, and at an endless number of speeds. I can play it in chocolate, strawberry, peach-mango, and wintergreen."

"How do you play a conversation in flavors instead of colors?" Tyrus asked.

There was a high-pitched squeal of audio feedback, then the Dormouse's voice came through the cat's speakers.

"Chocolate," Tyrus said, grinning. "That's awesome."

Celia knew it was impossible to hear something in flavors, but she could taste the sweetness of the words anyway. She tilted her head. "How did you record that when you didn't arrive until halfway through the party?"

"I didn't *show myself* until then. A good guest knows how and when to make an entrance. But I was watching and listening the whole time. Would you like me to play the part about tea party etiquette? I found it quite informative."

The earth trembled again, and a cloud of dust and splinters fell from the rafters. How long before the old barn collapsed completely?

"I don't think we have time for that," Celia said. "Could you just play the Hatter's part of the conversation?"

"Of course," Cheshire said. "I'll begin at the beginning."

They heard Tyrus ask if they could attend the tea party, and then the Hatter's voice came through the cat's speakers with perfect clarity.

"The three of you are most welcome," he said.

After that came the part where Celia stepped on the snail.

"Skip that," she said quickly. "Go to the next thing the Hatter said. Did you pick up all his comments?"

"Every one," Cheshire said, playing the part where the Hatter told them they had made excellent choices in chairs and suggested they choose their food wisely.

The Hatter explained that they didn't know the rules of tea party etiquette. They changed seats, had the entertainment, explained their problems, talked with Cheshire back when he had his squeak, got their hats, were surrounded by the cards, and finally were forced into the carriage.

"Did you notice any clues?" Tyrus asked.

Celia shook her head. "Let's try listening to the whole thing."

They listened to the entire tea party three times, replaying different sections to see if they'd misheard any parts. They analyzed the rules of etiquette and even debated if there might be some hidden meaning in the Dormouse's twisted version of Jack and Jill.

When they had resorted to playing the entire conversation in reverse, Celia knew whatever they needed wasn't there.

Cheshire turned down the volume as Tyrus thanked the Hatter for the party and the hats.

"The three of you are most welcome," the Hatter said one last time.

Celia ran her hands through her hair. "I should have done that."

"Done what?" Tyrus asked.

"Thanked him. I was so rude. I didn't ask if we could come to the tea party, and I didn't thank him for the hat."

"I'm sure he knew I was thanking him for all of us. That's why he said, 'The *three* of you are most welcome,' just like he invited us *all* to the party."

"Just like . . ." Celia sat up, something tugging at the back of her brain. It felt like when she was trying to figure out a hard part of a book. She had tricks to cope with her dyslexia. Could some of those skills help her figure out this problem?

She turned to the cat. "Could you change it up and try playing everything in wintergreen?"

"Good idea," Tyrus said.

Celia nodded as Cheshire began replaying the recording.

"The three of you are most welcome," the Hatter said, inviting them to the tea party. The words had a definite greenish sense—like a garden in springtime or a field of clover right after it rained—and the change seemed to help.

"Weird," Tyrus said. "That's the same thing he said at the end of the party."

"Very weird," Celia said. It had to be a coincidence, right? "What was the second thing he said?"

Cheshire fast-forwarded.

"Excellent decision," the Hatter said after they had taken their seats.

Celia held her breath. "What is the second to the last thing the Hatter said?"

"Excellent decision," the Hatter said again, this time with a snarl as the jack put away his sword.

She put her hand to her mouth. "How could I have missed that? But it's not possible. I mean, how could he?"

"Missed what?" Tyrus asked. "Is it a clue?"

"I think it might be *the* clue."

She turned to the cat. "Play only the exact words the Hatter said—cutting everything else out—from the beginning of the party to the end."

"You might be on to something," Cheshire said.

The Hatter's words shot out in rapid succession.

The three of you are most welcome.
Excellent decision.
Choose wisely.
They don't know the rules.
I'm afraid the party is over.
First things first.
Bravo!
Now it's your turn.
I see.
How can I help you?
Yes.
Return time.
Yes.
How can I help you?
I see.
Now it's your turn.
Bravo.
First things first.
I'm afraid the party is over.
They don't know the rules.
Choose wisely.
Excellent decision.
The three of you are most welcome.

"Do you hear it?" she asked, writing numbers in the dirt on the floor with her finger.

1-2-3-4-5-6-7-8-9-10-11-12-11-10-9-8-7-6-5-4-3-2-1

"The first line is the same as the last line," Celia said,

excited. "The second line is the same as second to last. He repeated everything he said in reverse order. Except for one line."

"I've heard of patterns like that," Tyrus said. "There's a word for it. I don't remember what it is, but I think the most important part is usually the line in the middle." He circled the number 12 that Celia had drawn in the dirt.

"Can you play the twelfth thing the Hatter said?" Celia asked Cheshire.

"Return time," the Hatter's voice said.

Maybe it was the wintergreen flavor helping her concentrate or maybe it was just that she was listening for it now, but Celia was almost sure she heard a greater emphasis in the Hatter's voice.

She and Tyrus stared at each other, eyes wide. "Return time," they said together.

CHAPTER 25

The Missing Time

*"In that case," said the Dodo solemnly, rising
to its feet, "I move that the meeting adjourn, for the
immediate adoption of more energetic remedies—"*

"I can't believe we figured it out," Tyrus said, strutting around the barn with a huge grin on his face. "I feel like Sherlock Holmes, or Hercule Poirot, or pretty much everyone in *The Westing Game.*"

Celia gave him a look, and he shrugged. "It's one of my favorite mysteries. I've read it like a hundred times. This millionaire, Sam Westing, dies and . . . never mind. What does 'return time' mean?"

"As a verb, 'return' can mean to go back to a location, feeling, earlier state, or to turn one's attention to," Cheshire said. "It may also refer to voting results, sports activities, cards, architecture, or profits. As a noun—"

"That isn't helping," Celia said.

Cheshire blinked his big green eyes. "If one doesn't wish an answer, one shouldn't ask a question."

"But that's not the answer we need," Tyrus said.

"Then perhaps you asked the wrong question."

They stared at each other as rain began to fall outside and lightning slashed the sky. It was the perfect time for an aha moment, but although Celia was sure they'd discovered the Hatter's clue, she had no idea what to do with it.

"I don't know what the right question is. We were talking about Tyrus and me going home, but I don't think that's what this is about. I feel like the Hatter wants us to do something."

Tyrus rubbed his jaw. "In the book, the Hatter tells Alice that he and Time quarreled and now it's always six o'clock, which is why the tea party goes on and on."

"Like they're caught in a trap," Celia said.

"But when Alice meets them, they're already stuck," Tyrus said. "That would mean they'd been in the trap before Charles Dodgson's visit."

"Or does it?" Celia steepled her fingers, thinking. "You said Mr. Dodgson wrote *Alice's Adventures in Wonderland* as a history of what he'd seen. But you also said he might have written it to help us. If he knew we would come back here, maybe he inserted clues into the book as well."

She pressed a fist to her forehead. "What if he knew the queen was going to trap the Hatter? Or, maybe it had already happened and that was part of why he left. The tea party scene could be in the book specifically to warn us about the trap. So maybe he also left a clue about how to break it. What else do you remember from the story?"

"Hmm." Tyrus folded his arms, head lowered in concentration. "When Alice first arrives, they are trying to fix—" He looked up, a shocked expression on his face. "Do the initials 'R.e.' mean anything to you?"

"I don't think so. Why?"

"In the book, when Alice arrives at the tea party, they are trying to fix a pocket watch that has crumbs in it. That's what gets them talking about time in the first place. Barrister Entwhistle said that Charles Dodgson gave his grandfather a pocket watch as a reward for pulling him out of the ocean. What if we have to take that same pocket watch to the Hatter?"

Outside, the wind howled, driving the rain through the barn doors, and the three of them moved deeper into the dark.

"How would an old pocket watch break the trap?" Celia asked.

"I don't know, but the initials R.e. were engraved on the back of the watch. It could stand for something."

"Something like 'Roderick Entwhistle'?" Celia exhaled. "Nice try, but sometimes the obvious answer isn't the right one."

"Except the initials were already on the pocket watch when Mr. Dodgson gave it away. When we were in prison, Barrister Entwhistle said Charles Dodgson gave his grandfather an engraved gold watch, who took the name Roderick Entwhistle— *because* of the watch."

Celia dropped back against the wall. "That is . . . *brilliant*."

"It is?" Tyrus asked. "I mean, yeah, it totally is. Why?"

"*R* and *e* are also math symbols."

Tyrus laughed. "The math nerd strikes again."

Celia ran to the bag the king had given them and was relieved to find her top hat inside. "Here," she said, pointing to a capital *R* on one side. "*R* represents the set of all real numbers. And *e* stands for Euler's number, which is one of the most famous irrational numbers in math." She turned the hat until her finger rested on a small gold *e* nearly hidden by the headband.

"Real and irrational," Tyrus said. "Sort of like the balance here between logic and fantasy. Something from our world combined with something from this world. That must be it. Mr. Dodgson knew the watch could break whatever spell the queen placed on the Hatter."

Celia remembered the dark circles under the Hatter's eyes, the run-down house, the piles of broken plates and dishes. "They've been stuck in one continuous tea party all this time, waiting for someone to rescue them."

"What are we waiting for?" Tyrus said. "We saw the rabbit with the watch the first day we got here. He probably still has it."

"Do you mean White?" Sylvan squealed.

Celia looked down at the rabbit, remembering that the White Rabbit wasn't the cute flustered one from the book, but a monster that had attacked Tyrus the first day they arrived in Wonderland.

"Do you know where he lives?" she asked.

"Y-yes," Sylvan stammered. "But we *can't* go there. The White Rabbit isn't the only one you need to worry about. There are"—Sylvan gulped—"others."

"Others?" Celia repeated, a tremor tracing her spine.

"This is a bad idea. Really bad. You don't understand. No rabbit ever goes near White's house, especially not his garden."

"I don't care," Tyrus said. "We have to get that watch and save the Hatter."

This sounded exactly like something from one of his books, but for once, Celia agreed. She was terrified of meeting White Rabbit again, and maybe they couldn't save Wonderland, but trying was better than sitting around a wet barn waiting for the world to end.

Tyrus was already heading toward the writing desk. "Tell us how to get there, Sylvan. Cheshire, you stay here; we don't want your gears to get wet. Meet up with us when you can."

"Goodbyes only prepare us for future hellos," Cheshire said. "But be careful."

Celia grabbed her top hat. She didn't want to get it wet, but she wanted to be wearing it when she saw the Hatter again. This time, she wouldn't forget to thank him.

A few minutes later, they were in the air. She was sure they'd get lost in the storm, but despite her obvious terror, Sylvan knew the way. Soon they were flying toward a large house that looked even more ramshackle than the March Hare's.

As they circled the building, Celia noticed a vegetable garden with a realistic-looking wooden scarecrow hanging from a pole.

"Is that a puppet?"

"Marionette," Tyrus said. "See the strings and handles hanging from its limbs?"

"Mary Ann," Sylvan whispered so quietly they could barely hear her.

Celia felt her little rabbit friend quivering as she held her close.

"That might be even creepier than the Duchess's songs," she said, clinging to the side of the desk.

The house looked like the least breeze could blow it over, and they were in the middle of a massive storm. There weren't any lights on inside the house, but the large windows seemed to be watching them.

Tyrus circled the desk and landed on the far side of the garden. "If he's asleep, maybe we can sneak in and out before he even knows we're here."

Celia hoped he was right. Meeting the White Rabbit in the middle of a field was bad enough. Dealing with him inside his haunted-looking house would be terrifying.

CHAPTER 26
The Rabbit's Den

"There goes Bill!"

"There is something seriously wrong with those carrots," Tyrus said as they crept through the plants.

"They're c-corrupt," Sylvan said, her tiny body shivering. "If you ate a single bite, you'd become like him."

"We won't," Celia said.

But it wasn't just the carrots; it was all the vegetables. From overhead, the garden had looked normal—lines of green, yellow, and red planted in rows across the yard. But up close, it was easy to see how the orange tops of the carrots stuck out of the ground and bulged and twisted. Odd lumps clung like blisters to the melons, and the tomatoes dripped a foul-smelling liquid.

She didn't like the idea of walking through the mutated garden, but they had all agreed it was best to stay out of sight as they approached the house. Although the rain was tapering

245

off, the muddy field sucked at Celia and Tyrus's shoes and Sylvan's paws as they walked through it.

They pushed through cornstalks with withered ears and leaves that seemed to whisper as Tyrus and Celia passed by.

Trying to touch as few of the plants as possible, Celia looked over her shoulder at the huge wooden puppet looming over the field. It appeared to be a woman, with a pale frowning face, long dark hair woven into two tight braids, and hands with jointed fingers that were twice as long as normal. Clothed in a dark pinafore and white blouse, she swayed gently in the breeze. Water dripped from her hair and the strings hanging from her neck.

"Who would use a giant puppet as a scarecrow?" she whispered.

Tyrus gave a quick glance and shuddered. "Not sure if it works on crows, but it scares me."

As they neared the edge of the field, Celia spotted something crawling around the side of the house.

Dropping to their knees, they watched the creature drag its thick body across the ground. It lumbered forward with slow deliberation on its four stubby legs. A long, heavily scaled tail flattened the grass behind it.

"What is that thing?" Tyrus murmured.

Celia squinted, trying to make out its shape. It appeared to be six or seven feet long, not counting the tail. "I think it might be an alligator."

"It's not," whispered a helpful voice. "It's a lizard. His name is Bill. He likes to eat little children."

Celia and Tyrus turned to see the marionette kneeling

behind them, her dress pulled up to reveal a pair of jointed wooden legs.

"My name's Mary Ann," the marionette said.

Celia tried to swallow, and a dry clicking sound came from her throat. "Hi, M-mary Ann. We were just coming to visit the, uh, White Rabbit."

The marionette's jaw clacked open, revealing perfectly white teeth. "Mr. Rabbit doesn't take visitors. He doesn't have the time." Her rattling wooden laugh sounded like bones clicking together. "That's a joke."

"It was, um, very funny," Tyrus said, his glasses fogged up so badly Celia wondered how he could see anything. "We were just hoping we could borrow his p-pocket watch."

"Borrow?" Mary Ann giggled, sending chills up Celia's neck. "White doesn't share his clocks, and I'm afraid the two of you are out. Of time, that is."

Rising gracefully to her feet, the marionette grabbed Celia and Tyrus and lifted them into the air.

"Let me go!" Tyrus yelled.

Mary Ann flung him deep into the garden, where he landed with a thud.

Celia tried to squirm away, but the marionette was incredibly strong.

"You can't fight against me," Mary Ann whispered, her eyes boring into Celia's.

Tyrus groaned, pushing himself to his feet.

Sylvan hopped through the garden. "Get her strings."

Celia looked up at the cords connected to the puppet's

arms and legs. If she could grab the handles, maybe she could stop the monster. But her arms had no strength.

"Those aren't for controlling me," the marionette said, her teeth clattering as she spoke. "They're for controlling you." Mary Ann dropped Celia to the ground, face-first in the mud.

"Can't. Move," Celia said. Forcing the words from her mouth took all the strength she had.

"Sure you can," Mary Ann said. She yanked the wooden handles, and Celia's body jerked upright. Another tug and her arms snapped out in front of her, hands open. "Give your friend a hug," the marionette said with a high-pitched giggle. "A very *hard* hug."

Celia felt her legs moving forward, her hands opening and closing, but none of it was her doing. She tried to stop, to turn around, but her body's movements were completely out of control. "Run," she growled through clenched teeth at Tyrus as her hands reached for his neck.

"No way." He ducked under her arm and charged at Mary Ann. The marionette swung at him with her free hand, but he dropped to the mud, out of her reach. Grabbing her leg as he slid by, he held on and twisted.

"What are you doing?" Mary Ann shouted as the hook connecting her lower leg to the upper slipped free. With only one leg to stand on, the marionette lost her balance and started to fall.

Celia felt the control on her slip, and she spun around. One of the wooden handles the marionette was holding turned, wrapping string around Mary Ann's wrist.

"Stop it," Mary Ann called, trying to pull loose.

Celia grabbed at the marionette's strings, twisting them in a hopeless tangle of knots. At the same time, Tyrus yanked on Mary Ann's limbs, pulling one hook after another loose until she was nothing but a pile of tangled limbs wrapped in string.

"You'll pay for this," Mary Ann howled.

"Be quiet," Celia said, hoping the White Rabbit hadn't heard the commotion in the garden. She quickly shoved one of the disgusting tomatoes in the marionette's mouth.

"Nice job," Tyrus said.

"Nice job, yourself," she said to Tyrus as the three of them snuck out of the garden and across the lawn to the rabbit's front door. "That was awesome the way you twisted her leg off."

Tyrus grinned. "I definitely don't remember anything like that in the book."

A brass plate next to the front door once read W. Rabbit, but now the plate was tarnished, and someone had scratched out the word "Rabbit," replacing it with "Rabid."

Tyrus forced a smile onto his face but it looked more terrified than brave. "Should we ring the bell?"

"Let's not," Celia said.

Inching the door open, they stepped inside, and entered a clockwork nightmare. Every inch of open space was covered with timepieces. Kitchen clocks, alarms clocks, cuckoo clocks, the terrifying cat clocks with moving tails and shifting eyes. Clocks under glass domes sat on grandfather clocks surrounded by dozens of wall clocks. The noise of thousands of ticking hands, clicking gears, and swinging pendulums sounded like a plague of locusts.

According to most of the clocks, it was almost midnight.

"Where do we even start?" Celia asked. There had to be at least a hundred pocket watches in the living room alone.

"No clue," Tyrus said. "But let's stick together. The last thing I want is to be alone in the dark and run into—"

"The owner of the house you're breaking into?" asked White Rabbit, walking down the stairs. "I must say, I'm quite impressed you got past Mary Ann. She's usually quite good at stopping unwanted visitors. She sometimes keeps them in the cellar to play with."

Celia and Tyrus turned to run just as a horned creature with pebbled black skin crawled through the front door.

"Visitors," the beast croaked, licking its jaws with a purple tongue. "Yummy."

White pulled a gold watch from his vest pocket. "I imagine you are looking for this." He let it spin on its chain, revealing the letters "R.e."

Celia, who had never been so scared in her life, nodded. "We just need to borrow it long enough to—"

"Please?" Sylvan begged, blinking her big eyes. "The Rabbit family needs your help."

"I'm afraid that's not possible," White said, pausing halfway down the stairs. He wiped a muddy glove across the fur of his chin, leaving a dark smear. "This is a one-of-a-kind item. Not from here, oh no, no, no. I could never part with it."

"We'll give it back as soon as we're done with it," Celia said, but the rabbit was already shaking his head.

Claws clicked across the wooden floor in time with the

ticking of the clocks, and Celia and Tyrus edged away from the lizard closing in on them.

"Wait," Tyrus said. "There's something important you need to know about that watch."

"My watch?" the rabbit said, looking down at it with bloodshot eyes.

Tyrus licked his lips, eyes darting from side to side. "The thing is," he said, slowly moving toward the stairs. "You see, Mr. Dodgson owned the watch, and, well, he didn't take very good care of it."

"Right," Celia said, catching on to what he was doing. "He spilled juice on it at breakfast and got eggs in the gears. I'm surprised it still works."

White held the watch at arm's length as he examined it for any sign of food. "It looks fine."

Sylvan nodded as Tyrus climbed the first step. "It *looks* fine," the rabbit said. "But everyone knows it runs a little slow."

Tyrus edged closer. "Which means if you've been using it to . . . keep . . . time . . ." Just as the minute hand on the clock to his left clicked to the top of the hour, he screamed. "You're late!"

"No!" the rabbit screamed as a thousand clocks all began chiming midnight at the same time. Bells rang, tiny birds popped out of their doors and tweeted, chimes clanged.

Tyrus darted forward, snatched the watch from the rabbit's hand, and tossed it to Celia. Together, the three of them turned to run, but Bill the lizard blocked their path to the front door. As they started for the back, Mary Ann stepped out of the kitchen, reattaching her left arm. White bounded down the stairs. They were surrounded.

"Get my watch!" the rabbit howled.

Mary Ann grinned, stretching her long fingers toward them. "Which one would you like, Bill?"

The lizard scrambled forward, teeth-filled jaws snapping.

Celia shoved the watch into her pocket and felt something squishy already there. Pulling her hand out, she saw her fingertips were stained blue. "You want something to eat?" she screamed, flinging the berries she'd saved from the bush outside the butterfly's home into the lizard's mouth.

Bill snapped his jaws shut, coughed, and began to shrink.

"Oh, my whiskers and toes!" the White Rabbit howled. "Get them, Mary Ann."

The marionette charged forward, but Sylvan darted under the puppet's legs, sinking her sharp rabbit teeth into Mary Ann's wooden ankle and pulling.

As Mary Ann fell, Celia snatched up Sylvan in one arm. "Come on!" Together, she and Tyrus raced by Bill, who was the size of a puppy and still shrinking, and onto the front porch.

"Come back!" White howled, chasing after them, but they were already racing back through the garden to the writing desk. As they climbed on and Tyrus grabbed the controls, something tugged at Celia's foot. She looked down to see the tiny lizard's jaws clamped on the toe of her shoe. With an annoyed grunt, she kicked it away, and the creature flew over the cornstalks and into the night.

Laughing wildly, Tyrus shouted, "Well, there goes Bill!"

CHAPTER 27
The Broken Trap

"Come, we shall have some fun now!" thought Alice.

As the sun finally began to rise above the small cave where Celia, Tyrus, and Sylvan had spent the night hiding out, hundreds of animals swarmed from the forest as though fleeing unseen beasts. It was morning, and, though the earthquakes and lightning had stopped, the sky was a dark green color that felt even more ominous. Strange sour-smelling breezes started and stopped, blowing first in one direction, then abruptly switching to the opposite.

"They're all trying to flee Wonderland," Sylvan said. "They can sense something terrible is about to happen."

"Let's just hope the Hatter knows some way to help," Celia said.

Tyrus wanted to go straight to the Hatter once they had the watch, but Celia said the idea of traveling at night was a bad idea. Now that they could see, the three of them covered

253

the desk with brush and tree branches and set out through the woods to the March Hare's house.

"You ever wonder how our clothes grew and shrank with us when we went to see Kat?" Tyrus asked. "Or what happened to them when we turned into slugs?"

"Nope." Celia shoved her hair up, trying to get the top hat to stay in place, but it kept slipping down over her eyes.

"I mean, is it magic or just normal Wonderland physics? In the book, Alice's clothes grew with her, so I'm thinking physics." Tyrus pushed his unicorn derby into place. "Think the Hatter will be surprised when we bring him the watch? Or will he be expecting it?"

She stared at him. "Don't you ever stop talking?"

He shuffled his feet. "I talk when I'm nervous. Or I read. But I don't have any books, so . . ."

"*Are* you nervous?" Sylvan asked.

"Sure," Tyrus said. "Aren't you?"

Sylvan nodded.

Tyrus rubbed his glasses on his shirt. "What if there's an ambush? Or what if the Hatter doesn't want us to bring him the watch? Or what if the watch doesn't work?"

"We'll just have to keep our eyes open and deal with whatever comes," Celia said.

As they rounded the corner of the hare's house, she tensed herself for an attack. But the only ones there were the Dormouse, the March Hare, and the Hatter, exactly the way it had been before.

Careful not to step on any smaller creatures who might be about, Celia approached the table.

"No room," the March Hare said, stuffing a biscuit into his cheek. "Besides, the party's nearly over."

"Which means it should be about ready to start," Tyrus said.

"May we join you?" Celia asked, holding her hat in place as she bowed to each of them. "I've heard the Dormouse tells excellent stories."

The Dormouse lifted his head from the table, a slice of treacle tart sticking to the side of his face.

> *Mary had a little clam*
> *A little lobster too*
> *She brought them both to school one day*
> *And put them in a stew*

"The three of you are most welcome," the Hatter said, watching Celia closely.

She approached the table. "I know the rules of tea etiquette are rather specific, but I'm afraid I didn't bring any loose hardware, I don't know the secret handshake, and I'd prefer not to slap anyone. But if it's all right, I'd like to give you this."

She reached into her pocket and took out Charles Dodgson's watch.

The March Hare gasped. The Dormouse woke up and rubbed his eyes.

Slowly, the Hatter removed his boots from the table and stood. As he looked from the watch to her, Celia thought she saw his shoulders relax ever so slightly.

He shut his eyes for a moment, taking a deep breath. "That

is a . . . *much appreciated* gift. Would you be so kind as to wind it completely and set the time to six o'clock?"

"Okay?" Celia had expected something a little more dramatic, but if that's what he wanted, she would do it. After winding the watch and setting it to six, she tried to hand it to him.

He held up a finger, head bowed.

Feeling foolish, Celia looked at Tyrus. He shrugged. She held the watch, waiting for someone to say something, until the minute hand moved to 6:01 with an audible *click*.

The Hatter looked up, grinning in a way she'd never seen before. The skin on his face didn't look quite as drawn, and the circles under his eyes weren't as dark. "That may have been the finest minute of my life."

"Is it . . . *over*?" the March Hare asked.

"It is." The Hatter laughed. "May I never drink another cup of tea again."

"May I never take another nap," the Dormouse said, looking the most alert Celia had seen him.

"May I never fetch another sugar cube or clear a broken plate," a small voice shouted. Celia looked down to see Ceremony, the snail, yank off his tuxedo jacket. "I quit!"

"May I never dance on the table again," said the March Hare. "Oh, who am I kidding?" He jumped up on the table, kicking cups and saucers in every direction.

Sylvan wrinkled her nose and laughed. "He's doing the Bunny Hop."

"The *Hare* Hop," the March Hare said with a glare.

"To no more tea parties," the Hatter said, throwing a cup to the ground and stomping it under his boot.

"The trap is broken then?" Tyrus asked.

"It is." The Hatter hurried around the table and pulled them both into a tight embrace.

"We didn't know if we would be able to figure out the clue," Celia said.

"I never had a doubt," Sylvan said.

The Hatter chuckled. "Neither did I. Charles said it might be one person who would come through the door next, but he thought it would be two. Either way, he knew whoever came would possess the talents to return time."

Celia grinned. "I forgot the last time I was here, but I wanted to thank you for our lovely hats."

"I hope they fit," the Hatter said.

Celia thought about mentioning that the sizes were wrong but decided it was the thought that counted. "They're perfect."

The Hatter nodded. "I pride myself on fitting the hat to the hattee." He looked up at the swirling green sky and frowned. "I'd love to talk more, but we must hurry. Things are coming to a close and, with the trap broken, they will be here any minute."

"What's coming to a close?" Tyrus asked. "And who's coming?"

The sound of hoofbeats and boots filled the air along with a deep howling. The wind began to blow, swirling dust devils into the sky.

"Go somewhere safe," the Hatter told the March Hare and the Dormouse.

The March Hare closed his hands into furry fists. "I'm not leaving you."

The Dormouse picked up a scone. "Let me at them."

Sylvan picked up a piece of broken plate. "We'll stay and fight too."

"You'll fight," the Hatter said. "But not here." The howling grew so loud it was hard to make out his words. "You must get the key."

"We don't know where it is," Celia shouted.

The Hatter pulled them close. "Wait till night, then go to the castle. When you get there, you must raise the stakes."

Celia shook her head. "I don't understand. Why would we go back? What are we looking for?"

"You'll know it when you see it," the Hatter said.

At that moment, four columns of cards, organized into spades, diamonds, clubs, and hearts, marched around the side of the house, swords drawn.

"You are all under arrest by order of the queen," shouted a king of diamonds.

The Hatter squeezed Celia and Tyrus's shoulders. "The fight will not be easy, but know that you each possess everything you need to come out victorious."

With that, he reached into his cloak and pulled out a pair of matching jade scissors. "For Wonderland and the freedom to believe," he shouted, rushing into battle.

"For the freedom to dance," the March Hare shouted, kicking a ten of diamonds so hard it dropped its sword.

"For the freedom to tell stories," the Dormouse said,

pouring a steaming pot of tea over the jack of spades's head. The jack clapped a hand over its eye and ran away screaming.

As the cards fell back under the onslaught, the howling grew so loud it sounded like a train was on top of them. A black tornado dropped from the sky, scattering the cards everywhere. When the dust cleared, a huge knight clad in black-and-gold armor stepped forward. A golden *A* and a club were emblazoned on his chest, and he carried a spiked mace that looked like it weighed a hundred pounds.

"Look out," Celia screamed, starting to rush forward.

"Leave now," the Hatter said to her, grinning. "Your fight is yet to come." With that, he whipped off his cloak. As the ace of clubs swung his mace, the Hatter ducked neatly under his arm. He stuck out a boot, swung the knight around, and knocked him to the ground.

Roaring in rage, the rest of the cards swarmed over the Hatter.

Just before he disappeared under the attack, the Hatter winked at Celia and shouted, "Use your heads."

CHAPTER 28

The Hidden Key

Alice had begun to think that very
few things indeed were really impossible.

Celia clutched the sides of the desk as they flew through the darkness. The storms, earthquakes, and winds had been replaced by a stillness so complete even the brush of air against her face felt stale and lifeless. The sense of a fuse burning had been replaced by the anticipation of a bomb sucking in all the air around it before exploding outward.

"I'm sure this is a good idea," Tyrus said, his voice quivering.

"Are you?" Celia asked.

"No, but if I keep telling myself that, I'm hoping I will." He looked back at her. "He's all right, don't you think?"

"Of course," Sylvan said. "He's the Mad Hatter. How could a bunch of playing cards hurt someone like him?"

Celia closed her eyes, trying not to remember seeing the Hatter falling beneath more than a dozen sword-wielding soldiers.

Tyrus steered the desk to the right, and the lights of the castle came into view. "Any idea where we go next?"

"None at all," she said. They'd spent the day hiding and discussing the key's hiding place, but the only thing they knew for sure was that the Hatter had said they would know it when they saw it.

She chewed the inside of her cheek. "I've been thinking. Once we find the key—if we do—I'm hoping we can use the box to save Wonderland *and* get home, but if we can only do one . . ."

"You want to go home." Tyrus nodded. "I understand, and I'll go with you. This isn't our fight."

Sylvan pressed her paws to her eyes but didn't say anything.

Celia swallowed, gratitude welling up inside her that Tyrus would want to stand by her. She shook her head. "I've decided I want to use it to save Wonderland."

The little rabbit's ears stood straight up.

Tyrus blinked. "But that would mean we'd never get home." He took Celia's hand. "Maybe the king was right. If we go home and seal the door, maybe the queen will change things back on her own."

"She won't," Celia said, testing the words on her tongue and in her brain. They felt right. "Her temper is too big for that. She'd rather see all of Wonderland destroyed than back down. You heard the Hatter. Charles Dodgson knew we would come. He left us whatever is inside the box so we could make things right here."

"This isn't our fight," Tyrus repeated.

She knew he didn't believe that. He was just trying to keep her safe. "Maybe it should be. Think of everyone who has tried to help us. Do you think Hatter would back down if it was *our* world that needed to be saved?" She squeezed Tyrus's hand. "It's time for us to stand up for the people who can't help themselves."

"You *are* The Celia," Sylvan said, her tail quivering with excitement. She turned to Tyrus. "And you are too!"

"Thanks," Tyrus said. "I think."

They stopped talking as they flew over the castle walls, afraid they might be overheard by the guards posted there, but the cards were looking outward not up.

They glided near a row of greenhouses and landed the desk silently. Sticking close together, they crept past the glass walls. Inside was line after line of rosebushes—all red, all the same variety and height.

"The Hatter said to raise the stakes," Tyrus whispered. "Smashing all these would probably do the trick."

"It would also get us caught immediately," Celia said. "I'm not sure what he meant, but I don't think it was that."

They moved from one building to another, checking for cards, then hurrying on, looking for some sign, something that would scream out, "The key is here!" She didn't want to think about what they would do if they circled the entire grounds without finding anything.

"We'll know it when we see it," she muttered under her breath.

"We'll know it when we see it," Tyrus repeated.

"I'll know it when I smell it," Sylvan said, hopping beside them.

Stepping out onto a wide grassy field, Celia recognized the croquet court, and a pang of guilt burned her insides. "I'm sorry for the way I treated you when we first came here," she said. "It felt so good to have someone like me for who I am that I didn't think about how you were feeling."

"I'm the one who should apologize," Tyrus said. "Coming to Wonderland and seeing all the weird creatures and strange buildings is like a dream come true for me. But I know it's been hard on you."

He held out his hand, fingers curled into a fist, but his little finger extended. "Whatever happens in the future, how about we both try to see it from the other person's side. Pinky promise?"

She linked little fingers with him. "Pinky promise." She gave him a playful smirk. "If we weren't on a mission to save Wonderland while being hunted by a deck of cards, I'd totally challenge you to a game of midnight croquet."

"Only if you promised not to lecture me about the physics of one ball striking another and the importance of placing . . ." His words died away as he looked around. He began to laugh. "This is it."

Sylvan and Celia followed his gaze, trying to figure out what he'd seen.

Tyrus tugged his hat down on his head. "When the Hatter told us to raise the stakes, he wasn't talking about increasing risks or placing a bet, he was talking about . . ." He pointed to the court.

Celia looked where he was pointing, remembering the queen's words as she had explained the game. "The hoops are called wickets, and the wooden poles are called . . . stakes." She laughed. "Tyrus, you're a genius."

He removed his hat and bowed. "And you thought I wasn't paying attention when you and that nasty woman were hitting hedgehogs."

Celia pulled him into a hug. "I'm so glad you were."

Tyrus bit his lip. "Could it really have been here all this time with no one discovering it?"

"The queen said the royal court has been in place for a hundred and fifty years." Sylvan giggled. "She'll be furious when she discovers the key has been under her *feet* this whole time."

"Well," Tyrus said, "what are we waiting for? Let's pull those things up and find out what's underneath."

They ran out on the court together, not worried about damaging the perfect grass or knocking over a wicket. When they reached the wooden pole at one end of the court, Tyrus bent and yanked at it.

Nothing happened.

"Let me try," Celia said. Grabbing the pole with both hands, she tugged as hard as she could. It didn't budge.

"Maybe it's like the Sword in the Stone," Tyrus said. "Only King Arthur can remove it."

"King Arthur isn't here," Celia said. "We'll have to figure this out on our own."

Sylvan studied the fields, her nose twitching. "The Hatter

didn't tell you to raise the stake; he told us to raise the *stakes*. What if you pull both of them up at the same time?"

"Of course," Celia said. Quickly, she hurried to the other side of the court. "When I count three, we pull." She grabbed the stake in front of her as Tyrus did the same. "One . . . two . . ."

On the count of three, they both pulled. Celia felt the stake in her hands rise smoothly out of the ground. At the same time, a circle of grass in the center of the court rose up and split open. Dropping the stake, she raced to the opening, arriving at the same time as Tyrus and Sylvan.

Lying in a hole in the dirt, without a trace of dust or grime—as if it had been placed there a moment before—was a small black bag.

"Open it," Tyrus said.

Celia shook her head. "You're the one who solved the puzzle of the stakes. You should be the one to do it."

"But Sylvan figured out we had to pull both at the same time."

Sylvan lowered her head, the tip of her bunny nose blushing. "We figured it out together. Let's open it together."

Facing one another around the hole, in the still night, surrounded by perfectly placed lines that had been there since Charles Dodgson had first drawn them, they knelt and picked up the bag.

"For Charles Dodgson," Celia said.

"For Wonderland," Tyrus added.

"For the honor of the Rabbit family," Sylvan finished.

Together they opened the sack, revealing a crystal key that glowed with a faint pink hue.

Tyrus withdrew the key from the bag and turned it in front of his eyes before handing it to Celia. It seemed to vibrate slightly in her fingers.

"The Hatter was right," she said. "Mr. Dodgson did want us to find this."

As they stood, blinding lights flashed all around them, turning the night to day.

The queen marched out, surrounded by dozens of her cards. "Thank you for recovering my property," she said with a smirk. "I'll take that."

CHAPTER 29
The Questionable Pilot

"For it might end, you know," said Alice to herself,
"in my going out altogether, like a candle."

"You can't have it," Sylvan said, baring her teeth as she backed away.

"I can, and I will." The queen walked toward them, her cards circling to the left and right to cut off any chance of escape.

Celia's top hat slipped down over her eyes, and she pushed it back. "How did you find us?"

"Child, please." The queen held up a beautiful mirror, turning it so they could see themselves reflected in its surface—not their faces, but from the top—like a bird flying overhead. "I've been watching you the whole time. I knew if I waited long enough, you'd find the key for me."

"Then you've seen what you're doing to Wonderland," Tyrus said. "How you're destroying it."

"I'm not doing anything to Wonderland," the queen snapped. "This filthy place has always been a cesspit of the broken and the unfit. Think of the people you've met since you arrived. A flock of foul-mouthed birds, squabbling over who can enter their pathetic village. A kleptomaniac rabbit. A woman who can't decide whether to be kind or hateful and her pig of a son. Not one of them could do in a lifetime what I accomplish in a single day. Not one of them understands who they are and how to fit in."

"Is that why you attacked the butterfly?" Celia asked. "Were the patterns on her wings not straight enough for you? Were her antennas not perfectly parallel?"

The queen scowled at the hole in her grass as Celia, Tyrus, and Sylvan backed across the croquet court.

"Poppycock. No doubt those webs of hers failed because of years of neglect. Like the rest of this pathetic land is failing. Don't think she was any more perfect than the rest of the outcasts—unable to decide whether to crawl or fly. To possess such great beauty and hide in a hole in the ground is a waste. To have access to all the information in the world and do nothing with it disgusts me. She was another pathetic failure who deserved what she got."

Celia's eyes burned. "She was one of the kindest creatures I've ever met. The only reason you look down on her is because she wasn't as power-hungry as you."

"I've had enough of this conversation," the queen said, snapping her fingers. "Take the key and have all three of them executed."

Celia held the key above her head. "One more step and I'll break it."

"Will you?" The queen quirked an eyebrow. "The one

thing that could get you home? The one thing keeping you alive?"

"You're going to kill us anyway," Tyrus said.

The queen paused. "Who would have expected logic from the boy? But you're right." She tugged at the heart-shaped pendent around her neck, frowning. "Very well. I'll make a deal with you. Give me the key and I will allow you both— and your rabbit friend—to live. What's more, I will take you back to your world with me. Isn't that what you wanted in the first place?"

"What would happen to Wonderland after you're gone?" Sylvan asked.

"It is not my concern," the queen said. "I'm tired of this game, and honestly, I don't think you could break the key even if you tried. Do we have a deal?"

Celia shook her head. "No. I've seen far more good outside this castle than I've seen in it. Our world has just as many outcasts as this one does." She reached for Tyrus's hand and squeezed. "I thought I wanted to fit in. I thought having all the numbers in a line, all the equations neatly summed up, was the most important thing. But I was wrong. If this is the way you treat your world, I'd rather die than have you reach mine. I think Charles Dodgson would have felt the exact same way."

"Charles Dodgson was a fool," the queen snarled. "He related to the misfits here because he was just as broken. He had one of the greatest mathematical minds I have ever seen, and yet he spent hours drinking tea and making up nonsense rhymes. It's what drew him here in the first place. The same way the two of you were pulled here. Because you are broken."

She strode toward Celia and Tyrus, eyes glittering. "I offered him everything—power, money. I offered him this entire world in exchange for the simple gift of the power to travel as he did—and he refused. Now give me the key!"

As the queen lunged toward them, a crash of shattering glass sounded from their left. Everyone on the croquet court turned to see a dark shape flying from the direction of the greenhouses, which were now nothing but shards of broken glass.

Sylvan ducked her head. "It's the gryphon."

"No," Tyrus shouted. "It's the writing desk."

Celia looked up to see the wooden furniture flapping toward them, twisting and looping like a drunk bird. But who was steering it?

A huge glowing grin appeared out of the darkness, followed by two green eyes. "Grab on or get out of the way," Cheshire called. "They both have an equal chance of success."

Celia picked up Sylvan and grabbed the desk as it swooped by. Tyrus was right behind her.

"No!" the Queen of Hearts screeched. As she leaped up to grab them, Celia's foot kicked against her mirror, shattering it.

"Boy, did we ever need you this time," Tyrus told Cheshire with a sigh of relief.

The cat winked. "A good friend knows."

"Get us out of here," Celia said, clinging to the desk as the queen howled below them.

Tyrus pulled himself up.

"You may want to take the controls," Cheshire said. "It appears I am a better philosopher than a pilot."

"Which way?" Tyrus asked, switching places with Cheshire. He turned toward the castle walls, which were now filled with cards pointing bows, spears, and catapults in their direction.

"We have to find the golden box," Sylvan said. "The one with the keyhole in it."

Celia pointed to the window they'd flown out of what felt like months earlier. "Take us back to the king's invention room."

Dodging arrows and spears, they barely managed to make it through the window without taking anyone's head off on the stone sill. The landing was harder than usual, but at least they were all in one piece.

"How do we find the box?" Tyrus asked.

"I believe the key itself may help you with that," Cheshire said.

Celia looked down to see that the key had begun to glow. As she moved it left and right, the glow increased and decreased. "It's like playing hot and cold."

The sound of running boots came from the stairs outside the room.

"It would be in your best interest to leave before they get here." The cat opened the crate of toy frogs. When he set a frog on the floor, it took three leaps before flicking out its long tongue with an explosive bang.

Cheshire nodded at the smoking hole in the wall with a satisfied grin. "I shall endeavor to delay the cards while you make your escape."

As Tyrus moved to open the door, he bumped into the

rocking horse. It reared back and then rocked forward with a realistic whiny. He tilted his head. "You don't think . . . ?"

"I think we found a ride," Celia said, climbing on the horse. "This time, I drive."

CHAPTER 30

The Royal Return

"No, no!" said the Queen.
"Sentence first—verdict afterwards."

"Faster!" Tyrus shouted, pressing his derby to his head as they rocked down a hallway, slid around a corner, and see-sawed their way up a winding staircase.

"If you want to go faster, rock harder," Celia called, checking the key to make sure they were going in the right direction. She pointed the key left and it glowed brighter, just as a full house of kings and jacks appeared in front of them.

Squeezed between the two of them, Sylvan clung to the back of Celia's jacket with her paws and feet. "That way," she called, pointing to a narrow door.

Celia steered the horse into the door, knocking it open. A lobster wearing only a towel looked up in surprise. "Sorry!" she shouted before riding away.

Spotting a wide corridor behind a partially closed set of tapestries, she grabbed the horse's reins and rocked for all she was worth, sending them shooting down the hall.

"Cards behind us," Tyrus called.

"Shoot the flamethrowers," Celia yelled.

"You want me to use a flamethrower on a deck of cards in the middle of a castle?" Tyrus asked, clinging to the back of the rocking horse.

"Unless you want to get caught and beheaded."

He grabbed the nozzle from the holster on the horse's side, narrowed his eyes, aimed, and squeezed the trigger. Directly behind him, the cards skidded to a halt, then scattered as they searched for somewhere to take cover. The flamethrower gurgled and kicked in Tyrus's arms, nearly throwing him from the saddle.

Large rainbow-colored spheres expanded from the opening, floating lazily down the hallway.

"It doesn't shoot flames, it shoots bubbles!" Sylvan yelled.

Celia glanced back and scowled. "That's less than helpful."

Elbowing one another and laughing, the cards reformed and continued the chase. The deuce of clubs ran straight at the first large bubble. It closed around him with a snap and floated into the air. The next two bubbles encased a six of hearts and an eight of diamonds. They, too, sailed upward, spinning head over heels.

The eight of diamonds jabbed his sword at the translucent wall, but his blade bounced back as if the bubble was made of thick rubber. A ten of spades tried to dodge the next bubble, but it followed him and gobbled him up before bouncing down the stairs.

"Maybe not as useless as they seem," Tyrus said, firing another round of bubbles at the cards.

Swinging the key back and forth, Celia continued in what she thought was a northeasterly direction, but a moment after the glow grew brighter, the key began to dim. They paused in the middle of a ballroom, trying to get their bearings.

"Why are we stopping?" Tyrus asked, searching for something to shoot.

Celia shook her head. "I think the box is moving."

"How could it?" Tyrus asked, aiming at a pesky four of hearts. As Tyrus fired the bubble gun, the four ducked around the corner. The bubble paused, bounced up and down, then followed the card around the corner. A moment later, they heard a muted scream.

"I could really use one of these at school," he said.

"Spread out," the queen's voice called from nearby. "I want that key! Fail me and you'll all be dealt to the farthest reaches of Wonderland."

Sylvan's ears twitched. "We have to go."

"I know." Celia rotated the key slowly north, west, south, and east. None of them glowed more brightly than the other.

"Maybe it's broken," Tyrus suggested.

"It was working fine a minute ago." She raised her hand, and the key flared magenta. "It's above us."

"The tower," Tyrus said. "We passed a staircase a few seconds ago."

Celia wheeled the horse around and rode back to the stairs. But the staircase proved too narrow for the horse's rockers.

"We'll have to go on foot," Celia said.

As they jumped off the horse and ran up the stairs, shouts and footsteps behind them made it clear the cards were close.

Gasping for breath, they raced around and around the spiral staircase until Celia began to wonder if they'd ever reach the top or if this was a trap.

Her legs ached and her lungs burned when they finally reached a landing with an arched doorway. Rushing through, they found themselves standing on a balcony high above the castle grounds.

"Where's the box?" Tyrus asked, looking around.

Celia held up the key. Before she could check its glow, dozens of cards raced through the door behind her.

"Grab her," the queen said, stepping out onto the balcony.

Celia moved to the wall and dangled the key over the edge. "I'll drop it."

The queen nodded to the jack and ten of spades. The cards grabbed Tyrus and lifted him up.

"Let him go, or I swear you will never find out what's in the box," Celia said, her breath catching in her throat.

The queen smiled. "Go ahead. Throw the key over the side."

Celia gripped the key, her hand shaking. Could she do it? Could she destroy the last hope for Wonderland, and maybe the only chance she and Tyrus had of ever seeing their families again?

The queen clasped her hands behind her back, her face the epitome of arrogance. "Of course, should you drop the key, the next thing you will see is your friend going over the wall after it. I don't know whether the key will survive the fall, but I assure you, *he* won't."

At her signal, the two cards dangled Tyrus over the wall. It was at least a hundred feet to the ground.

"D-don't give it to her," Tyrus said, his voice trembling.

Sylvan's ears dropped. "Give it to her. I couldn't stand to see either of you hurt."

As Celia brought her hand back, the key flashed pink. The balcony was empty, so where was the box?

"I'll take that," the queen said, extending her hand.

Celia jerked the key away, and Tyrus yelped as the cards prepared to drop him.

"Okay," Celia hurriedly told the queen. "You can have the key. But you have to promise you'll let us all go."

"That time has passed," the queen said. "If you had cooperated before, I would have taken the two of you with me to your world. Now your choice is to keep the key and watch your friend fall to his death, hoping it will be quick and relatively painless, or give me the key and know that your beheading will be swift and efficient."

Celia dropped her head, knowing she had lost.

Running footsteps echoed from the stairway, and a small figure stepped through the door. "Darling," the king said, panting and clutching something to his chest. "Is everything all right? I heard shouts and thought—" He noticed Celia and Tyrus. "You found them."

"Of course, I found them," the queen snapped. Then, noticing what he was holding, asked, "Is that my box?"

"One of the cards told me to bring it to you," he said, his eyes shifting from his wife to the key.

"Yes, yes." The queen snatched the key from Celia's

fingers. "Take the girl to the guillotine and chop off her head at once. Throw the boy over the wall."

Celia gasped. "No! You said you wouldn't."

"I didn't give you a monarch's promise, though, did I?" the queen said with a wicked smile.

The cards holding Tyrus leaned farther out over the wall.

"Are you sure that's wise?" the king asked.

The queen raised a perfectly shaped eyebrow. "Whatever are you talking about?"

The king bowed his head, trembling. "It's just that, you haven't actually opened the box yet. Perhaps it would be"—he licked his lips—"wiser to wait until you're sure it works."

"What do *you* know about wisdom?" she said, before waving her hand at the cards. "Very well. Hold off on killing them." She snapped her fingers at her husband. "Give me the box."

"Of course." He began to hand it to her, then paused. "I almost forgot. I have a gift for you." He reached into his pocket and withdrew a gold bracelet studded with tiny ruby hearts.

"Another trinket?" she said, contempt dripping from her lips. "I am about to be the most powerful woman not just in this world but in every world I travel to."

"Of course, my dear, but first . . ." Moving with surprising quickness, he reached out and snapped the bracelet around his wife's wrist.

Her eyes grew wide, and her mouth opened, but no words came out as she collapsed to the stone floor.

"Your Majesty," the leader of the cards said, kneeling at her side.

The king straightened and addressed the cards. "Set that boy safely back down."

"But the queen," the card said.

The king plucked the key from his wife's fingers. "Take her to her room," he stated with surprising authority. "She has passed out from the excitement of finally getting what she wanted, but she'll be fine after a little rest. As your king, I command you and the rest of the cards to wait for us in front of the castle. Do not make me tell you again."

"Yes, Your Majesty," the card said, turning and disappearing down the stairs with the rest of the cards.

Once they were alone, the king grinned and wiped his sleeve across his perspiring forehead. "That was too close."

CHAPTER 31

The Box's Contents

"You ought to have finished,"
said the King. "When did you begin?"

Sylvan looked down the stairs where the cards had taken the queen. "Is she . . . ?"

"Only sleeping," the king said. "The jewelry I've been giving her draws away her power."

"Won't she be angry when she wakes up?" Tyrus asked.

"Furious," the king said with a nervous twitter. "But by then the two of you will be long gone."

"What about you?" Celia said. "She'll blame you for giving us the box."

"I'll deal with that," the king said. "I've been preparing for this moment for quite some time. What we need to worry about now is getting the two of you home." So close to the box, the key glowed an almost blindingly bright rose-red.

Celia looked at Tyrus and Sylvan, who nodded together. "We've decided we want to use the power for something else," she said to the king. "Something more important."

The king frowned. "What could be more important than getting the two of you back where you belong and shutting the door once and for all so my wife can never come to your world?"

Sylvan hopped forward. "They are going to save Wonderland."

The king frowned. "Who are you?"

"Sylvan Rabbit," she said proudly. "Descendant of your original timekeeper, White Rabbit."

Tyrus nodded, his face calm but determined. "We want to fix everything the queen messed up."

Setting the box and key on the wall beside him, the king looked at each of them in turn. "I'm afraid I don't understand what you mean by 'fix.' What is wrong with our world?"

"Nothing," Celia said at once. "I mean, nothing like what the queen thought was wrong with it. We love how quirky everything is here. The crazy characters, the talking animals. We love how you can grow big or small but still fit in."

Tyrus nodded. "We love how someone can be both a boy and a pig without being judged. We love how the Duchess can be both happy and angry without anyone saying that makes her a bad mother. How a mouse can decide to become a lawyer one day without anyone telling him he's not good enough or smart enough."

Celia laughed. "I'm even learning to appreciate bad puns and roads that take the most winding routes to get where they're going."

"Yes, yes," the king said, beaming. "That's the power of imagination, the strength of fantasy. My wife never understood it, but it was one of the things Mr. Dodgson loved most about this world."

"He shared that love in his stories," Tyrus said. "People in our world have been inspired and uplifted by Wonderland for over a hundred years. Charles Dodgson may be gone, but Wonderland will live on forever."

The king straightened his jacket, looking the most regal Celia had ever seen him. "I am honored to have impacted your people in such a manner."

Celia nodded. "But there was always a balance of logic and imagination in Wonderland. I think that's one of the things we love so much about the stories. For every nonsensical poem, there is a mathematical formula. For every bunch of crazy birds, there is a Cheshire cat making wise comments. For every baby that turns into a pig, there is a philosophical caterpillar."

"We don't trust that the queen will restore that balance," Tyrus said. "So we're going to use the power from the box to do it ourselves."

"That won't be necessary." The king picked up the box and the key. "I think it's time for you to go."

"We told you we aren't leaving," Celia said with a growing sense of unease.

"We're going to save Wonderland," Sylvan added.

The king's eyes narrowed, his mouth an angular slit. "Wonderland doesn't need saving. It is perfectly fine the way it is. The only thing broken is this castle. And that will soon be remedied."

Tyrus held out his hands. "May we have the box, please?"

"I don't think so," the king said. "I was hoping you would open the doorway, but since you seem determined not to, I will have to do it myself."

Like the final pieces of a puzzle sliding into place, Celia realized what she should have seen all along. "The queen hasn't been attacking Wonderland. *You* have."

Sylvan shook her head. "Why would he destroy our own world?"

"*Fix,*" the king snarled. "I've been fixing Wonderland, turning it into the world it always should have been, if my color-inside-the-lines wife hadn't been in power for so long. I didn't see that until an outsider visited our world. Didn't realize how much she had pushed me to the background."

Celia collapsed against the wall, feeling light-headed. "Why would you want to steal the logic?"

"You *are* slow-witted," the king said. "I wasn't stealing the logic. I was destroying it. Without the constraints of logic to hold it back, Wonderland is free to become a world of pure, undiluted imagination."

"The queen must have seen what you were doing," Tyrus said.

The king guffawed. "She's never cared what happened outside her walls. All that mattered to her was keeping her grounds perfect. That, and getting to your world once I convinced her that ruling Wonderland wasn't enough."

"But she turned into a monster at dinner," Tyrus said. "We saw her."

The king laughed. "It never occurred to my wife that the jewelry I was giving her allowed me to syphon away *her* logic any time I wanted. What you saw was the dark part of herself she tried to keep hidden—the non-logical part."

Reality smashed Celia in the stomach, pushing the air out of her lungs until she feared she might faint. "You were the word creature—the hauntstrosity. You attacked your own citizens."

The king smiled, and for a moment his skin turned into a smoking mass of words that coiled like a hungry snake. "I contain every possibility of every story, every world, every character or creature you can imagine," the word monster hissed. "And many you can't. It was a small sacrifice to make, compared to all the 'logical' beheadings I've stopped my wife from committing."

The word *KING* swirled out of the myriad sentences, and the smoke turned back into the King of Hearts. "When you opened the doorway in Dodgson's diary, I came so close to entering your world I could smell the millions of possibilities there—the things I could create once I destroyed your logic the way I have in Wonderland."

"Give us the box and key," Tyrus demanded, stepping forward.

"Never," the king snarled, clutching the items to his chest.

"With your cards outside the castle, we have you outnumbered," Celia said, stepping up beside Tyrus. "We don't want to take them from you by force, but we will if we have to."

"I've never been large in stature," the king said. "It's one of the reasons my wife felt comfortable pushing me around. But you're wrong about having me outnumbered."

The sound of flapping wings came from overhead, and

Celia turned to see two fierce-looking gryphons land on the wall behind her and Tyrus. A gust of wind slapped her hair against her face as a blur of spinning darkness morphed into the ace of clubs.

"She has her spies, and I have mine," the king said. "And don't expect any help from your cat friend. I dismantled him myself before coming here." He inserted the key into the box. "I won't execute you unless I have to. That has never been my way. But it's time to open this and finish what I started."

"No!" Celia cried, but a pair of sharp talons jerked her and Tyrus back against the cold stone of the wall.

Sylvan leaped toward the box, but the king backhanded her, slamming the rabbit into the wall, where she collapsed to the ground.

Celia and Tyrus watched in horror as the king turned the key. A surge of bright red light surrounded the box, the king, and everything on the balcony.

The king opened the box.

Celia held her breath, waiting for an explosion or a flow of energy. Instead, the light slowly faded away until everything looked just as it had before.

"What's this?" the king asked, pulling a plain envelope from the box.

"It's a letter," Tyrus said.

"It must be directions to the real power." The king ripped the envelope open, pulled out a single piece of paper, and examined both the front and back, before bursting into startled laughter.

"Always the trickster," he said. "How I wish the queen was

awake to discover that the 'power' she has craved all these years is nothing more than a last poke in the eye from our precious Mr. Dodgson."

"What does it say?" Celia asked, leaning forward.

The king flipped the paper around so she could see it before letting it float to the ground.

In the center of the page was a hand-drawn heart.

In the center of the heart, in Charles Dodgson's careful script, were written two words:

U Matter

CHAPTER 32

The Little Trip

*"Give your evidence," said the King; "and don't
be nervous, or I'll have you executed on the spot."*

The king let the beautiful box clatter to the ground.

He looked at the key, shook his head with a wry grin, and smashed it against the wall, where it shattered into a thousand tiny crystal shards. "It would have been nice if the box opened a doorway to your world, but once I destroy the last of the logic from Wonderland, I'll have more than enough power to open it myself. The good news is that you'll get to stay and witness my final victory."

"You can't!" Celia screamed. She tore away from the gryphon's talons, ripping the sleeve of her jacket.

Before she could reach the king, he pulled a scepter from his robe. "I believe it is time for you both to experience my full power. Perhaps it will help you to see how insignificant you really are."

Celia's stomach flip-flopped as a cloud of words flew from the end of the scepter and formed a spinning tunnel that sucked her and Tyrus into it. She tried to fight, but before she could turn away, the word *SCHOOL* flashed before her eyes.

• • •

She was walking through Kat's cocoon again, only somehow it was completely repaired. Drops of information raced down golden wires making the walls appear to move. She knew it was impossible that everything could had been repaired after the fire, but then so much had felt impossible lately.

"Hello?" she called, walking through the golden hallway.

Reaching the end of the tunnel, she expected to step into the wire-filled cavern. Instead, she entered a classroom filled with books and kids.

"Who are you?" Kat demanded, looking up from an empty desk.

Celia had to think for a moment before the words came to her. "Celia Lofton," she said, pushing the top hat up out of her eyes.

"You're late," the butterfly said, standing and writing Celia's name on the dry-erase board. The marker gave an ear-piercing squeak.

At least Celia thought it was her name. It was one of the first patterns she'd learned to recognize, long before she understood that her inability to read had a name. But now the letters all looked like alien symbols.

"I'm . . . s-sorry," she stuttered. "I'm a student new. I mean a new student."

Several of the kids snickered at her mistake, and she felt her face heat up.

"Where are your supplies?" Kat asked with a sneer.

Celia opened her empty hands; she hadn't brought so much as a pencil.

"Take your seat," Kat said, waving her majestic wings in annoyance. "As you can see, we're in the middle of a test."

She wanted to ask the teacher how they could be taking a test on their first day. She hadn't studied for whatever it was, and even if she had, she wasn't good at written tests. But the butterfly was already returning to her desk, which was now covered with a stack of reports. All the covers read "Celia Lofton" and "Dyslexia" in glowing red letters.

The only empty seat was in the middle of the room. Prime territory to be called on. She looked for Tyrus, hoping he was in her class. Instead, she saw the Queen of Hearts. She was wearing her gold tiara and a school uniform.

"Don't sit by me," she growled. "I don't want to catch your stupid."

"Keep your infected brain away from me," said one of the girls who had stolen her clothes from the gym locker at her old school.

"Idiot," muttered a boy who'd been in her history class.

"Outcast," hissed another student.

"Stand in the back," snarled the Duchess. "We have no room for your kind here."

Celia stumbled to the back of the room, her stomach churning at the sight of the books on the shelves. The letters in the titles jumped from one spot to another, never staying in place long enough to read.

"Time to go over the results of the test," Kat said, walking to the front of the class. "Question one. What chance does a girl who can barely write her own name have of accomplishing anything of value?"

"None," said the Duchess.

"Correct," the butterfly said, showing one of the glowing red reports to the class. "She didn't want any of you to know that her brain is broken."

The students burst into laughter, turning to stare at Celia. She dropped her head in shame.

"Question two. Does a girl who, even when she plays video games, spends all her time with outcasts, deserve to have friends?"

"Obviously not," Cheshire said with a hideous grin.

"Last question," the butterfly said. "Does a girl this stupid, this broken, this illogical, deserve to exist?"

"I'm not stupid," Celia whispered, tears streaming down her cheeks.

"Are you sure?" Kat asked as smoke began to rise from her wings. "If you'd been smart enough to figure out the king was destroying logic, you could have warned me. If I'd known in time, I could have turned off my connections and taken down my wires, before everything burst into flame." Fire licked at her beautiful wings, turning them to ash. "Ask yourself this— since you are responsible for my death, do you really deserve to live yourself?"

Still facing forward, the Queen of Hearts twisted her neck around to smile at Celia. "Off with her head!"

Tears streaming down her face, Celia raced out of the room and found herself in a school cafeteria.

• • •

Tyrus was being held by a pair of muscular boys in tight T-shirts that read "Books Are for Babies."

A group of students screamed taunts in his face as they threw food at him. They all had melting faces like candles that had been left out in the sun too long.

"You're weird," screamed one girl, pelting him with a carton of milk that exploded against the front of his shirt.

"You're not like us," shouted another. "You don't fit in."

Tyrus pushed his unicorn hat on, as a boy darted forward and smashed an egg into his face.

"Is this your bike?" yelled a redheaded boy, wax dripping from the corners of his lips as he held up the broken remains of the Cheshire cat.

"Leave him alone," Celia screamed. She clawed at the boys holding Tyrus's arms, but her fingers passed through them as if she were a ghost. She turned and spread her arms, trying to shield him from the food, but the refuse flew through her body.

Wrestling away from the boys—egg running down his cheek—Tyrus turned and fled the cafeteria.

"Wait," Celia yelled, but he didn't stop. She followed him down a long hallway with yellowing tiles. Each intersection had a pole covered with signs, all flashing DANGER in bright red letters.

At last, he threw open a pair of double doors and raced inside. As Celia followed him, her stomach clenched. It was the library—the one room in the school she dreaded more than any other. Trying not to look at the words that screamed out from every wall, she forced her way inside.

Tyrus was standing in the middle of the room, surrounded by librarians. But instead of people, these librarians were marionettes. Their loose joints clattered, and their teeth clacked as they chanted at him.

"The only friends you have come from books, because you don't deserve real friends."

"Your own life is so pathetic you have to live in stories."

"Even the characters in your books don't like you."

White Rabbit's servant, Mary Ann, knocked down a pile of books that had been stacked under a sign that read "Fantasy." The pages began to flip on their own.

A hobbit with wide, hairy feet jumped out of one book. "We don't want you on our quest."

A robed girl climbed from another and waved her wand in his face. "You wouldn't survive a day in our world."

"Loser, loser, loser," the librarian marionettes shouted as Mary Ann made Tyrus dance and twist from the strings connected to his arms and legs.

"Stop it, stop it, stop it!" Celia howled, charging into them.

• • •

All at once she was back on the balcony with Tyrus. The night air felt hot on Celia's face as she turned to see a familiar figure in a dark suit.

"I'm so disappointed in the two of you."

"Charles Dodgson?" Tyrus asked.

"I trusted you with my most valuable possessions, left you

my diaries, gave you every clue I could, and look what you've done." He pointed at the upside-down box and the shattered key.

"We tried," Celia said. "We really did. But we thought the queen was . . . and when we out king the found." She licked her lips, trying again. "I mean, when we found out the king was—"

"You failed," he said, dark eyes flashing. "Because of you, Wonderland is going to be destroyed."

He waved his hand, and Celia and Tyrus were standing on the wall of the parapet, looking down at the ground far below. All they had to do was take one step and their problems would be over for good.

"Go ahead," Charles Dodgson said, placing his hands on their backs. "The two of you don't matter. Not at all."

CHAPTER 33

The Uneven Balance

"How dreadfully savage!" exclaimed Alice.

Celia shut her eyes and reached for Tyrus's hand. Charles Dodgson was right; she had failed. She had ruined everything. All it would take was one small step.

"Use your head," a voice whispered in her ear.

She looked around, but no one was there.

She lifted one foot. As her balance began to shift, she felt a phantom hand grip her shoulder. "The fight will not be easy. But know that you each possess everything you need to come out victorious."

Who had said that? She thought she should remember, but her brain felt muddled. "I don't possess anything," she whispered.

"What did you say?" Tyrus asked, pushing his hat down.

Celia shook her head, and her top hat wobbled.

I pride myself on fitting the hat to the hattee.

She pulled her hat off her head, really looking at it for the first time. It was true her hat was covered with math symbols while Tyrus's had all the elements of imagination he loved. But was that what the Hatter had been talking about? Or was there something more to it?

Would the Hatter—the *Mad Hatter* she'd been hearing about since before she was old enough to walk—give her a hat that didn't fit?

What if what she needed wasn't math at all?

"Give me your derby," she said, clutching Tyrus's hand in a death grip.

Tyrus took off his unicorn derby and gave it to her with a confused look.

She placed it on her head, and it slid into place as if it had been made for her. Shutting her eyes, she imagined herself in a few years, graduating from college with honors. Her mother was in the audience, beaming. She saw herself sometime later standing beside the desk of a young boy who looked up from a math book with an expression of dawning understanding.

"Do you see it now?" Celia's future-self asked.

"Yes," the boy said with a grin. "You make it so easy. This changes everything."

Like stars blinking on in the night sky, she saw a dozen different possibilities streaming out before her. A career, a family, teaching a math class, even one of her holding a novel with her name beneath "Written by" at the bottom.

Is this what Kat had meant when she told Celia to stop trying to be someone else? She didn't need to hide who she was. She could be proud of it.

She shoved her top hat into Tyrus's hands. "Put this on."

He did, and it fit perfectly.

"I don't read books because I *have* to," he said, in a stunned voice. "I read them because I *want* to. Simple logic says that reading isn't a sign of weakness, it's a symbol of strength." He tipped the top hat at the same jaunty angle the Hatter had worn his. "I'm a reader and I'm proud of it. Going on adventures with imaginary characters teaches me how to succeed in my own adventure. Reading makes me a better person, a better friend." He nearly lost his balance, and Celia had to pull him back.

"Good for you," she shouted.

Then she jumped from the wall back onto the balcony and snatched up Charles Dodgson's letter—the words "U Matter" seeming to burn on the paper.

"We *do* matter," she screamed at the man in the dark suit. "The *real* Charles Dodgson knew it, and he sent us here to win this fight."

For a moment, the fake Charles Dodgson stared at them with a surprised expression. Then he swirled into a cloud of smoke that once again became the king. As the king lifted the scepter above his head, Celia and Tyrus both grabbed it and, for a moment, she thought they were going to be able to tear it away.

"It's too late!" the king howled. Clouds of orange, red, and purple swirled around him in a vortex of crackling energy, knocking Celia and Tyrus to the floor. "You've already lost."

Spreading his arms wide, he floated from the turret and into the air. All around him, imaginary creatures appeared.

Dragons belched fire, swooping into the night. Unicorns, chimeras, and goblins scampered across the grounds.

"No more lines or angles or squares," he cried, stretching out his hands. Clouds of glowing green light hissed from the castle and into his fingertips as the perfectly square building changed into a fantasy palace. Spires jutted into the air, gem-covered domes sparkled into existence, and walkways sprouted in every direction.

"No. More. Roses," he howled. More glowing green lines hissed from the perfectly laid out gardens as the red roses were replaced with swaying yellow flowers three stories high that snapped startled birds from the air.

Bushes cut into the shapes of fantasy creatures gamboled and danced in the moonlight. Gnomes climbed from the ground, carrying picks and shovels. Cackles and screams filled the air as demons and gorgons battled each other. Witches swooped by on brooms only to be attacked by packs of harpies.

Celia and Tyrus backed toward the doorway just as a cloaked figure stumbled up the stairs, holding the Cheshire cat in his arms.

"Quite the show," he said, with a tip of his hat.

"Hatter!" Tyrus called.

"Are you all right?" Celia asked, noticing a dried line of blood coming from the corner of his mouth and a cut over one eye.

The Mad Hatter groaned as he set the cat on the floor. He touched the cut and grimaced. "Tea parties were definitely less stressful, but I'll be fit with a few days of rest." He tapped the unicorn hat on her head and smiled. "I see you finally worked out whose was whose."

"I heard your voice when we were on the wall," Tyrus said. "It told us we possessed everything we needed to be victorious."

"Did it?" Hatter smiled. "I've told that rebellious thing to stay with my tongue, where it belongs, but it has a mind of its own. Quite awkward when it tells secrets."

Celia picked up Sylvan, afraid she was dead, but the steady rhythm of the rabbit's heartbeat drummed beneath the silky fur.

Sylvan blinked open her eyes, slowly. "Celia?" she whispered. "What's happening?"

"I don't know," Celia said. "But I'm glad you're okay."

She looked at the king floating over the castle grounds, but he didn't seem to care about them anymore. The cloud of imaginary creatures surrounding him grew bigger by the second, the storm rising in volume alongside it.

"We tried to stop him, but he's been stealing the logic," she said to the Hatter, raising her voice.

"So uncivil of him."

"He's going to destroy Wonderland."

Hatter scratched his jaw. "Perhaps you two should do something about that."

The Hatter's voice carried perfectly well, despite the storm, but Tyrus had to scream to be heard over the wind. "Do what?"

Outside, the storm cloud was spinning faster and faster. In the center of it, the king howled and giggled as if he was the mad one. A jagged crack formed in the sky, and the glowing green light zapped into the darkness.

"He's opening a doorway to our world!" Celia screamed. "Once he's destroyed all the logic in Wonderland, he's going to do the same thing there."

The vortex of energy spun so fast it started sucking creatures into it. One of the gryphons was pulled off the wall, and the ace of clubs disappeared into the night.

Hatter tilted his hat down to shade his eyes. "Logic *can't* be destroyed. It's like . . . What do you call the things in your world that hold papers together?"

"Rubber bands?" Tyrus asked.

"No." The Hatter shook his coat and a small house with wings buzzed out; it was immediately sucked into the whirlwind.

"Tape?" Celia suggested. "Paper clips? Glue?"

"Carrots?" Sylvan chimed in.

"Perhaps it was rubber bands after all," the Hatter said. "Anyway, logic is like that. You can stretch it to a point, but eventually it snaps back. The logic the king has stolen has to be stored somewhere. If you could get it and return it to all of the creatures in Wonderland in the next"—he pulled out the barrister's watch and studied it—"let's say fifteen minutes, give or take, you might be able to stop him."

Tyrus shook his head. "There's no way we could get all the creatures here in time."

"I can," Sylvan said, her voice gaining strength. She leaped from Celia's arms and onto the parapet wall. Her fur blowing in the storm, she stomped her feet as hard as she could. For a moment, nothing happened. Then, barely audible above the storm, additional thumps sounded. "The Rabbit family will spread the word. We'll get everyone here in time."

"Now we just have to find the stolen logic," Tyrus said.

Celia slapped her forehead. "I know where it is." She turned to the Hatter. "You and Sylvan and Cheshire meet us in the courtyard."

Together, she and Tyrus raced down the stairs and jumped back on the rocking horse.

"Where are we going?" Tyrus called as Celia steered them down the halls.

"To the only place the king can hide his secrets," she said over her shoulder. A few minutes later, they reached the room with all the king's inventions. Celia leaped off the rocking horse and grabbed the glowing green globe she'd noticed the first time they'd been there.

The green inside the glass ball was the exact same color of the energy the king had been stealing outside. The orb pulsed and glowed in Celia's hands. Quickly, the two of them jumped back onto the horse and rode it to the castle entrance.

By the time they stepped outside, the crack in the sky behind the king was wider than ever. Liquid lightning poured out of it like a waterfall, and an enormous dragon made of flames flew around the king's head.

A hand dropped onto Celia's shoulder, and she turned to see a circle of cards running up to surround them. A trio of cards held the Hatter, Cheshire, and Sylvan prisoner.

"You aren't going anywhere with that globe," the ace of clubs snarled at Celia.

"They captured us before we could open the gate," Sylvan said, tears streaming down her face. "The Wonderland creatures are locked outside."

"And that's where they'll stay," the ace of clubs said.

"Let me go," Tyrus shouted, trying to pull away from their grasp.

Celia kicked and slammed her fists against the cards, but it didn't seem to affect them.

The only person who didn't appear upset was the Hatter. He fluttered his hands in the air in mock terror. "Oh, no. You managed to solve every other puzzle you faced, but I suppose the two of you will never solve this problem."

Tyrus scowled at the Hatter's sarcasm, but Celia thought the Hatter might be sending them another message.

She thought back to all the puzzles they'd solved since they arrived—the crocodile's test, the math knots, the sluggishness antidote, getting into the Duchess's house, the Hatter's riddle. At the time, they'd only seemed like a series of obstacles they had to get past, but was there more meaning to them?

"What did the tests have in common?" she mused. "The riddles we solved?"

"Nothing," Tyrus said as the Hatter raised an eyebrow. "Unless . . . it's not the puzzles that had anything in common but how we solved them. Every time we solved a problem, we did it together—your logic and my imagination."

Hatter's grin was nearly as wide as Cheshire's. "Too bad Charles didn't leave you anything powerful in that box of his."

Something small and gray flapped slowly onto his shoulder. It looked like the ugliest moth Celia had ever seen, with twisted feelers, a warped head, and tattered wings that looked almost burned.

She frowned, then gasped. "*U matter.* Not y-o-u the word, but the letter *U*, which in math, stands for the union of things together."

Tyrus nodded. "Kat said we couldn't save Wonderland, but by working together, we could make a change."

Kat! Celia looked at the gray creature on the Hatter's shoulder. "I know the change we can make."

Holding the glowing green ball together, they lifted it toward the moth-like creature.

"Stop!" the ace of clubs commanded. As he lunged for the ball, the tiniest wisp of green slipped from the orb, and the gray moth changed into a beautiful butterfly.

"Thanks," Kat said, fanning her restored wings. "I'll take it from here."

As she flew up over the cards, a line of green floated from her to Cheshire. The robot cat shifted in the arms of the card holding him, and his eyes opened. "I feel . . . different."

"You're a real cat again!" Tyrus shouted.

The card dropped Cheshire in surprise, but the cat landed gracefully on his feet.

The ace of clubs finally snatched the glowing ball, but he couldn't stop the light pouring out of it. Lines of green began shooting down like fireworks from one creature to another on the other side of the gate—the crowd spreading as more arrived—until the ace was left holding an empty globe.

"I suggest we all step inside," the Hatter said. "This is apt to be messy." He looked up at the king, who seemed to have finally realized something was wrong. The crack was closing as the cloud around him began to swirl with streaks of green.

"Never mind; there isn't time." Hatter took off his top hat, dropped to one knee, and leaned over Cheshire. "Right about now, I would suggest ducking."

At that moment, a tremendous bang shook the air. The glowing crack snapped shut. Nearly all the imaginary creatures the king had created rebounded toward him with a crescendo of howls, screams, and screeches.

Celia dropped to the ground as the energy vortex blew outward, sending green jelly everywhere.

The king gave one surprised screech, then plummeted to the earth.

Tyrus, who had been walking forward to get a better look, was covered in green slime. "Awesome!"

The Hatter shook his head. "That logic stain is never going to come out."

CHAPTER 34

The Political Party

Alice had got so much into the way of expecting nothing but out-of-the-way things to happen, that it seemed quite dull and stupid for life to go on in the common way.

"Runners, take your places," the Dodo called with great importance.

"Where do we line up?" Tyrus asked.

There didn't appear to be a lot of organization for the Great Caucus Race, as they were calling it. Birds, humans, and animals of all shapes and sizes filled in spots along the course, which wound around the croquet court, wrapped between the greenhouses—currently boarded over until repairs could be made—and turned directly into the stables—now housing a contentious manticore and a baby dragon as well as the royal horses—before returning to the starting line.

"I don't think it matters," Celia said. "I'm not even sure there are any rules. That duck is riding an ostrich, and the clams are all strapped to roller skates."

Tyrus set his feet, arms cocked. "I knew I should have

brought the rocking horse. I could have taken out half of the other racers with bubbles."

The race began, despite not having a countdown or a starter's gun. One moment the contestants were standing still, and the next they were running, hopping, riding, skating, and flying around the course.

"Yeehaw," Tyrus whooped, joining the fray.

Celia and the Hatter watched the race for a few minutes before heading toward the tent-covered tables piled high with goodies and treats, all of which had been paid for from the royal treasury.

"How will they know when the race is over?" she asked.

"When the last person stops," the Hatter said. "There will be much debate about who won, prizes will be handed out, and then, after a while, it will start all over again. Caucus races are rather predictable that way."

As he reached for a buttered croissant, Celia slapped his hand. "What happened to the rules of etiquette?"

"This is a political party, not a tea party," Hatter said. "Rules of etiquette do not apply, and common courtesy is optional at best."

It had been three days since the king's plan to overthrow Wonderland with raw imagination had failed. Since that time, some things had begun to return to normal. Others appeared to be permanently changed. The castle had ended up as a crazy combination of boxy cubes and fantastical swoops and curves.

The cards had tried painting the new yellow flowers red, but the flowers kept biting the tips off the paintbrushes until everyone agreed they were probably best left the way they were. The croquet court had been completely restored, and the flamingos and hedgehogs had been there all day—this time as players, not equipment.

The biggest change, though, had been the decision to replace the queen and king as the rulers of Wonderland. A general election was scheduled for the end of the week, although Celia wasn't sure how smoothly the voting process would go.

"Are you sure democracy is right for Wonderland?" she asked, stepping into the shade of one of the many large-striped tents that had been put up for the occasion.

"It's the best form of government for the mad," Cheshire said from under a table. "And we're all—*squeak*—mad here."

Celia patted the cat's head. "Oh, no, your squeak is back."

"Not at all. I was just giving the Dormouse a ride."

"Thanks for the lift, gov'na," the Dormouse said, hopping off the cat and onto the table where he landed in a tin of biscuits. "Good luck in the election," he called, pulling back the lapel of his jacket to reveal a flashing "Hatter for President" pin.

"I thought you weren't running," Celia said, glancing at the caucus race where the birds and rodents had banded together to try to overtake the marsupials.

"I'm not," the Hatter said. "It's taking all my time and energy to get the millinery business up and running again. Hat customers can be quite a disloyal lot when you've been stuck in a tea party as long as I have."

Cheshire blinked. "And yet, according to the latest polls, you lead all other candidates by more than forty percent. Your next closest opponent is a lory running on the promise of free pudding for all."

"Pudding is formidable," the Hatter said.

Celia recognized a far less terrifying White Rabbit and a human Mary Ann, who were sharing a celery tart in an out-of-the-way corner. Mary Ann looked more comfortable without her strings and screws. White's teeth were back to normal, and his eyes were no longer red, but they still had a slight glaze to them.

"Are they going to be all right?"

"Perhaps. Or perhaps not. All things come to an end in time." Hatter glanced toward Kat, who fluttered onto the table and picked up a giant chocolate chip cookie, only to discover the "chocolate" was a family of small brown beetles.

"Sorry," she called, lowering them back to the table.

"A common mistake," the beetles called, trundling off toward a tiny set of swings and slides set atop a jam roly-poly.

Sweating and out of breath, Tyrus joined them. "I need to get in better shape."

"Finished already?"

Tyrus grabbed a tall glass of knickerbocker glory and dug into it with a spoon. "Just taking a break for a minute. Those roller-skating clams are brutal. They throw elbows as they skate past."

"I didn't know clams had elbows," Celia said, watching him devour the sundae.

"Neither did I," Tyrus said around a mouthful of ice cream. "But I have the bruises to prove it."

Celia picked up a slice of banana-and-toffee pie, checking

for insects before taking a bite. It was a surprisingly delicious combination. "How did the king manage to survive the fall?"

Cheshire flicked his tail. "Interesting fact about political leaders—most of them are made up of at least twenty-five percent rubber. It's shocking the tumbles they can take and still manage to bounce back."

"He has an excellent set of doctors working on him," the Hatter said, sampling a bowl of creamy lemon-flavored fluff. "He demanded all of his soldiers and men care for him, but when they failed to put him together, we sent for an out-of-town crew rumored to have done excellent work with a cracked egg in another kingdom."

"Egg-cellent," Tyrus said with a laugh.

Celia wiped whipped cream from his face with her thumb. "Are the king and queen really gone then?"

"Royal families never completely go away," the Hatter said. "They just become less relevant. A few of the cards left the castle to join the queen in exile, but once the inhabitants of Wonderland discovered the shenanigans their leaders were up to, their rule effectively came to an end."

Tryus set his empty sundae glass on the table. "I don't understand how returning the logic made everything"—he opened his hands, which were still stained a faint green, miming an explosion—"go blam-o."

"It's quite simple," the Hatter said. "All living things have a balance, whether it's an individual, a family, a community, or a world. The balance is never perfect because there are constant swings as situations change. But push too far in one direction and eventually the pendulum will swing back—often quite violently."

Cheshire nodded. "For as long as the king and queen ruled Wonderland, they balanced each other out. She is loud, brash, and very logical. He is quiet, devious, and quite imaginative. The two of them fit our world perfectly. When Mr. Dodgson visited us, the queen realized for the first time that she could expand her rule to other worlds."

"She'd had glimpses of such worlds from time to time in her looking glass," Hatter said. "But until she met someone from one of those worlds, she'd didn't understand how close they were. That's when the king hatched his plan to take over Wonderland. He convinced his wife she was too important to rule only one world, when in reality he was planning on being the one to go through the doorway."

Tyrus nodded. "And she locked you in time, to pressure Mr. Dodgson to take her through the doorway?"

"Quite so," Hatter said. "Mr. Dodgson wanted to break the curse she put on me, but he could see that as long as he remained, she would continue to use her power to hurt those he cared about. I believe he had an inkling that her quest for power was having a counterreaction on the king."

A family of walruses carrying "Hatter Is Tops" signs lumbered by, and the Hatter edged away nervously.

"He knew his time was short. If he stayed in Wonderland much longer, he might never be able to leave. He promised me that one day someone else would come from his world to restore balance to Wonderland. And here the two of you are."

A large herd of rabbits headed in their direction. Hatter nodded. "I believe someone would like a word with you."

As Celia and Tyrus turned, two of the most ancient-looking rabbits Celia had ever seen stepped forward. Their fur was almost completely gray, and one of them had a bald patch between his ears, but both were smiling.

Sylvan came bouncing up behind them. "Great-Great-Great-Grandfather Gotland and Great-Great-Great-Grandmother Gabali, these are Tyrus and Alice." She clapped a paw over her mouth and giggled. "Sorry, I mean Celia."

Tyrus shot out one hand to the rabbits. "A pleasure to meet you both."

The bald rabbit wrinkled his nose. "Pheasants and Easter toes?"

Grandmother Gabali shook her head. "The pleasure is all ours. We can't thank the two of you enough for saving Wonderland."

"All we did was make a change," Tyrus said.

Celia pointed at Sylvan. "And none of it would have been possible without her help."

Grandfather Gotland tugged at the back of his sagging pants. "We've got big plans for this little one. She's going to be the new Commissioner of Conjunctivitis. Or is it the Mayor of Malocclusion?"

Grandmother shook her head and chuckled. "We brought you both a present from the whole family."

Sylvan handed Celia a pink box wrapped with a red bow. "It's a carrot cake."

"Had a little bite on the way over," Grandfather said. "Quite tasty."

"You did not," Grandmother said, her mouth dropping open.

The old rabbit winked and nudged his wife. "It's a going-away present."

"Where are you going?" Celia asked.

"Not us," Grandfather said. "You. The cheese clock says it's time for the pair of you to return home. I figured you knew."

With hugs and waves, the rabbits turned and hopped back to join the party.

Celia tried to force a smile but couldn't quite get it to stick.

"What's wrong?" Hatter asked. "Does carrot cake not agree with your stomach? It could be a gluten allergy. Or a case of wanderlust. Carrots always give me that."

"It's not either of those," Celia said. "It's just . . ."

"The rabbits said it's time for us to go home," Tyrus said. "But we can't. We'll never get to see our own world again. We'll never see our families."

"Whyever not?" Hatter asked. "You aren't losing your vision like poor Barrister Entwhistle, are you?"

"It's not our vision," Celia said, smiling at the mouse who was telling a group of entranced gnomes a story so complex that his words wound nearly all the way to the top of the castle. "It's the box."

"We thought there would be something inside that would help us return home."

The Hatter looked at them as if waiting for the joke. When neither of them spoke, he threw his green cloak over his shoulder. "I'm surprised after everything you've accomplished, the two of you would still underestimate the greatest power in Wonderland."

CHAPTER 35

The Sad Farewell

"Well, I sha'n't go, at any rate."

The night of the election, Celia and Tyrus stayed up with Hatter, March Hare, Dormouse, Cheshire, and Kat until the last of the votes had been counted. Not surprisingly, Hatter won by a landslide.

At least that's what the lory's supporters claimed. Shortly before the voting had closed, a small aftershock had sent dirt tumbling down a hill, temporarily blocking one of the polling stations. They were demanding a recount, which would take at least a week.

"The only reason Judge Dodo hasn't already named you the winner is because he doesn't want to lose the bird vote in the next election," Cheshire said from where he was curled up on the table.

"Personally, I hope the lory wins," Hatter said. "Politics is for the birds."

The March Hare buttered a croissant. "You're still a shoo-in to win. Or, in your case, a hat-in."

Celia looked at Kat, perched silently on a teacup. "Are you feeling all right? You haven't eaten anything."

Kat smiled and stretched her stained-glass wings. "Butterflies' lives are short, and mine has been longer than most. I'm afraid it is coming to an end."

Tyrus pushed away his plate, his eyes welling up. "You're dying?"

"Not dying," Kat said. "Only changing. Being a caterpillar was intriguing. Being a butterfly was enlightening. I can't wait to see what comes next."

"But Wonderland won't be the same without you," Celia said, feeling like a fist was squeezing her heart to pieces.

"It won't be alone," Kat said with a mysterious grin.

Hatter removed his top hat—bright orange with frog eyes and a spray of jaunty peacock feathers on the side—and set it upside down on the table before him. Something moved inside, and five beautiful blue caterpillars crawled out onto the brim.

Tyrus leaned forward to get a better look. "Are those . . . ?"

One of the caterpillars raised its head to look at Celia, blinked its eyes, and asked, "Who are you?"

"You had babies!" Celia cried, clutching her hands to her chest.

"Three hundred and forty-two," Kat said. "Hare has offered to raise them until they're old enough to be on their own."

The March Hare dropped his croissant. "I what?"

Hatter drummed his fingers on the table. "Much as I'm enjoying our conversation, I'm afraid it's time."

"Can't they stay a few days more?" Dormouse asked, sipping from a steaming cup of tea. "I'd like to hear more of Tyrus's stories. Those elves and dwarves are fascinating creatures—if a bit unbelievable."

"I'm afraid not," Hatter said. "The two of them are already feeling a bit sticky. If they stay any longer it might be impossible to pry them out."

Although Celia had known this time was coming, she still felt a lump in her throat. "Thank you all for everything you've done for me. I feel like a different person."

March Hare squeezed her arm and shook his long ears. "But not like the queen, fortunately. I don't imagine it would be pleasant to feel like her." He handed both of them a paper bag. "Cherry tarts for the trip home."

"Thanks," Tyrus said, sniffing the bag.

Dormouse wiped his eyes. "In honor of your departure, I have prepared a story of courage, friendship, lessons learned, and dairy products."

He placed his hands behind his back, small furry chin trembling.

> *Hey diddle doodle*
> *There once was a poodle*
> *Who furnished his house*
> *With cheese.*

"Oh," he cried, burying his face in his paws. "I'm too sad to finish it."

"There, there," March Hare said, pouring tea on Dormouse's head.

"Thank you all for helping me believe in myself," Tyrus said. "And helping me understand that it's okay to be different."

Hatter reached into his pocket and pulled out Charles Dodgson's watch. "Thank you for bringing this to me. I offered it to Barrister Entwhistle, but he said his family no longer needs a timepiece to define them. He thought it might come in handy for the two of you down the road."

"Thank you," Celia said, imagining how her mother would react to seeing Charles Dodgson's watch.

"I'd offer you a gift," Cheshire said, flashing his wide grin. "But the true gift is in giving, which means I would only be giving myself a gift if I gave one to you, and since selfishness is—"

"Hush," Kat said, patting him gently with one wing. She studied Tyrus and Celia. "I once asked if the two of you knew who you were. Do you know now?"

"Yes," Tyrus said.

"I think so," Celia added.

"Do not forget it," the butterfly said. "Even when others may cause you to doubt."

Celia and Tyrus stepped forward and pulled them all into a hug—careful not to crush Kat.

When they finally let go amid sniffles and red eyes from everyone, Hatter put his hat back on his head. "You have the letter?"

Celia took it out of its envelope and studied the words

"U Matter." It was hard to imagine that more than a hundred and fifty years earlier the author of the Alice in Wonderland books had left it specifically for them.

She turned it over in her hands. "I know what it means as far as saving Wonderland, but how does it help us get home?"

"The simplest way to discover where one is going is to remember how one arrived where one is," Cheshire said.

Hatter winked. "Well stated. Do the two of you remember how you got here?"

"Celia solved a math problem she found in Mr. Dodgson's diary," Tyrus said.

Hare dipped a cookie in his tea. "You weren't there at the time?"

"Of course, he was," Celia said. "He made me drink from the bottle when—"

She and Tyrus stared at each other.

"You're saying it wasn't only math that opened the door," Celia said.

Tyrus nodded. "It wasn't just the bottle, either."

Cheshire grinned. "It was the two of you, working together. Logic and imagination combined will always be greater than either one alone. And change is the strongest when created together."

Tyrus rubbed his glasses on his shirt. "We could have opened a door back to our world any time we wanted?"

"It's astounding how many times we believe we are locked out of our greatest dreams," Hatter said, "when we have but to turn the knob."

"But . . ." Celia began before really thinking about it.

There had been moments when both she and Tyrus each wanted to leave Wonderland, but it was never both of them at the same time.

She looked at Tyrus. "Are you ready? To go home?"

"I am." He reached out and gripped her hands. "Let's do this together."

Celia furrowed her brow, staring at their entwined fingers. "I'm trying to remember the math."

Tyrus bit his lower lip. "I'm thinking of a doorway to . . . Narnia." Celia's gaze snapped up, but he was grinning. "Kidding. I'm imagining a doorway home."

For a moment nothing happened, and Celia was afraid they were doing something wrong. She squeezed her eyes shut, concentrating as hard as she could. "I don't think . . ."

Then she smelled it. Movie popcorn, the beach . . .

She opened her eyes in time to see a tunnel of spinning colors swirling slowly shut. She reached out to touch the Hatter's hand one last time, but he was too far away.

"Don't forget the power of cooperation when you return to your world," he said, his words beginning to fade.

"Goodbye," Celia called. "Thanks for . . ."

But they were already gone.

The Fitting Epilogue

"Oh, I've had such a curious dream!" said Alice. And she told her sister, as well as she could remember them, all these strange Adventures of hers that you have just been reading about.

Cheshire's grin was the last thing I remembered seeing before the rainbow tunnel closed.

I looked for Tyrus, afraid he hadn't made it with me. But there he was, falling or floating—or both—by my side.

"It was real, right?" I asked. "I mean, I'm not going to open my eyes and discover it was all a dream, right?"

"Not unless I dreamed it too," Tyrus said, his cheeks dimpling. "I have a great imagination, but not that great."

Our words, which had started out as cartoon bubbles, changed back to real sounds. The corduroy jacket the crocodile in the Arithma Sea had worn shot past us. Only this time it was going down, which, I suppose meant that we were falling up.

"How are we ever going to go back to normal life after this?" I asked. Tyrus didn't even have to answer. I smirked. "I know, I know. Books."

A moment later a pair of worn bunny slippers hopped past alongside one of the Duchess's horrible paintings. Tyrus tried to grab one of the slippers, but they jumped nimbly away from him.

He scratched the back of his head. "About the whole not-being-friends-at-school thing. Does this change that?"

"I don't think we can be friends," I said. He reached for his glasses, but I pulled his hand away, gripping it tightly in mine. "Because we are going to be *best* friends. In middle school, in high school, and in whatever comes after that. We've been to Wonderland together. Plus, we've committed library crimes. You don't throw away something like that."

I couldn't help laughing at his relieved look.

The colors around us began to spin faster.

"We have to decide what to do about Mr. Dodgson's chest," Tyrus said. "I mean there are three more diaries in it, and—"

Before he could finish his sentence, we thumped to the ground in my mother's office. Everything looked the same as it had when we left. Peeking out the door, things seemed to be going on as though we'd never been away.

Tyrus reached for the open diary on the desk, but I slammed it shut and put it back inside the chest with the other diaries, wrapping the whole thing back in the brown paper. He might not know what to do with the diaries, but I did.

It felt strange walking back into the library. I gave my mom the Rabbit family's carrot cake, saying it was from a happy library patron, but she still made me read three chapters of a novel before I could leave. Of course, Tyrus had plenty of opinions on what book I should choose, but I didn't even mind—much.

He and I spent the last few days of summer vacation talking about math and reading, logic and imagination. We played video games together and told each other riddles.

And on the first day of school, we dug a hole in the yard behind my house. When it was nearly two feet deep, I picked up the package I'd wrapped in so many layers of tape and plastic I could barely see what was inside.

"Are you sure we have to bury them?" Tyrus asked. "It feels wrong."

I bit the inside of my cheek but forced myself to stop. "Do you want to take a chance that someone else might open a doorway to Wonderland? Maybe mess things up all over again?"

"No," he admitted. "But we don't even know what's in the other three diaries."

"And I don't want to know. One caused us more than enough trouble. The world has managed to live without them for a hundred and fifty years. Maybe in a couple more centuries someone will find these. Fortunately, we won't be around when that happens."

Still, as I slipped the chest with the four wrapped diaries into the hole, I couldn't help feeling a twinge of curiosity. The math in the first book had been world-changing. What kinds of equations might be in the other three? An elixir of eternal youth? How to change lead into gold? A guide for instantaneous space travel? A cure for cancer?

For just a moment, my hand lingered on the heavy

package, and I imagined taking the tiniest peek at what was inside.

I jerked my fingers away. I didn't care what was in those books. I was never going to look at them again.

My certainty grew stronger with each pile of dirt I dropped into the hole until, at last, it was filled. It was a wonderful feeling to pat down the last shovelful of earth, pushing the grass back into place so no one would ever know it had been disturbed.

Mom felt bad about not being able to drive me to school on the first day, but I told her Tyrus and I would be just fine on our own.

We stopped when we reached the first row of buildings. Unlike my old school that was one big building filled with hallways, Bernal middle school had a bunch of individual classrooms connected by outdoor walkways. Watching hundreds of kids I didn't know laugh and joke together, I felt my stomach cramp.

"You okay?" Tyrus asked.

"I think I'm going to puke," I said.

He nodded at the phone sticking out of my pocket. "There's always Minecraft."

"There's always another book," I said, gesturing at his giant backpack, and we both cracked up.

"You sure you want to do this?" he asked.

"No," I admitted, trying to calm my breathing. "But I think I have to."

A janitor with a name tag that read Cebrowski glared at us. He had a scruffy gray beard and hair that stuck up on the sides of his head like rabbit ears. "Better hurry, you two. Don't want to be late on your first day."

"Right." We laughed as we trotted to class.

We'd both signed up for Advanced English first period. I knew it would be hard, but I'd done harder things. We walked to the room together.

"Everyone will need a copy of *The Red Badge of Courage* by Stephen Crane," the teacher was saying as we stepped through the door. "That will be our first book of the semester."

"Crane is no Lewis Carroll," Tyrus whispered.

"He's no Dormouse either," I said, still feeling torn between breaking out into hysterical laughter and throwing up in front of the entire class.

"Take your seats, please," the teacher said as we paused by his desk.

I curled my fingers until my nails bit into my palms. I could do this.

"Excuse me," I said, intentionally not looking at any of the other students. "Could I say something to the class first? Please?"

In the days leading up to this moment, I'd imagined the teacher telling me not to interrupt his lesson, laughing in my face, sending me to the office, and a million worse and more far-fetched things.

Looking at me, he must have seen something in my eyes. "Go ahead," he said with a nod.

As the bell rang for the start of class, I stood in front of the whiteboard.

I'd practiced exactly what I wanted to say, over and over,

until I had it memorized. I'd carefully written it down, study-ing each word. I took a deep breath, turned to look at the thirty or so students in front of me . . . and froze. Every word I'd practiced jumbled inside my head like leaves on a windy day then blew straight out, leaving cold, terrifying, black emp-tiness.

The kids waited, glancing from me to each other. Someone slid their desk, making a squeak that sounded like it could be heard around the world. I remembered Cheshire's squeak and felt a little more brave. Prying my tongue from the roof of my mouth, I forced my lips to move. "The reason why I am here is . . ."

Nothing. I had absolutely nothing. Maybe in Wonderland I was something special—here I was only a girl who couldn't read and built video-game castles no one would ever see. I shook my head, closed my mouth, and turned to walk to my seat when an explosion shook the class.

Okay, maybe it wasn't an explosion, but, in the deathly silence of the room, it sounded that way.

Tyrus had dropped his backpack. The zipper split open and books flew everywhere. Several of the kids snickered, and I quickly bent to help him gather them, but Tyrus only stood and grinned.

"I'm new here, but my name is Tyrus Weller, and I'm a bookaholic."

More students laughed, but this time it was *with* him not *at* him.

"Hi, Tyrus," several of the kids replied.

Tyrus took off his glasses. "I have so many books in my

house, my parents have given up buying shelves for them. Now we just make bookshelves out of books and put more books in them. I have so many copies of my favorites that I can lay them side by side and read an entire chapter without having to turn a page."

"Right on," somebody in the back shouted.

"I take books with me everywhere I go—even to the bathroom," Tyrus continued.

"Too much information," laughed a girl in the front.

Laughing so hard I was almost crying, I had completely forgotten why I was there until Tyrus turned to me and said, "This is my friend, Celia Lofton. I've only known her for a little while, and I know you don't know me, but in that time, I've discovered that she is the bravest person I know. She has something very important to tell you."

He slipped something cool and metal into my hand, threw his backpack over his shoulder, and whispered, "Remember who you are."

Peeking into my hand, I saw the golden gleam of Charles Dodgson's watch. I remembered everything I was going to say. More importantly, I remembered who I was.

"My name is Celia Lofton, and I am dyslexic. What that means is that my brain works differently from many of yours. Just like some of you have braces or need glasses to see, I need more time and use technology to read, write, and spell."

I took out the reading pen I'd been so afraid for anyone to see and held it up in front of the class. My heart was pounding—not from fear this time but from excitement.

"This might look like a tiny lightsaber, but it's actually called a reading pen. I use it to learn words I don't know."

Tyrus nudged me in the side, and I looked down to see he was holding open a copy of *Alice's Adventures in Wonderland*.

I turned on the pen, checked the setting, and ran it across a word I didn't recognize.

Quadrille, the pen read aloud. *A square dance performed typically by four couples and containing five figures, each of which is a complete dance in itself.*

"Cool," said a girl in the front row.

"I want one of those," said a kid in the back.

I smiled. "I used to be embarrassed by this because I thought people would believe that I'm not smart. I'm not anymore. Dyslexia is a part of who I am."

That Night

Although the moonlit air of my backyard was not at all cold, I felt a clear chill as I stood looking at the spot where Tyrus and I had buried the lost Wonderland Diaries. Goose bumps rose on the backs of my arms, and I clasped the novel I was holding to my chest.

"I'm not going to dig you up," I whispered to the package under the ground.

I waited a moment, listening for a mysterious voice or some sign of movement in the earth near my feet, but the only response was the *ree-deep* of a frog hiding in the grass.

A soft breeze ruffled the hair on the back of my neck, and I pictured Charles Dodgson bent over his desk on a night like this one, scribbling onto the page of one of his leather-bound journals. Out of all his writings, he'd chosen to hide only those four. Clearly, he didn't want anyone to see them.

And yet, everything that happened in Wonderland proved

he not only wanted me and Tyrus to read his diary, but he'd expected us to. Had he used his code in the other three? I felt an overwhelming urge to find out. I'd just crack open the cover of the second diary. It would just take a moment or two to pull up the sod, burrow into the loose dirt with my hands, and—

"No," I said, backing away. "I don't care what he wrote in the other diaries or why. I have more than enough adventure in my life here and now."

I turned and walked back to the well-lit safety of my house, promising myself I'd stay away from the temptation of the buried package. I'd never think about the books or the secrets that might be hidden in them, never consider the fact that six years after he'd written *Alice's Adventures in Wonderland*, he'd published a second book set in a completely different world.

Just because one diary led to a fantastical world didn't mean the others did too, and it definitely didn't mean Charles Dodgson wanted us to go there.

Opening my back door, I inhaled the scent of greasy burgers and appreciated the normalness of the fast-food wrappers spread around the counter. I dropped the book I'd been holding onto the kitchen table. I didn't bother looking at the cover. I knew it as well as I knew the title I'd seen at least a thousand times in my life.

"*Through the Looking-Glass, and What Alice Found There*," I muttered under my breath as I headed to bed. "By Lewis Carroll."

Acknowledgments

In 2018, before I had written a word of this book, I was having lunch with the wonderful Heidi Gordon and Lisa Mangum. I happened to mention that Charles Dodgson (aka Lewis Carroll) kept detailed diaries, but four of them disappeared after his death. "Wouldn't it be cool if—" I started. I'm not sure I got any more words out of my mouth before they both said, "We want it!" Bless you both, along with Chris Schoebinger and everyone else at Shadow Mountain, for believing in this project and guiding it into what it has become.

Thanks to my agent, Michael Bourret, for his constant support, encouragement, wisdom, and snarky humor. Don't know that I could survive the crazy world of publishing without you.

Kevin Keele, who provided the amazing artwork for this novel, Richard Erickson and Sheryl Dickert Smith, who made everything look gorgeous—thank you, thank you, thank you. (To all the kids who tell me how much they love the amazing covers of my books, these are the people who make the magic!)

Thanks to Rachael Ward, whom I may have driven crazy with my eccentric typesetting requests for this book, and Callie Hansen and Troy Butcher who are both marketing geniuses.

Writing is a lonely business and much of the time it can

feel discouraging, but I am so grateful for my many, many author friends who are never competitors but always cheerleaders. You are the best.

A special shout-out to some wonderful friends of mine who deal with dyslexia every day and who gave me wonderful feedback on what it is like to be dyslexic or to be the family member of a dyslexic person. Anything I got right is thanks to them; anything I messed up on is purely my fault. Thanks Hannah Fackrell, Julie Whipple, Travis Behunin, Heather Brand, Miranda Ferguson, Loralie and Landon Pearce, Erin Draper, Sandra Sorenson, Judy Casper, Kimberly Berg, Becca Secor, Dustin Hansen, Rebecca and James Blevins, and the members of the Utah Decoding Dyslexia Facebook group. Also, my great BETA readers and friends, Jackson Porter and Matt Hayes.

Finally, thanks to my amazing family who make this whole writing thing possible. My kids—Erica and Nick Thurman, Scott and Natalie Savage, Jacob and Maura Savage, and Nick Savage. My grandkids—Graysen, Lizzy, Jack, Asher, Cameron, Declan, and little Michael. My dad, Dick Savage, who has always read all my books and given me great feedback. My sister Deanne, who read an early draft of this book and made it much better. My sister Kathy, and my brothers, Craig and Mark. And my many nieces, nephews, cousins, and in-laws who put up with "Weird Uncle Scott."

And most of all, my amazing wife, Jennifer, who is my partner in everything I do and the biggest supporter an author could ask for. You are my life!

Author's Note

I know you picked up this book for the story and not to read a bunch of authory stuff from me. But I wanted to mention two things that became more and more important to me while I researched and wrote this book.

First, before I started writing this book, I had only an inkling of what it might be like to be a dyslexic person. I knew that it made reading harder, and I had a general idea that letters switched places on the page. What I learned from interviewing dyslexic people and reading about the subject opened my eyes in ways I couldn't have imagined, and I gained so much respect for the people I met and read about. They are true heroes.

I also learned about coping mechanisms taught by amazing teachers, specialists, librarians, and, most of all, by the parents who fight for their children every day. In this story, I tried to represent some of what I learned. A real conflict for dyslexic children is the desire to succeed while not wanting to appear different to their friends. That was a hard part of the story to write, and I hope I did it justice.

If I didn't capture dyslexia the way you have experienced it, or if the things I wrote are not the way that you see them, I apologize in advance, and I would love to hear from you at scott@jscottsavage.com. Also, if you like what you read, I wouldn't mind hearing that either!

If you are unfamiliar with dyslexia, I'd recommend doing some additional research after you finish this book, and maybe take a moment to recognize your dyslexic friends and the amazing people who support them. For more information, check out the International Dyslexia Association at www.dyslexiaida.org

Second, I have to take a moment to recognize the genius of Charles Dodgson, aka Lewis Carroll, and his amazing books that I used as the source material for this novel. These days, it seems most people know about *Alice in Wonderland* from the movies, but there is so much more depth to his stories. He really was an amazing mathematician, a genius wordsmith, a brilliant mind, and one of the key founders of books written for children. Do a little research on him and you might understand a little better why I consider this work a love letter to him and his books.

Discussion Questions

1. Celia doesn't want anyone at her new school to know that she is dyslexic because she is afraid they will think she is different. At the end of the book, she stands up and tells the class about her dyslexia. What made her change the way she feels?

2. When Celia first meets Tyrus, she thinks they can't be friends because she doesn't like books and he doesn't like video games. Why is it important to get to know people who have different interests than you do?

3. In the Arithma Sea, Tyrus realizes they need to look at the math problem in a different way to solve it. How does looking at everyday problems in a different way help solve them?

4. The Duchess has two sides—one angry and one kind. Do you ever have times when you feel angrier or happier than normal? Why is it okay to have different feelings on different days?

5. Celia and Tyrus use a combination of logic and imagination to solve many of the Wonderland puzzles. Do you consider yourself more logical or imaginative? How might using both logic and imagination help to create a better world?

6. Kat tells Celia and Tyrus that they should be proud of their

differences inside of trying to be like everyone else. Why is it important to be proud of who you are?

7. The Cheshire cat says, "The simplest way to discover where one is going is to remember how one arrived where one is." How does knowing how you got where you are help you figure out where you are going?

8. At first Tyrus uses the library to hide from bullies. Later, he says that reading makes him a better person and a better friend. How have books changed you?

9. Celia and Tyrus decide to bury the rest of the diaries without reading them. If you had the diaries, would you read them or bury them? Why?

TURN HERE

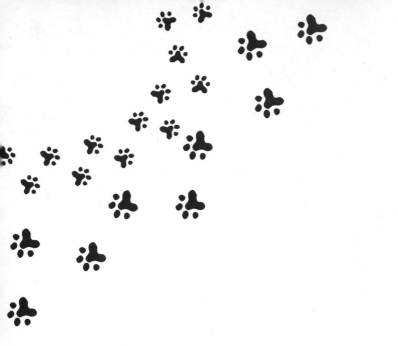

"Any change yet?" the March Hare asked as he and Hatter strolled through the castle grounds.

Hatter removed his top hat and prodded his head with two fingers. "A bit squelchy at the temple." Something squeaked, and he pulled a small blue caterpillar out of his hair. "Sorry about that."

Lowering Kat's offspring back into his hat, he quirked an eyebrow at the hare. "Perhaps I'll avoid the swollen head common to newly elected politicians."

Hare offered him a red rubber bottle with a carrot-shaped stopper.

"Ice pack?" Hatter asked, licking a stray bit of cupcake frosting from his lapel.

"Humility pack. At the first sign of ego, apply twice an hour to the forehead, backhead, lefthead, and directly on the tongue." Hare wriggled his nose. "It's butterscotch flavored."

Practical and tasteful," Hatter said. As he tucked the gift
is cloak, sunlight flashed from beneath a rosebush that
had survived the king's curse. He reached through the branches
and pulled out an ornate hand mirror with a large crack in its
surface. "The queen's magic looking glass."

"It's broken," Hare said. "That's seven years' bad luck. Or
is it three years of missed appointments? I can never . . ."

Hatter stared into the slightly murky lens of the mirror,
wondering if it still showed other worlds, when something
white flickered like a ghost across its surface. His stomach
flipped, and for a second, he had the distinct feeling of being
in two places at once. Of being two . . . *people* at once.

March Hare rubbed his paws across his eyes. "Odd. I feel
somehow *less* than before."

"Yes," Hatter said, frowning intently into the mirror that
now only showed his reflection. "Very odd indeed."